There was absolute silence

Becki held her breath, listening for a repetition of the sounds that had sent them into the woods. When the voices came again—only after she'd waited a long time—they were much nearer.

If they were going to be caught, if they were going to die, she thought, there were a couple of things she wanted to do first. Had wanted to do for months. Her mouth opened, and her tongue touched the stubbled softness at the corner of Deke Summers's lips.

Touched. Caressed. Traced along the line of his upper lip. Enjoying the feel and taste of his skin.

She hesitated, trying to find again the courage that had allowed her to put her mouth against his. "I've been wanting to do that for a long time." She whispered her confession, the sound of the words only a breath. "Longer than you can possibly imagine."

He made no verbal response, but his blue eyes continued to study her face. Then, after an eternity, his head began to lower. She opened her lips, welcoming.

She had wanted Deke Summers to kiss her, but she was surprised by how thoroughly he did it.

Dear Reader,

You've told us that stories about hidden identities are some of your favorites, so this month we're happy to bring them to you, in the all-new HIDDEN IDENTITY promotion.

Gayle Wilson leads off this sure-to-be-popular miniseries with the enigmatic Deke Summers, a man whose very life depends on how well he can keep secret who he truly is. But Deke makes one mistake: He falls in love.

We're proud to announce that Gayle has won the Colorado Romance Writers Award of Excellence for her first Intrigue novel, *Echoes in the Dark*, which was also a Maggie Award finalist. *The Redemption of Deke Summers*—richly emotional and intensely suspenseful—is the finest book yet from this immensely talented author.

We hope you enjoy it—and all the books coming to you in HIDDEN IDENTITY.

Regards,

Debra Matteucci
Senior Editor & Editorial Coordinator
Harlequin Books
300 East 42nd Street
New York, NY 10017

The Redemption of Deke Summers

Gayle Wilson

Harlequin Books

TORONTO • NEW YORK • LONDON
AMSTERDAM • PARIS • SYDNEY • HAMBURG
STOCKHOLM • ATHENS • TOKYO • MILAN
MADRID • WARSAW • BUDAPEST • AUCKLAND

For Rebecca Gay,
Who makes me very proud that she bears my name

And for the girls
Who help to keep me sane

ISBN 0-373-22414-1

THE REDEMPTION OF DEKE SUMMERS

Copyright © 1997 by Mona Gay Thomas

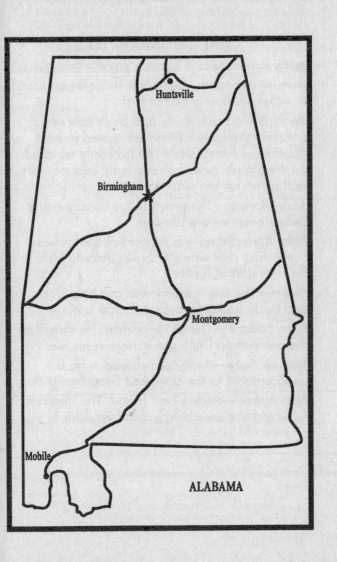

Huntsville

Birmingham

Montgomery

Mobile

ALABAMA

CAST OF CHARACTERS

Deke Summers—A man on the run from more than his memories, but it is their darkness that threatens to finally defeat him.

Becki Travers—Her life had been safe and ordinary until Deke Summers moved in next door. Now the violence she had only watched on the nightly news has suddenly become very real...and far too close to home.

Josh Travers—The pawn in the deadly game Deke's enemies are playing.

Mike Beauchamp—Is he part of the faceless conspiracy that wants to bring Deke to face their version of justice?

Mary—The only person who can help Deke and Becki find Josh before it's too late.

Luke Ballard—Deke's ex-partner, he should be the one person Deke can trust with his life.

Vernon Petty—Mary's boyfriend, who is unacceptable to the close-knit Beauchamp clan.

Nita Fisher—Becki's best friend. The question is: would she ever betray that friendship?

Prologue

Deke Summers slid the ten-dollar bill across the counter to the tall gray-haired man behind it.

"Ten dollars worth of regular," he said. His voice was soft, but the accent was right, the slow cadence of his childhood found again in the months he'd spent in the South. He had known there would be nothing in his speech to draw unwanted attention, and that was important. As always, he needed to blend into his background like the shadows melted into the dark corners of this room.

"Pump's on," the owner answered, opening the cash register drawer to deposit the ten, the bell loud in the quiet dimness of the small filling station.

"Thanks," Deke said.

He turned from the counter and walked to the screen door and then through it to the outside. There had been nothing in the exchange that had triggered any alarms, no instinctive recognition of threat, but he had used this station at least three times in the months he'd lived in the small Alabama town of Muscova, and he knew that was pushing the limits.

Last time, Deke thought as he disengaged the hose from the old-fashioned tank. This was the last time to show his face here. He didn't want to become familiar to anyone, recognizable, a memory.

The silence he had left behind him in the station didn't last long. The combat boots in which the tall man crossed the wooden floor were touched around the soles with mud, dried and hardened, out of place with their military-style gloss, and his footsteps echoed across the pleasant gloom of the small room. He no longer noticed the smells that surrounded him, the wooden floor itself permeated by years of gasoline fumes and the odor of the sweeping compound that was sprinkled over it weekly in an effort to remove grease and stains. The owner stood behind the screen door that had just banged shut, eyes slightly narrowed against the brilliance of the afternoon sunshine.

He watched as his customer unscrewed the gas cap on the mud-splattered pickup and began to fill its tank. The man stood beside the truck, left forearm resting against the cab's roof, his stance throwing into prominence the muscles in the broad shoulders and long back, clearly revealed by the thinness of the navy T-shirt he wore. The sun glinted on his downturned head, highlighting platinum streaks that blended through the darker gold. Ancient jeans, riding low on his narrow hips, followed the line of well-developed thighs and calves, bunching slightly over the tops of scuffed work boots, worn heels testifying to their age.

The man inside, concealed by the darkness of the sheltered interior, did not refocus his attention when he was joined in the doorway. The newcomer took a long drink from the green glass bottle he had removed from the refrigerated case in front of the counter, tilting his head back as he swallowed, the muscles in his throat moving smoothly under the tanned skin. He reached across to the revolving rack and pulled down a narrow package of peanuts, ripping open the cellophane with his teeth. He carefully poured the stream of nuts into the dark liquid in the bottle he held, and only then did he allow his eyes to find whatever it was on the other side of the screen that had attracted the attention of the station's owner.

They watched in silence as Deke Summers finished filling the truck, allowing the gauge to inch upward to the ten-dollar mark. He replaced the hose and the cap of the tank, each movement carried out with a powerful, fluid grace that was not lost on the men inside the building.

"You know him?" the newcomer asked, taking another swig of the soda, allowing a few of the bobbing peanuts to enter his mouth with the liquid.

"I ought to," the original watcher said softly. "Somehow I know I ought to."

The eyes of the one with the bottle returned to the man outside, who was now climbing into the truck. They watched, again in silence, as Summers started the pickup, the ancient motor coughing in protest a couple of times before it caught. He put it into gear and pulled out onto the empty blacktop. They watched as the truck disappeared behind the heat waves shimmering upward from the asphalt.

"Always pays with cash," the tall man said. "Don't use a card or ask to make a bill."

"A lot of people pay with cash," the other said dismissingly.

"Something ain't right," the owner offered.

It was as far as he could go in expressing aloud what he had felt from the first time the stranger had come into the store. It was like when you were in the woods, in a stand or hidden by the foliage, and despite the care you'd taken, you suddenly felt something was there, watching from the dawn darkness with eyes you couldn't see. Something dangerous. It had been that same weird feeling. Maybe it was *his* eyes. Pale blue. And cold. The kind of eyes that could look through a man.

"Somewhere..." the owner said, and then he hesitated, knowing he was making a fool of himself, but the feeling was too strong to deny and had been building now for weeks. "Somewhere I've seen his face before. And I ought to remember where."

"It'll come to you," the other man reassured, smiling, and then he downed the last of the concoction in the green bottle and set it on the counter beside him, along with a folded dollar bill he'd fingered out of the front pocket of his jeans.

"I don't ever forget a face," the tall man said, his hand

automatically pushing open the screen for his companion to step through; then he allowed the door to close behind the departing customer. He put his hand flat against the pocket on the side of the camouflage pants he wore, to feel the reassuring bulge of his cigarettes. As he lifted the flap to reach his smokes and the disposable lighter, he pushed open the screen door with his elbow. He stood on the covered porch, watching the second customer leave with far less interest than he had expended on the first.

He lit his cigarette, allowing a deep, satisfying draw before he removed it from his lips, using his thumb and forefinger to hold its unfiltered length. Eyes squinting against the rising smoke, he tried to think where he had seen that face. Unconsciously, he shook his head, no closer to remembering than he had been from the first time, several weeks ago, when he had noticed the cold blue eyes. Finally his hand lifted, bringing the cigarette back toward his mouth.

Suddenly the automatic motion was arrested, and it was not until the smoke drifting upward began to sting the widened eyes that he moved again. He pitched the half-finished cigarette into the dirt between the narrow porch and the gas tanks. He stepped down with one foot and ground it out beneath the rounded toe of his boot.

He opened the screen door, hurrying now, retracing his journey across the echoing boards to the small office where he kept his business records. It was not to the neatly organized file drawers he headed. Instead he punched on the switch of the computer system that covered a substantial portion of the desk, incongruous in the confines of the rural station.

There was no hesitation in his search, no fumbling to retrieve the information he sought, obviously comfortable with the technology. And when he had found what he was looking for, he took a moment to relish it.

"Son of a bitch," he said softly, his deep tone touched with awe, unaware of the small smile of triumph that lingered at the lined corners of his mouth as he began to take the steps to utilize the information he'd discovered. "I told you I don't *ever* forget a face."

Chapter One

"Sleep tight," Becki Travers said firmly, pulling the sheet up over the pajama-clad body of her six-year-old son as she bent down to drop a kiss on his nose, "and don't let the bedbugs bite."

"You forgot to kiss Bear There," Josh said, holding up a disreputable-looking teddy.

"A ploy," she accused, ignoring the one-eyed bear, large patches of its plush skin worn off from a couple of generations of cuddling, to turn determinedly toward the door.

"Prayers," he reminded, not bothering to hide his satisfaction as the word halted her progress.

"You really are an awful child," she said, but she recrossed the short distance between them.

"Because I want to say my prayers?" Innocence dripped from the question, brown eyes wide and dark with feigned hurt.

"Because you will use any excuse to put off going to sleep. And you know it. Okay, but it better be something beyond 'Now I lay me down,'" Becki threatened, sitting beside him on the edge of the narrow bed.

"A good prayer," he suggested.

"A sincere one," she corrected. "And not too creative."

"How can a prayer be too creative?" he asked, interested in the concept. "If you're praying for what you want, you

ought to be able to imagine whatever will make you happy
and ask for it."

"Shut up and pray," she ordered, knowing this entire conversation was delay-of-bedtime trickery.

Josh closed his eyes, dark lashes fluttering over the lightly
tanned peach of still baby-soft cheeks, and began to intone
piously, hands angelically folded over the leaping figures of
Batman and Robin on his pajama top, "Now I lay me down
to sleep, I pray—"

The prayer was abruptly cut off as his mother's fingers stole
under the sheet to gently nip his bottom.

"Ouch!" he said, indignantly.

"I will *not* have you make a mockery of praying. Do it
right or I'm gone," she threatened again. Dark eyes, almost
exactly matching hers, studied her face a moment, evaluating
the seriousness of the warning. She met his assessment with
her schoolteacher look, the one that said she meant business,
and finally his eyes closed again. He began to pray earnestly
for every relative he could think of, enumerating the slightest
ailment or problem that each had ever had and offering it up
for the Almighty's consideration.

Becki opened her eyes to watch his face, strands of the fine,
shining black hair falling over his forehead, lids squeezed
tightly together to hold them shut through the endless minutiae
of his litany. She was enjoying, despite her end-of-the-day
tiredness, being with him. Bedtime was very important for
them both. This was when they talked, shared things they
would never have told another member of the very extended
family he was praying for so fervently.

She sometimes worried that they were *too* close, but she
had made a determined effort not to turn him into a mama's
boy. Josh had begun T-ball at four and would play soccer as
a seven-year-old in the fall. He went on fishing trips and va-
cations with aunts and uncles and cousins, automatically invited, thoughtfully included in the activities of the two clans
who loved him.

"And bless my Daddy, wherever he is. Amen," he finished solemnly.

"Wherever he is?" she questioned. That was a new phrase.

"How do you *know* he's in heaven?" he asked.

"Because I know."

"That's not an answer," he complained. "*How* do you know?"

"I *believe* he's in heaven," she amended.

"But you can't know."

"Some things you take on faith. You just believe in your heart they're true."

"But you don't have any proof?"

"Like scientific proof? Something I could show you?"

"Yeah," he breathed, agreeing that was the exact word. "Scientific."

"Nope," Becki affirmed. "Nothing scientific. Just a feeling that he's always watching over us."

"You still miss him?"

"What do you think?"

"Yeah," Josh said, too softly.

"Yes, ma'am," she corrected automatically, but when he didn't repeat the habitual correction, she knew something more was going on in the too-quick mind that functioned behind those dark little-boy eyes. "What's wrong?" she asked.

"I don't think I remember him any more. I try, but I don't think I do."

It hurt. The truth often did, but that was part of the bond they shared—being able to speak the truth.

"It was a long time ago," she comforted. "You were just a baby."

"But you remember?" he asked.

She knew his question was a desire for reassurance that if he couldn't, it would be all right. She was still remembering, still guarding the flame.

"Yes," she said. And then knowing there was more she should explain, she added, "It's all right if you don't remember everything. Just remember something. Pick out one memory and hold on to it. Like catching a firefly in a jar. And every once in a while, it will light up, and you'll remember.''

"When do you miss him the most?" he asked, his voice drowsy with the warmth of the bed, the comforting familiarity of his room and her presence, the sound of the tree frogs coming through the open screen window.

Her mind flickered errantly to the image of sunlight glinting in the blond hairs on John Evans's forearm this afternoon. The tips of his fingers had whitened, curling around the railing he had held on to as he squatted on his heels to look under the small deck, so dilapidated it was dangerous, which she had just hired him to replace. His hand had been strong and brown, the nails close trimmed and very clean. When he stood up, he had propped his arm casually along the top of the railing, looking up at her with blue eyes surrounded by a thick fringe of dark gold lashes, shading to white at their tips.

Her body had reacted, the feelings so unfamiliar they were almost unidentifiable, almost forgotten in the years since a man had touched her. In the years since she had wanted a man's touch. And the most disturbing thing was that it was not the first time it had happened. Her reactions to John Evans had caught her unprepared, without protection against emotions she had somehow thought she might never feel again.

"Mom?" Josh questioned the long delay.

"I don't know," she stalled. *Almost a lie,* she thought, honest with herself if not with him. But she couldn't tell her son that she missed his father most at times when she was aware of her attraction to another man, a man who was almost a stranger. A man who, by his every action, had made it clear he wanted to stay that way. Some other woman might understand the aching loneliness. Lonely for the intimate connections of mind and body and spirit that marriage had been for her. But not Josh, not for a long time yet. Not her family. And certainly not Tommy's.

"It's hard to decide. When do you miss him the most?" she asked instead of answering.

"When everybody's around," Josh said. "Like at the ball

park. When we win and all the dads are there, and everybody's hugging and high-fiving. When everybody belongs to somebody.''

His words recreated the scene he described, too vivid, almost with sound and color. The fathers reacting to the boys' victory with physical contact, unusual for some of them in their relationships with their sons.

"*I'm* there," she offered.

"You're a *mom*," Josh argued with undeniable logic.

"Chopped liver?"

"Close," he agreed, smiling up at her.

A certain type of loneliness, she thought. An indefinable sense of not belonging. She knew exactly what he meant. She had felt it even in the heart of their family. The babble of laughter and conversation surrounding her, so loud it was hard to hear what was being said. The house crowded with the odors of the covered dishes they'd all brought. Crowded, too, with standing adults, tea glasses or coffee cups in hand, waiting to be called to dinner. Crowded with children, flitting dangerously between them, cautioned sharply by first one aunt and then another.

She and Josh were always included, loved and wanted she never doubted, but sometimes the aloneness was more intense there than anywhere else. Seeing the wordless invitation, given and accepted, in the eyes of a couple who had been married only a few months. Or the soft, unthinking curve of an older, work-hardened hand over a too generously rounded bottom and the knowing, unthinkingly sensuous smile of reaction. Or the tender, caress-in-passing touch of arthritis-swollen fingers in a partner's white hair. And then she wished she were anywhere but there. An outsider. Not by choice, but by circumstances.

"Don't cry," Josh said, reaching up to touch her cheek. "Aunt Charlotte will send you to the counselor if you let her know you *ever* cry."

They both laughed, hers a little damp and relieved. She was glad they could joke about the incident. When her managing sister-in-law had arranged Josh's visit to the school counselor without consulting her, Becki had, despite her love for her brother, expressed her anger over Charlotte's interference in no uncertain terms. Since then the relationship had been strained.

"Yeah?" she asked, smiling at him. "Aunt Charlotte and whose army?"

"She means well," Josh said.

She wondered if he had heard someone say that or if the thought and expression had, as seemed to happen too often, simply formed in that almost adult consciousness. Too grown-up. Not by choice, but by circumstances.

"I know," she agreed. She leaned down to kiss the rounded cheek, the delicate skin smooth under her lips. "Go to sleep. Sunday school tomorrow."

"Are we eating dinner at Granny's?"

"God willing..." she began and stopped, waiting for him to complete his great-grandmother's favorite expression.

"And the creek don't rise," he obliged, giggling.

Ritual. Surrounding the daily pattern of their lives with warmth like a quilt, pieced and stitched by loving hands. Softening the sometimes harsh reality of the outside world she watched on the nightly news. It held that world at bay, keeping them safe and secure in a place that seemed unchanged and unchanging.

"I love you," she said.

"I love you, too."

Leaning down, she kissed Bear There and raised the sheet enough to slip the teddy in close beside the small, solid warmth of her son's body. She recrossed the path she had begun before and flicked off the overhead light, leaving behind only the dim glow of the Batman night-light...like a firefly captured in a summer jar.

BECKI TRAVERS'S SIGH as she settled down into the chaise longue the following Wednesday afternoon was loud enough to evoke sympathetic smiles from the four women who were already enjoying the fan-induced breeze on the screened-in porch at the back of Nita Fisher's sprawling old farmhouse.

"Get your exams graded?" Nita asked, shifting her glass of lemonade on the table between them to make room.

"Only first period's," Becki answered, closing her eyes and easing a little deeper into the cushioned wicker.

"How'd they do?" Dianne Handley questioned.

"Like they thought school was already over, and we were just going through some archaic formality."

"You're just too *hard*, Ms. Travers," Donna Jackson said, drawing the *hard* out, her voice becoming a prolonged whine.

It was an effective mimicry, and one they all recognized.

"I just don't know how you expect the little darlings to have a social life with all the work you require," Dianne mocked.

"My daughter's a cheerleader, you know," Barbara Thompson added, "and what with the games and the practices, she just don't have time to do all that work y'all pile on."

A collective groan showed that Barbara's accurate impersonation of that particular parent had led to an instant identification.

"And all those big ole novels you want 'em to read...," Barbara continued, adding more drawl. "Why, you act like you think those things might show up on the AP exam or somethin'."

"Just pure *unreasonable*," Dianne agreed sarcastically.

They all taught some honors-level classes, and this was what they heard every year. Since Becki taught AP English, she came in for more than her share of complaints, but she had really been disappointed with the quality of the essays on her seniors' final exam, so she didn't want to talk about students or their parents, although both were familiar topics when they got together.

"I have a *novel* idea," she said. "Let's talk about something besides school."

"Now there's a conversation stopper," Nita argued. "What do you suggest? The weather?"

"Hot as hell," Dianne offered. "I think that about covers that subject. Next?"

"How about what I'm going to fix for supper tonight?" Donna suggested.

"What's wrong? Your car broken?" Nita asked.

They all laughed. Their mothers might still cook a meal every night, but their generation often gave in to the reality of working all day, of families scattered over the community when supper time came, and of the availability of fast food.

"I guess we could eat at the ballpark. Margaret's got a game," Donna conceded.

"Josh at your mother's?" Dianne asked, lifting the sweat-dampened hair away from her neck.

"Mike picked him up after school for practice. He'll drop him off at home when it's over," Becki explained.

"How's the deck coming?" Nita asked. There was some nuance of tone underlying the question that produced small, knowing smiles on several faces as they waited for an answer.

"Fine," Becki said.

"Fine?" Nita repeated. "That's it? Fine is all you've got to say?"

"What do you want me to say? The deck's coming along fine."

"And how about buns of steel? How's he doing?" Barbara asked. Her teasing grin was open.

"Mr. Evans?" Becki questioned innocently.

"No, Mussolini," Donna said with disgust. "Of course, Mr. Evans. Who else do we know that fits that description?"

"Not me," Becki admitted. "I spend too many hours sitting on mine grading papers. Buns of mush."

"*You* should worry," Barbara said. She was the oldest of the five, and middle age, four children and a sedentary job had taken a toll she readily admitted to.

"I do," Becki agreed, grateful that her attempt to change the subject had worked, "but not enough to seem to be able to do anything about it."

"You make me sick," Nita said. "There's nothing wrong with your butt. Men don't like bony women. Trust me."

"Just look at the magazines. And the movies."

"Breasts and hips. I'm waiting for those to come back in style," Dianne said plaintively.

"And you've been waiting now since what? About 1959?" Nita jeered.

Again, the comfortable laughter of old friends. The other four were married, but since the group seldom did anything as couples, Becki had never felt like an outsider. They were an unofficial support group, female, but not necessarily feminist. They liked men, and although sex was almost never a topic, they openly admitted their devotion to the men they lived with, so they also felt free to discuss the things about the males in their lives that drove them up the proverbial wall.

"And you neatly avoided my question," Nita reminded. "So how's the poster boy for the strong, silent type?"

"Strong and silent?" Becki offered, smiling.

"Cut the crap, Bec. You trying to tell us you don't talk to the guy? Late afternoon sunsets in the backyard. You slip into something soft and sexy, fix him something long and cool, take it out to him and...?"

"I hired Mr. Evans to rebuild my deck because it was so rotten it was about to fall down. We don't talk. I don't fix him anything to drink. He brings his own thermos. And I certainly don't bother to slip into something sexy."

"Why not?" Donna suggested. "You might be surprised at his reaction."

"I'd be surprised if he bothered to look up from sawing and nailing," Becki said truthfully.

"That doesn't sound too promising," Dianne said.

"Trust me. Our relationship is strictly professional."

"But *you* might like it to be a little more personal?" Nita asked, watching her face.

There was a long pause.

"I don't know," she admitted finally.

"Does he turn you on?" Nita asked bluntly.

"Turn me on?" Becki repeated, laughing, relieved at the break in the tension that had grown as they had waited for her answer. "What decade did you get stuck in?"

"Okay, whatever the current terminology is. Does he do it for you?"

Again Becki hesitated. These were feelings she'd never before openly articulated. It had taken her a long time to admit them to herself. To confess them aloud seemed a betrayal of Tommy, but these were her closest friends. If she couldn't talk to them, then there was no one. And she somehow needed to verify that what she felt when she was around John Evans wasn't all that unnatural.

"Yeah," she said. "Yeah, he does."

"Well, thank goodness," Barbara said softly. "I was beginning to worry about you, honey."

"It just seems wrong, somehow. Like I'm betraying my marriage vows. I know that's crazy. At least with my mind I know it, but..."

"Tommy's been dead a long time, Bec," Nita said when she didn't go on. There was no teasing in her voice now. "There's nothing wrong with you still being alive."

"Then you don't think it's...unnatural? The way I feel?"

"Not by a long shot," Donna said. "And if it's any comfort, I'll admit that he turns me on, too. When he was building the girls' playhouse, I 'bout wore Sam out. He made me promise to stop reading those historical romances. Little did he know..."

The comment trailed off in the shouts of laughter that followed that confession. Becki laughed, too, relieved that nobody thought it was strange that she was aware of the good-looking man living next door. Still, she was glad when Barbara's daughter Angelon came out on the porch to ask permission to use her mother's car. And when she left, the conversation moved on to other topics, eventually coming back to the high school where they taught. It was their common bond, and they seldom strayed far from what went on there, despite the fact that the academic year was almost over.

She sat and let the conversation and their friendship swirl comfortingly around her, occasionally throwing in a comment, but mostly content just to listen. Aware again, in their acceptance of what she'd said about John Evans, of how much these friendships meant to her.

WHEN SHE GOT HOME, at least half an hour before baseball practice was scheduled to end, she put her briefcase on the kitchen table and walked to the sliding-glass doors in the den. She edged aside the curtains enough to look outside where a new deck was emerging from the load of wood the local building-supply company had delivered on Monday.

John Evans had already torn down the old deck and hauled the rotten lumber away in the rattletrap pickup he drove. He had been working methodically for three days, arriving before she and Josh left for school and working until darkness forced him to stop.

She was surprised to find two heads bent over the board lying across the sawhorses. The blond one she had expected, but the dark raven's wing fall of Josh's bangs, so close to John Evans's head they were almost brushing against one another, took her by surprise. Despite her natural curiosity as to why her brother would have delivered Josh at home at least thirty minutes before he should have, she stood inside, watching the interaction of the two, who apparently had no idea she was here.

"Two and a fourth," John Evans said, the tape measure he held stretched carefully along the board.

Josh made a small mark with a thick carpenter's pencil. The procedure was repeated on the other side of the one-by-four and Josh again was allowed to make the mark. When the man straightened, returning the tape to its pocket in the cloth carpenter's apron he wore, the little boy looked up into his face, apparently for approval of what he had helped to do.

Becki held her breath, hoping. *A smile,* she thought. Or maybe a quick tousle of Josh's hair with one of those beautiful hands she'd admired on Saturday.

"Good job," John Evans said softly. No smile, no touch.

The little boy didn't smile either, the moment apparently too serious for that response. He nodded, and then the spell was broken. Evans turned to find the electric saw and Josh stepped out of the way, pressing his small back into the board-and-batten of the house. She realized that must be what he'd been told to do while the cuts were made, to stand at a safe distance, and no one ever had to give Josh directions twice.

She released the breath she had been holding and watched the man employ the saw against the board they'd measured together, his movements quick and sure. When he'd finished the cut, he put down the saw and picked up the board to fit it in place. As he began to nail it in, Josh moved closer to watch. The blue eyes of the man lifted at the movement—granting permission, perhaps. Josh certainly responded as if he had, edging nearer, seeking a better vantage point from which to watch the competent hands employ the level and then complete the nailing.

Becki eased up the latch of the door and pushed it open. She couldn't step out because the planks of the new deck had not made it this far. There was still only a void in front of her. The noise of the opening door attracted the attention of the two workers, and both pairs of eyes tracked upward.

"Hi, Mom," Josh said.

"Hi, yourself," she answered, nodding at John Evans, who met her eyes politely before turning away to select the next piece of lumber from the stack on the ground. "What are you doing home?" she asked Josh.

"Bobby Phillips broke his thumb and practice ended early."

"And Uncle Mike brought you home? Without checking to see if I was here?" she asked. She couldn't believe her brother would be that careless. Mike had no kids of his own, but surely he would realize you didn't drop off a six-year-old at an empty house, no matter how bright that six-year-old was.

"Mr. Evans was here. He told Uncle Mike it was okay. He needed to check on Bobby."

Becki automatically sorted out the masculine pronouns. She

glanced at John Evans who was laying the board he'd picked out over the horses.

"It seemed to be an emergency." He offered the explanation without looking up.

"Thanks," she said softly. If she asked Josh any other questions, it would appear she was ungrateful for Evans's agreement to look after the child. Or that she didn't trust him.

She knew Josh well enough to know that he would like nothing better than an opportunity to spend some time with their neighbor. He'd probably managed to convince Mike this was a good idea, told him that they were friends or something. And after all, this man had lived next door for more than three months. Mike probably figured she knew a lot more about John Evans than she really did.

"You better come in and get your bath," she suggested to her son.

"Just a little while longer, please. Just while John's cutting. I'm doing the marking, and he's going to let me measure the next one. Aren't you, John."

"Mr. Evans," she corrected.

"He said I could call him John," Josh argued.

"How about Mr. John," she suggested.

"Mom," Josh protested.

"Why not?" she asked reasonably. Children did not call adults by their first names. That was one of the rules, and Josh was certainly aware of it.

"We tried that," John Evans said, his eyes rising to meet Josh's, "but we decided it sounded like something you'd call a hairstylist."

A *joke,* she realized in amazement. He had just made a joke, and although she was too shocked to respond, Josh giggled appreciatively. She watched the minute reaction of that hard mouth to Josh's laughter, and then his gaze returned innocently to the board he'd selected. She noticed he hadn't taken out the tape, and she knew it was because he'd promised Josh he could do the measuring. All they were waiting for was for her to go inside and get out of their way.

"Fifteen minutes," she said, tacitly admitting defeat.

"Thirty," Josh suggested.

"Don't push your luck," she threatened, sliding the door closed. Once inside, safely separated by the curtains from the masculine conspiracy, she allowed her own smile. Mr. John *did* sound like a hairdresser, she admitted. She was still smiling when she opened the refrigerator to see what looked possible for dinner tonight.

It was longer than the thirty minutes Josh had begged for before she opened the sliding door again. John Evans was kneeling on the edge of the finished section of the deck, which extended halfway across the door opening now. Josh, who was on the ground, was holding a level against the board, which Evans was attempting to lever into its proper alignment so he could nail it into place. Neither looked up this time at the sound the door made.

She waited without speaking while they completed the job. Evans put in the last nail and eyed the bubble of the level himself. "That's it," he said softly, and only then did Josh place the tool on the finished portion of the deck and look up at her. She hadn't realized how dark it had gotten while she'd worked in the kitchen. And she hadn't examined her motives in preparing a meal that was far more elaborate than those she usually fixed for the two of them.

The cut-up chicken she'd bought the previous day was frying in the cast-iron skillet on the back of the stove, and she had boiled several ears of corn Nita had shared from her garden. There was a bowl of leftover green beans warming in the microwave. She had sliced the best of the tomatoes that she'd had ripening on the kitchen windowsill, and corn muffins from a quick-mix package were already in the oven, just beginning to turn golden on top.

"You need to come in and wash up for supper," she said to Josh. "It's almost dark." Maybe reminding him of the fact that Evans wouldn't be working much longer might prevent any stalling.

"Are we having fried chicken?" Josh asked.

She knew the smell had floated out into the dusk through the opened door.

"And corn on the cob," she tempted. Two of his favorites.

"And there's plenty?" Josh's question was hopeful. It was an expression he'd heard all his life, relatives urging them to stay, their offered hospitality sincere. *Y'all stay for supper. There's plenty.* And there always was. She knew Josh was praying she wouldn't let him down.

"There's plenty," she affirmed, and saw the depth of the relieved breath his small body took before he turned to Evans, standing silently on the finished part of the deck. She couldn't see her son's eyes as he looked up at the man who, given the boy's position on the ground, would certainly loom larger than life in the shadowed gloom of twilight.

"Would you like to stay for supper, Mr. Evans?" Josh invited.

Unbelievably, Becki felt her throat tighten at the hopefulness with which the child issued the invitation. There was nothing she could do to protect him if John Evans refused, and she realized that in the waiting silence she, too, was holding her breath.

"I can't," the man said softly.

Another breath disturbed the small chest in the striped cotton knit shirt.

"But thanks for inviting me," John Evans added, perhaps reading the disappointment in the face raised so expectantly to his.

"You ask him, Mom," Josh urged.

She realized what he was thinking—that Evans was simply being polite, waiting for her invitation. Josh had been taught to accept no social engagement without the agreement of the mother involved.

"You're more than welcome, Mr. Evans. There really is plenty, and we'd love to have you join us."

The pale blue eyes, luminescent in the dusky shadows, lifted from their concentration on Josh's face to the doorway where she stood. Becki knew she must be little more than a silhouette, a dark shape against the light behind her.

"Thank you, ma'am," John Evans said, "but I already have plans."

"Some other time, then," she agreed. "I better check the chicken. Come on in, Josh," she suggested casually. She walked back into the kitchen with its pleasant smells of supper almost ready. She left the door open for Josh and deliberately didn't look up from turning the crisply browning pieces of chicken when she heard it close. She listened to his slow footsteps cross the room behind her and finally, distantly, to the sound of water in the bathroom lavatory where he would be washing his hands.

She took the muffins out of the oven, and scooping a few out of the tin, she split them to insert a pat of margarine. She put those on a plate she took out of the cabinet rather than into the napkin-lined basket she'd already set out on the counter. That was for company, and there would be no company to share tonight's meal.

What did you expect? she asked herself a little bitterly. John Evans had made it clear in the months he'd lived next door that he didn't want anything to do with being neighborly, with being friends. She'd set Josh up for this disappointment tonight, frying chicken and letting the aroma leak outside like some kind of bachelor lure. All she'd accomplished had been another rebuff for her son.

She stuck the long two-pronged fork she had used to turn the chicken into one of the thighs with more force than was necessary, taking it out of the hot grease to place it on the paper towels that lined the platter. She had to push the chicken off the prongs with her finger.

"Damn," she said, raising the forefinger she'd just burned to her mouth to suck it better, a habit from childhood.

"He doesn't like me, does he?" Josh's voice came from behind her, from the doorway of the hall that led to the front of the house.

She didn't turn around, but speared another piece of

chicken, her stinging finger still in her mouth. She only took it out to answer, "Of course he likes you. He let you help measure. He told Uncle Mike he'd watch out for you. He just had other plans for supper. The invitation was a little impromptu."

"Then we can ask him again? Give him more warning?" Josh asked, the hopeful note back in his voice.

"We'll see," she said noncommittally.

"That means no," Josh said.

"It *means* we'll see. If the opportunity comes up. You don't want him to think we're pushing him to be our friend."

"Because you don't have a husband?" Josh asked bluntly.

Smiling, she fished the last piece of chicken out of the skillet and turned off the stove. She carried the chicken platter and the plate with the muffins to the table, where she had already placed the corn and tomatoes. She turned back to retrieve the beans from the microwave. Josh sat down at his place, and Becki put a slice of tomato, a spoonful of beans and a small ear of corn on his plate as she answered.

"Maybe Mr. Evans thinks I'm interested in acquiring one," she said, smiling at her son, "and he's been selected."

"I wouldn't mind," Josh said softly.

"If I acquired a husband?" She was a little surprised at the openness of that confession.

"If it was him."

She sat down opposite him, wondering how to respond to that.

"Mr. Evans doesn't act like he wants to be my *friend,* Josh, much less my husband. You can't make people be friendly if they don't want to be. He's a very private person. You know that. And just because he didn't want to have supper with us tonight doesn't mean he doesn't like you. It may mean that he doesn't know how to..." She hesitated, trying to think of a word that expressed the idea without criticism. "To interact with people. He seems to like being by himself. Some people do. And that's his right," she reminded him. "I don't want you bothering him. You can't *make* someone be your friend, no matter how much you like them. You know that from school.''

''I know,'' he agreed softly.

His head was down, eyes on his plate. He had picked up his fork, and with one tine he was tracing the design nature had implanted in the tomato slice. Using her fingers, she reached across the table to place a buttered muffin on his plate and then a drumstick from the chicken. He glanced up, dark eyes full of regret, and she smiled at him.

''I just wanted him to come,'' he said.

''I know. I know you did, and I'm sorry that he couldn't. Now eat your supper.''

She served herself, and they ate a few minutes in silence. She tried to examine her own feelings. What had been her motives in inviting the man next door to dinner? Whatever they had been at the time, she had to admit that she had set her son up for this disappointment. She had known how he felt about John Evans. She might not understand why, but she at least was aware of his feelings. And of her own, she thought. She had even admitted them to her friends this afternoon, and remembering that conversation, she felt the hot flush of embarrassment. Like some kind of lovesick teenager. Daydreaming about a man who had made his disinterest obvious.

She didn't think she had sunk to that level, but maybe she had. The first attractive man she'd come in contact with in years, and she invited him over for an intimate dinner for three. No wonder he'd shied away. Somewhere within her self-disgust, she recognized the flaw in that castigation of her behavior. She had had plenty of opportunities to be attracted to men in the past couple of years. A decent interval after Tommy's death invitations to date had been issued, and bruised by the disinterest of the man next door, the memory of their number was flattering.

She worked with a couple of unattached males. There were a few single men, widowed or divorced, involved in the program at the ballpark. She hadn't had to think twice about turning down their invitations, and there was nothing wrong with any of the men who had asked her out. She just hadn't wanted to go. There had been no interest on her part, at least not until—

"I hit the ball good in practice today," Josh announced, breaking into her introspection.

"Did you?" she asked.

"All the way to the ditch at the back of the playground," he bragged, nodding.

She smiled, wondering how many legs and gloves that ball had rolled through on its way.

"That's great," she said.

"Uncle Mike showed me a new stance."

She put the other drumstick on his plate and half a muffin. At least they had found a safe topic. Something besides the mystery man next door. Even as she thought it, she questioned the phrase. *Mystery man.* Now, why in the world would she call John Evans that?

"And then I hit the ball the first time," Josh announced with satisfaction.

"Way to go," she said, softly, smiling at him, loving him so much it hurt her heart. She was grateful for the resilience of childhood, which had softened the disappointment of the refusal that had been so painful a few minutes ago. Josh would survive his infatuation with John Evans, she thought, secure in the love that surrounded him.

And so will I, she added determinedly. *And so will I.*

Chapter Two

Deke Summers put his head back against the reassuring solidness of the tree trunk behind him. It seemed to be the only steady thing in the night world that had begun to circle sickeningly around him. He knew that what he had done tonight wasn't smart, wasn't allowed within the careful confines of his existence, but the demons had all been howling and he couldn't make them shut up.

Nothing had worked, not even the hard physical labor he used to allow himself to fall into bed, finally exhausted enough to sleep. And he knew why. It had been four years—exactly four years today. Added to the guilt he had always borne was the realization that he had almost forgotten the date, had almost let it slip by without the familiar pain of remembering.

And he was losing the clarity of the memories. Sometimes he could recall nothing more than a flash of long black hair shimmering with light. Or an echo of laughter. But they were fading—at least the vividness. Sometimes he had to think about the shape of her face, try to re-create the feel of its fragile bone structure against his palm. And that was getting harder and harder to do. To re-create. To remember exactly how she had been before...

He closed his eyes, raising the beer to his mouth. He should have bought something stronger, he thought again, but the temptation to get blind drunk had been too much. For once, just once, to be allowed to forget. To silence the demons. To relax—only once—into the dark, comforting oblivion of alcohol.

Too dangerous, a sliver of his brain had reminded. Too dangerous. He wondered if he really cared any longer. There were times he thought he could feel himself coming apart, the images fighting for control of his mind, sometimes very close to winning. In the military they had come up with a name for that unraveling of the mind—posttraumatic stress syndrome. Too much fear. Too much danger. And more pain than the psyche could deal with. He wondered if he had already passed that point, if he were only operating now on some primitive instinct for self-survival. Unbidden, an image flickered into his head, his usual control sufficiently inhibited by the alcohol to allow its formation.

The little boy next door. Black hair and dark eyes. Like hers. He was even aware of the confusion. Not like his wife's eyes and hair, although that was true. But like the mother's. The child's mother. Eyes dark enough to draw him in, like a vortex whirling in space. Compelling. Pulling him. Except—

He shattered the picture deliberately, breaking it into a million pieces by opening his eyes. He raised the can to his lips again and realized it was empty. He crushed it with one hand and then lobbed it at the tree directly in front of him. It struck with a sharp, satisfying clang, and Deke Summers grinned, the movement unfamiliar, the muscles it required almost atrophied from disuse.

Take that, you bastards, he thought. *Damn demons.* Strike ten or was it nine? The baseball analogy had somehow made sense when he'd started chunking cans at the tree, at the demons. But now he couldn't remember the count, and he didn't want to try to figure out how many cans were left. He fumbled into the darkness beside him and was relieved when his fingers encountered metal, cool and damp with condensation. They automatically found the pull-tab and opened it, the sound it made small and sibilant in the darkness, pleasant compared to the clang of the cans hitting his target. He wondered briefly if anyone had heard them, but the soothing night sounds had already begun again around him. He raised the fresh beer to his lips and didn't worry about it any more.

Somebody had to kill the demons, he reasoned drunkenly. *Somebody always had to do the dirty jobs. Somebody...*

BECKI TRAVERS HAD NOT been sleeping soundly. Something had already disturbed the safe, well-known darkness of the dead-end street they lived on. There were only two houses, built for the company executives when the red ore mine had opened. They stood together, tin roofs unchanged, their wooden exteriors painted and repainted by each generation of owners. Hers was the one at the end, edged against the tall oaks and pines of the ever ready-to-encroach woods.

But the sound had not come from that direction, and it wasn't repeated as she lay on her side, listening to the silence. She must have drifted back to sleep, deciding that whatever the noise had been, it did not represent danger, simply an anomaly in the normally peaceful darkness.

She woke with a start when Wimsey landed lightly on her back, his four-footed passage over her body quick, but startling her out of sleep. He had jumped down from the top of her old-fashioned bookcase-style headboard. That was where he slept—never allowing himself to become too accustomed to the inviting warmth and softness of her bed.

She had thought when she'd coaxed the battle-scarred tomcat to spend the first night inside that he would eventually cuddle beside her through the dark, lonely hours like the house cats of her childhood, their comforting weight and purring contentment enough then to keep the night monsters away.

Wimsey apparently had no such intentions. He would tolerate her food and her home, but his independence was too important to be surrendered in exchange for those paltry enticements. He had made his way in the world for a long time without her support, clearly evidenced by the marks he bore, and he obviously did not intend to be seduced into becoming some tame pussycat simply for scraps and a bed.

She sat up, trying to reconstruct the sound that had preceded

Wimsey's departure. No explanation for what she had half heard came to mind, and so she stumbled out of the bed in the darkness to follow the path the cat had taken down the hallway.

When she reached the kitchen, the pet door her brother had installed was still swinging. She didn't turn on any lights, inside or out, but tiptoed across the room to look through the glass panels at the top of the back door, the same door through which Wimsey had obviously just departed. It took her eyes a moment to adjust, although with the spill of moonlight washing the neatly mowed yards, it was really lighter outside than in her dark kitchen.

The tom seemed to move as smoothly as one of the cloud shadows that floated across the close-cut grass, but he was not stalking, not traveling in that low-crouching hunter's crawl from one concealing bush to another. He was padding swiftly, focused single-mindedly on something across her lawn and on the one next door. Her gaze followed his intended path and found the man, white T-shirt almost brilliant in the silver moonlight.

John Evans, she thought, her recognition instantaneous: broad shoulders, strongly muscled arms and sun-streaked hair, its fairness obvious even in the semidarkness. He was sitting on the ground, leaning back against one of the massive oaks that shaded the house he had rented. He held a beer in his right hand, and as she watched he lifted it to his mouth, head thrown back by that motion against the rough bark of the tree.

Searching still for whatever had awakened her, her gaze moved across the yard to another oak, directly in front of the seated man. Around its trunk lay crushed cans, their metallic gleam catching an occasional moonbeam that filtered through the shifting pattern of light and darkness made by the clouds.

Quite a few dead soldiers, she thought, the corners of her lips creeping upward. That had been what she'd heard, the noise that had awakened the cat. The sound of beer cans thrown, apparently with pretty good accuracy, at the targeted tree. She wasn't shocked at their number, although a glass of wine was about the limit of her own drinking. She had grown up with boys who thought a couple of six-packs and Saturday night went together like football and fall.

Her own brothers could down a few, the only evidence of their imbibing the laughter that rang a little louder and the jokes that flowed a little more off-color. Of course, that occasional celebrating, usually limited to an afternoon spent watching some prime SEC game they hadn't been able to get tickets for, was still carefully concealed from their mother, although the youngest son was now almost thirty.

A toot, she thought, still amused. *John Evans was having himself a Saturday-night toot.* And despite the fact that it seemed out of character—at least out of the bits and pieces of character he'd grudgingly revealed in the three months he'd lived in the run-down house next door—she smiled again. Maybe it would loosen him up. Relax him a little. Ease the constant wariness of those blue eyes.

At first, as she'd explained to Josh, she had attributed his standoffishness only to the fact that he was an attractive and apparently unattached male and she was the "widder woman" next door. But there was something else in his eyes, something moving behind the usual Southern so-polite-butter-wouldn't-melt act he automatically carried out. There was a lot more to John Evans, Becki had decided several weeks ago, than met the eye. A lot more than he wanted to reveal. And so far, she thought, leaning against the wood of her kitchen door, he had revealed almost nothing.

She watched the cat butt his head into the denim-clad thigh and then circle around to push against the man's arm. One of the long-fingered hands reached out to scratch the top of the scarred head. Wimsey raised his front feet off the grass, balancing a moment on his hind legs to allow the hand better access to that one spot he could never reach himself.

They certainly seemed to be old acquaintances, Becki thought. It had taken her almost two months of patient work to achieve the first caress the tom had allowed, and her own petting was still done at Wimsey's convenience. There were days when he approached her with the same determination he had just used to demand John Evans's attention and other days when he treated her as if she needed a bath and to brush her teeth, as if her presence strongly offended his delicate sensibilities.

The cat twined around the man's legs, finally putting his front paws up on the corded arm that was propped across the raised knees, the beer Evans was working on dangling loosely from his fingers. The man lowered his head and rubbed it against the tom's. She knew enough about cats to know that was a special sign of favor, a form of greeting felines employed between themselves—but only if there was a certain level of trust between the cats involved.

Eventually, as she watched, the can Evans was holding was crushed by the fingers of his strong right hand and pitched, overhanded, with unerring skill, to clatter against the oak, falling to join the others scattered around its base. Wimsey, who had been taking a moment to wash an apparently bothersome ear, shied away at the unexpected sound.

Seemingly unaware of the cat's frightened retreat, the man leaned his forehead against his knees, his hands locking, almost protectively, over the top of his head. His body seemed to curl inward into an upright fetal position. In the nighttime stillness, Becki could even hear the noise he was making, soft and yet strangely harsh. He was laughing, she realized. So bombed he was laughing—all by himself in the summer moonlight. At least he was that kind of drunk, she thought, smiling, and not the violent, pick-a-fight variety.

Apparently hearing the same strange noises, Wimsey approached the seated man again, this time more cautiously, once again wary. He pushed his broad, triangular face under Evans's arm, nosing upward. The man loosened his hands, reaching out with one to gather the tom under the belly and bring him into the warmth of his chest. He bowed his head again, this time resting his face against the softness of the cat's unresisting body.

It was, however, what Becki had clearly seen when the man

had reached for the cat, his face lifted briefly into the revealing light of the summer's moon, that created the sudden hard tightness in her throat. What she had glimpsed was the undeniable glint of moisture on John Evans's cheeks.

She put her forehead against the coldness of the pane of glass, and for some reason felt her own eyes fill. Men didn't cry in her world. Despite the talk of the sensitive nineties man, no one she knew would be comfortable watching a man cry. Especially a man like John Evans.

She couldn't explain how she knew that those tears were unusual, an unaccustomed release for the man who sat under the sheltering oak, holding the warm body of a living, breathing fellow creature against his chest. Perhaps that gesture had touched her heart because she, too, had at times used Wimsey's fur as a repository for her feelings. Cats respected secrets, and she had known he would never betray her emotional breakdowns. As he would not betray those of this man who, in the brief time she had known him, had seemed to be almost emotionless. Which she now knew he was not.

This was something she should not have seen. Some midnight violation of his privacy that she would not intentionally have made. There was nothing she could offer this man, crying alone in the darkness of the summer's night, the sounds he had made too harsh, too full of pain, a strong, masculine pain that didn't find the release of tears easy. There were no words of comfort he would want to hear. None he would accept. The best she could do would be to return to the bed she had left, leaving him to the primitive connection he had made with the scarred and wary tom.

She put her palm lightly against the glass, letting her fingers slide slowly down its pleasant smoothness. A gesture of farewell, perhaps. Apology. She didn't know. She only knew that she would never tell anyone what she had seen tonight—too agonizingly private to expose. What other secrets John Evans guarded behind that grimly beautiful face she might never know, but this one, at least, was safe.

SHE WOKE AT THE USUAL time, five-thirty, although Sunday's schedule would have allowed her to sleep much later. She no longer seemed able to sleep much past dawn. Maybe the press of responsibilities weighed too heavily on her. Her mother had often called her that—the responsible one.

She lay a moment, thinking about the previous night. Using her feet, she pushed the sheet off her legs, turning her face toward the screen window where the morning light was beginning to appear. She wondered suddenly if John Evans was still sitting beneath the oak that grew so near the property line separating the two houses. And for the first time she wondered if Josh had heard the cans hitting the tree, if he might possibly have risen to investigate those sounds as she had.

For some reason she didn't want her son to be aware of the painful drama she had watched unfold in the moonlight. She raised up enough to see the empty length of the headboard. Wimsey had not returned to finish the night here. She was glad that the cat was not the coward she had been, glad that he had chosen to stay with the man who had wept, alone and pitilessly revealed by the cold moonlight.

She rolled over and sat on the edge of the bed, slipping her feet into the terry slippers on the floor beside it. Rubbing her eyes, she retraced the path she had taken the night before into the still darkened kitchen, her slides making a soft dragging sound over the wooden floors. She looked out the glass of the back door.

There was no one there. No broad-shouldered figure sat beneath the oak, and she was relieved. However, the beer cans were still clustered like unnatural acorns around the base of the other tree.

Despite the fact that she had not taken time to pull on her robe, she took out the clean garbage bag she had put into the kitchen can the night before, and carrying it with her, opened the door and moved in the dawn silence across her lawn to the tree on the property next door. Bending, she began to gather up the evidence of John Evans's Saturday-night toot.

She had made some headway with the cans, a little surprised

at their number, when a hand touched her arm, bare and exposed in the sheer sleeveless gown she wore. She jumped, her startled gasp audible. Turning, she found herself confronting her neighbor. Unshaven, blue irises surrounded by a revealing array of red lines, still wearing the same aged denims and white T-shirt, John Evans stood unsmiling before her.

"What the hell do you think you're doing?" he asked.

"I didn't want Josh to see these," she admitted, blurting out the truth in her haste to make some explanation of why she was picking up his beer cans from his lawn.

The bloodshot eyes moved quickly to the windows of her house and then, still silently questioning, back to hers.

"I think he's made his fascination with you apparent," she added.

He could figure out the rest. She was protecting her son from finding out the man he had picked to admire, out of all the more acceptable male role models that surrounded him, had feet of clay. Josh had heard enough anti-liquor diatribes from the pulpit and from his grandparents and great-grandparents that she knew this would disturb him, despite her own knowledge that it probably didn't mean anything. She had seen no other evidence in the months Evans had lived next door that the previous night's binge was customary.

His lips tightened slightly, and he glanced down at the cans still scattered at their feet.

"Did I wake the boy?" he asked.

His voice was deeper, husky with early morning hoarseness. Or rusted from lack of use, she thought.

"His name is *Josh*," she said, a little challenging. He certainly knew that, although he usually avoided referring to him by name, tried to avoid addressing him at all. *You could at least have put out your hand and touched him the day he helped you measure, the day he so eagerly invited you to dinner*, she found herself thinking. *You touched the cat. Why not my son who thinks you're some kind of superhero? Why not respond in some way to a child who is trying so hard to reach you?*

His lips tightened again at her reminder that he knew the boy's name.

"Josh," he said softly, his concession surprising.

"No, you didn't wake him," she admitted. For some reason there was a tiny emphasis on the last word. She hadn't meant for it to be there, but it was, perhaps a residual anger from the rebuke she had intended. *You didn't wake "the boy," but I watched what went on out here last night. I spied on what you would certainly never want anyone to see.* She didn't think the decision to let him know that had been conscious, but he was astute enough to read her tone and to know what she'd just revealed.

"I'm sorry for the noise," he said after a pause, blue eyes still examining her face.

"It's okay. It wasn't really the cans that woke me," she clarified. "It was Wimsey."

"What?" he asked, confusion clear.

"Wimsey. My cat."

"Wimsey?" he said again, and despite the unsmiling sternness of his mouth, there was a trace of amusement in the question.

"Lord Peter Wimsey," she explained, an explanation she had made a score of times. Wimsey seemed such a strange name for the squat, powerful body and marred head of the tom.

"Because he's blond?" he asked.

He was the first person who had recognized the name, obviously familiar with the fictional English detective for whom she had named the ginger cat. She glanced up at him in surprise and found his gaze direct and openly amused now—direct and open for the first time since she'd met him.

"And elegant," she said softly. She was almost embarrassed to make that claim. But he was—the cat was powerful and elegant and able to take care of himself.

"An aristocrat," he offered.

"Maybe not, but at least smart."

He smiled at her, the movement beginning at the corner of

his lips and edging slowly across. Something turned over in her belly, shifting hotly. She couldn't quite decide if the sensation was pleasant, and while she stood, trying to figure that out, he spoke again.

"At least smart," he agreed.

She returned his smile, unconscious of the upward tilt of her lips, and became aware for the first time that she was wearing nothing but her nightgown. Aware because she could feel her nipples tightening, brushing upward against the soft, cool fall of the aqua nylon, its thinness offering little concealment of the body beneath. Or of its reaction.

She faked a shiver, crossing her arms over her breasts, using her hands to rub along the uncovered length of her upper arms. Her right hand carried with it the swinging white garbage sack with its cargo of cans. Their soft clink was a distraction, and his gaze moved to follow the sound. She felt rather than saw his eyes trace quickly over the low neckline of her gown, before they shifted again to her face.

"I'll get them," he said, holding out his hand for the sack.

She hesitated a moment and then, realizing that it really was his business, she handed him the bag, exposing again the shape of her breasts, pushing too obviously against the gown. She could feel the heat of her blush climbing under the skin of her throat and into her cheeks.

"Thanks," she said, suddenly breathless.

"I'm not going to hurt you," he said, his gaze following the upward creep of blood until it stopped, her cheeks touched with color beneath the smooth olive skin. "I'd never hurt you."

It was such a strange thing to say. She had not been afraid that he'd hurt her, despite the fact that they were alone in the faint light of dawn. Despite the fact that she knew he was still probably a little drunk. Even if he'd slept, as she had, after the incident she'd witnessed, he had drunk enough that he was certainly not yet stone-cold sober.

For some reason she didn't react when the hard, callused palm touched her elbow and then trailed slowly up her arm.

At least she didn't react outwardly. Except to stop breathing, savoring the glide of its caress. He held her eyes with his, waiting for her to tell him no, maybe, but the word wasn't in her head. It ought to be, she knew, her rational mind operating independently of her body. And it was her body, her physical reaction, that was in charge now. She was enjoying what he was doing. The feel of his hand. There was nothing unpleasant or frightening about it, no matter that there should be. She should not be allowing this.

"You're cold," he said softly. He halved the distance between them, still leaving space between their bodies, but he was close enough now that she could feel the heat of his. Pleasant. And his smell. Hot, like the sun he'd worked under all day yesterday finishing her deck. The masculine aroma of a clean body and honest work done in the out-of-doors. It was how the men of her childhood had smelled, like her grandfather had smelled when she was a little girl.

She didn't move away from him, didn't want to, didn't believe that her body was capable any more of stepping back from the warmth he offered. Instead, ridiculously, she remembered how it felt to be held, to be enclosed in strong arms and sheltered against a broad chest. Those memories should have only reinforced the idea of stepping back, of moving away from this man about whom she knew nothing, but instead they drew her, reminding her that this was the way men and women were supposed to be. And were supposed to feel.

His hand had stopped on her shoulder, and then it lifted to cup her face, his thumb sliding along her lower lip, his spread fingers gentle against her throat and the curve of her cheek.

She expected him to say something. Some compliment. Some inane comment, but when his mouth moved it was not to speak. It began to lower toward hers, opening slightly, so that his lips eased over hers and his tongue slipped inside her mouth. No preliminaries. Nothing but the desire that had sprung suddenly between them. She wanted his mouth on hers, and as it lowered to satisfy that longing, she was aware of her lips parting in anticipation.

Insane, her brain warned, but the images of the week during which he'd worked in her backyard, quick glimpses she'd stolen through the protection of the den curtain, intruded. Muscles moving smoothly in the broad shoulders and strong back, their strength tapering to a narrow waist. His long arms reaching upward or the perfect curve of his hip as he bent for materials. The grace of motion unthinking. Unaware of the audience.

His lips were soft, but his tongue was hot and demanding, pushing into her mouth and melding with hers, which was suddenly just as seeking, just as hungry, hungry from months of being aware of him and from years of being alone. Of living without the power of a man's embrace. Some women didn't need this, she knew, or at least they said that, but she had enjoyed the physical aspects of her marriage. And she enjoyed John Evans's kiss. Hot and tremblingly erotic.

He was trembling, she realized, his arms holding her now as if she were fragile, enclosed in the strength of his body, his mouth still examining hers, ravaging emotions she shouldn't feel, shouldn't need. She put her hand up, thinking she should offer some protest. It fluttered without purpose against his shoulder, finding the hard reality of the muscles that shifted under the soft cotton.

She couldn't *want* to touch him, she thought, trying to find some rationality, some reason, in the madness. Her fingers brushed over the roughness of his unshaven cheek, and then slipped naturally to the back of his head, threading into the fair hair, a little long and curling through her fingers, as if hungry for their touch. As his mouth had been hungry. And hers. *Needy. God, she was so needy.*

Her fingers automatically pulled his head downward, urging a closer contact between them, wanting more, unashamed now of the lift of her nipples against his chest. She felt the small, gasping inhalation he made when their pearled hardness touched his chest, but her own breath was harsh also, almost panting. Too revealing of what she felt.

His mouth left hers and traced downward, open, to her throat, the moisture it left on her skin hot. She turned her head to give him access to the low, exposed neckline of her gown. His lips moved, no longer floating over her skin, but pulling across it, wet and demanding. Her fingers locked in his hair, her body heaving suddenly with the depth of the breath she took when his mouth found the dark valley between her breasts. He hesitated, his lips lifting slightly away from her skin, allowing the cool morning air to touch where their sweet heat had been.

"Please," she begged softly.

"Please what?" he demanded, his mouth lowering again to her throat. "Tell me you want this."

"Yes," she said. *Insane,* her brain cautioned again. *This is insane. You don't even know this man. You know nothing about him. Nothing...*

Perhaps her body had stiffened. Perhaps she had made some involuntary or unconscious movement backward, away from him. Whatever she had done, she hadn't meant to do, but his head lifted. He stepped back, releasing her so suddenly that her trembling knees almost gave way. Her hand moved quickly to his shoulder to find her balance.

He was looking into the woods that stretched across from the two houses, absolutely still now, silent. Watching and listening. His wariness was back so strongly that despite the emotional turmoil in her body, she was aware of it. She glanced over her shoulder to the dense undergrowth he was staring into. She could see nothing, no movement. Only dawn stillness. There appeared to be nothing there to attract his attention. Nothing that demanded the searching intensity of the ice-blue gaze that examined every foot of the edge of the woods exposed by the road that ran between the houses and the forest.

"What's wrong?" she asked. She knew how Josh felt. Drawn to him and then pushed away. Like moth and flame. Burned, she thought, examining the analogy. Burning.

At her question, his eyes had returned to her face. Whatever had been in them before, its force frightening her for the first time, disappeared, deliberately controlled, restrained by his will. He glanced once more at the silent woods behind her, and then he met her eyes again.

"This is crazy," he said softly. "Get the hell out of here," he ordered, his voice suddenly harsh. "Get the hell away from me."

Bewildered, she stepped back, removing her hand from his body as if it had been physically scorched.

"What—"

"Go home," he ordered. "Now." He took her shoulder and turned her toward her own yard. The fingers that had been so gentle against her throat bit into her flesh now, grinding down into her collarbone, pushing her away.

"You're hurting me," she whimpered, too shocked to be angry, almost disoriented by the abrupt change.

"Good," he said, his voice savage. "Good," he repeated. "Just go home and stay away from me. Way the hell away."

He pushed her again and she stumbled, almost falling. His hand reached to catch her, automatically, and then he jerked it back, denying his help. His mouth was set in a thin white line and his eyes were almost black, the pupils wide and dilated inside a narrow rim of blue. Something beyond the previous night's binge was going on here. Something abnormal.

"What's wrong?" she asked, too accustomed to reading through teenage hostility to the pain underneath to believe she could be mistaken.

He blinked at her question, at the concern in her tone, perhaps, and then he looked down at the hand that had just pushed her.

"I'm sorry," he said. "More sorry than you'll ever know, but you have to go. Now."

When she didn't move, he looked up again and she didn't think she had ever seen so much pain. It was like looking into the eyes of a soul in hell, she thought.

"Please," he said.

Slowly she nodded, and then she turned and almost ran across the yards, stumbling up the new back steps of the deck he had so carefully and lovingly built. Behind her in the early morning stillness, she heard the crash, loud enough that she was afraid it would wake Josh.

She glanced almost fearfully over her shoulder. John Evans had thrown the white plastic garbage sack she had handed him against the oak, the cans she'd managed to gather before he'd interrupted her still inside. She had looked around in time to watch a few spill from the bag out onto the grass. Evans was standing, head lowered, just where she'd left him.

Turning, she hurried across the deck and fumbled a moment with the sliding-glass door. She stepped inside the dark house, closing the door behind her and leaning against it.

She didn't understand what had happened, but something certainly had. Whatever their relationship had been before, after last night and this morning she knew that it would never again be the same. She just wasn't sure right now whether that was good or somehow frighteningly terrible.

Chapter Three

"But three *weeks*," Becki protested, her hands occupied with filling the paper filter she had just inserted into her grandmother's coffeemaker. The rich aroma of freshly ground beans rose as she poured the coffee in, not bothering to measure, because she had done this so many times.

"Maybe four," her brother said. "We haven't decided. We don't want to be tied to any set itinerary. We just want to be free to explore, to move on after one night or to stay two or three if the area is worth that much time."

"He's too young," she argued, moving between him and the counter to fill the water container at the sink.

"Daniel's going," Mike said.

Caught by surprise, Becki hesitated in cutting off the water until the container began to overflow onto the stained white porcelain.

"He's not even six yet," Mike went on, "so you're going to have a hard time explaining to Josh why you wouldn't let him make this trip and Daniel got to."

"That sounds like blackmail," she accused, pushing the plastic container into its place in the coffeemaker with more force than was necessary and sliding the red switch into the "on" position.

"It sounds like the truth, and you know it. Don't make the kid a sissy."

"I haven't made him a sissy," she denied, suddenly angry. "You know damn well I haven't."

"Maybe not, but he's getting older now and letting him play ball isn't going to be enough."

"He's all of six years old," she said sarcastically.

"And he'll be seven next month. David and Joel are going, and they're only a little older. *And* Daniel," he reminded, his strongest argument, they were both aware.

"But camping out. Maybe if you weren't going to be camping all the time—" she began, only to be interrupted.

"Coffee ready yet, Miss Becki?"

She glanced up to find her sister's new boyfriend standing at Mike's shoulder, his empty coffee cup held out. He waggled it at her, as if to attract her attention, and she felt a trace of embarrassment. Like his insistence on calling her Miss Becki. She knew it was intended as a sign of respect, or his idea of politeness, but it was subtly out of place.

Vernon Petty had attended church with the family this morning, and like the other men he was wearing a white shirt and tie, but the tie was wrong, a little too wide, the material cheap. Becki hated herself for having noticed, so she injected extra warmth into her voice to make up for the fact that she had.

"Five minutes, Vernon. I just put it on."

"You call me when it's done," he requested, smiling at her, returning her friendliness. She knew that he was certainly smart enough to know that he had not quite been accepted by her family.

"Leave your cup, and I'll bring it to you," she offered.

"No, I don't want to put you to any trouble."

"It's no trouble. I'll be glad to."

"No, you just give a yell when it's ready." He nodded at Mike and then, carrying the empty cup, he went back into the noise of the dining room, leaving them alone in the oasis of quietness that the after-dinner kitchen had become.

Trying too hard, Becki thought. *Like a new kid at school, trying to fit in and not really knowing how.* She had sensed her brother's relief when Vernon left.

"We'll spend a few nights in a motel," Mike went on, picking up the argument that had been interrupted by Petty's intrusion. "The boys will be hungry for TV and pizza, and we'll want a hot shower."

"What if Josh gets sick? He's never slept outside more than a couple of nights."

"And he didn't get sick. How many times has Josh been sick in his entire life? He's the healthiest kid I know."

"Because his mother doesn't send him out to sleep in a tent for months at a time," she said, mocking the plan.

"For God's sake, Becki, be reasonable. You know we'll take care of Josh. If he gets sick, if any of the boys get sick, we'll get them to a doctor. Bill's a dad. He's an old hand at deciding when it's time to call the doctor."

"Have you told him?" she asked, her last hope. Maybe if her son wasn't already pumped about the trip, she could reason with him so he wouldn't be too disappointed about not being allowed to join his cousins.

"Bill and I agreed to talk to you first, but I'm willing to bet he knows from the other kids."

Which was probably true, she realized.

"And what am I supposed to do during those three or four weeks?"

"Get a life?" Mike suggested with a trace of sarcasm. "Something beyond grading papers and hovering over Josh."

Get a life. The phrase so carelessly thrown. Unbidden, the image of John Evans's mouth descending over hers this morning intruded. It was a little irrational, she knew, to be angry at Mike's unthinking comment. *Get a life,* she thought again, knowing that the advice would apply as well to the man who lived next door as to her own lonely existence.

"I'm quite content *hovering* over Josh, thank you," she said, tight-lipped. She knew he'd be able to read the anger in her voice. He knew her too well.

"Sorry if I hurt your feelings, but you're not cut out to be a loner, Becki Sue," Mike said softly. "We both know that."

It was his childhood nickname for her. It wasn't really her name, but it sounded so Southern that as a kid he'd decided it should be. This was double-name country. Thank goodness her mother hadn't done that to her. Whenever Mike had used the combination of names during their childhood, it had evoked an automatic cry of outrage and usually some physical retaliation.

They had always been close, not just in age but in temperament. And she still felt a special warmth for him, maybe because he was the only one younger than she and she had felt free to boss him around, or maybe because she had always taken care of him when they were children.

"I'll think about it," she said finally, the silence stretching as Mike waited for her answer.

"Think fast," he warned. "We're leaving Tuesday."

"Tuesday?" she repeated, her voice rising sharply. "That's a little rushed, isn't it?"

"Why not?" he asked, shrugging away her questions. "Bill and I had both decided not to teach summer school this year. None of the boys' teams made it into the play-offs. Nobody was chosen for all-stars. All of a sudden it just seemed like the perfect opportunity, which may never come again, given everyone's summer commitments. We've talked about going for a long time. You know that. When we realized this was the year it was finally possible, we decided to just take off. It'll give us all a reward, a break from the grind. The kids, too. They're pretty good kids, you know."

They *were* pretty good kids, she acknowledged, and so close in age that they were friends as well as first cousins. Stair steps. Joel and David both just turned eight, Josh almost seven, and Daniel the baby. But Daniel would be going with his dad, she thought, and that made a difference.

"And Mary's going to let Joel go? With just you guys?" she asked. She knew he would sense her weakening.

"She's already given him permission. Besides, it'll give her

some quality time with Vernon,'' Mike said. There was dis-
taste in his pronunciation of the name. Their sister's penchant
for unsuitable men was a frequent topic of conversation among
the brothers. Mary had divorced Joel's dad two years ago—a
move no one had criticized, given his inability to hold a job,
his near-abusive behavior—but her current boyfriend was not
considered by the men to be much of an improvement. Vernon
was a little rough-hewn for Becki's tastes, too, but she was
glad her sister had found somebody who seemed to make her
happy.

"I'd think you'd be pleased Mary, at least, has a life,''
Becki said, the memory of his comment still stinging.

"Okay. That crack was uncalled for, but for what it's worth,
I do wish you'd find somebody.''

"Maybe Vernon's got a friend,'' she teased, letting him off
the hook because she loved him so much.

"He does. I've even met a few of them, but they're all as
red as he is.''

"Don't be so critical.''

"I just think Mary can do better than that.''

"There's such a wealth of eligible men around here,'' she
said, letting him hear her disbelief. "Be thankful Mary's found
somebody.''

"Do I detect a note of envy?'' Mike asked, his dark eyes
studying her face.

"I don't know. Do you?''

"You want me to fix you up?'' he asked, his voice soft and
sincere.

"Oh, for goodness sakes, Mike, of course I don't want you
to fix me up. And by the way,'' she said, remembering, "is
that what you were trying to do when you dumped Josh on
my next-door neighbor? Trying to fix me up?''

Mike had the grace to look a little sheepish. "Warren Fisher
had mentioned the guy.''

"Warren?'' she asked, thinking about the embarrassing confession she'd made to her friends. She should have known the
attraction she'd admitted to would at least be shared with their

spouses. She found herself wondering what Nita's husband had suggested to Mike.

"While I was there, I just thought I'd check the guy out, Becki Sue. To see if he's..." Mike hesitated.

"Acceptable?" she finished for him. "Better than Vernon? Well, did he get the Beauchamp stamp of approval? Or are you going to send the rest of the crew out to give him the once-over?"

"Whoa. Calm down. I really thought you might be home and I could leave Josh, not have to take him to the hospital. Instead, I found Mr. Evans."

"And?"

"And what?"

"What'd you think?"

"He seemed okay. Josh thinks so."

"A bad case of hero worship," she admitted.

"And you're wondering if the guy deserves it. Or are you worrying because you think Josh's trying to replace his daddy?"

She didn't answer except for a small shrug of her shoulders.

"Then letting Josh go with us for a while seems the perfect solution. Maybe distance will lessen his fascination."

"But you'll be gone so long," she objected again. "And camping out the whole time—"

"There's nothing dangerous about what we're planning," he said patiently. "Drive west, enjoy the scenery, tour some of the attractions, camp out at night, teach the boys some survival skills along the way."

"Survival skills?" she echoed, shaking her head and smiling at an idea she thought ridiculous for such little boys. So damn macho.

"How to get along in the woods," he said. "In case they're ever lost. It could be invaluable. And it'll make us all feel safer about them on the next fishing or hunting trip."

"No hunting?" she asked suddenly, looking up into his eyes, which were smiling now because he knew he was going to get his way, that he had talked her around.

"Just sight-seeing. Just learning to live in the outdoors, to get along with nature."

"No guns," she demanded softly. She had been raised in a family where half the men were avid hunters, like Mike, and the other half thought hunting was about the most boring activity ever conceived. Although she had been carefully taught how to handle a gun by her father when she was growing up, Becki had always had an aversion to them.

"No hunting. It isn't that kind of trip."

"Okay," she said softly, not feeling that she really had a choice. "If Josh wants to go."

Mike put his arm around her shoulders and squeezed her tight. "Don't worry, Mama," he said. "Nothing's gonna happen to your baby boy."

"It had better not," she said, poking her finger into his chest. "If it does, you're dead meat, little brother. *I'll* do the hunting in that case."

"Ow," he said, backing away from her finger, but smiling. "That thing's dangerous," he objected. He tugged a strand of the shining midnight hair that almost touched her shoulders, curving softly around the oval face. "Don't worry," he advised, the dark eyes serious now. "I'll take care of Josh. And I'll see that nothing happens to him. That I promise you."

BECKI WAS SITTING on her den couch the following Tuesday night, feet up, a low-fat microwave dinner in her lap and the latest issue of *Newsweek* magazine, which had come with today's mail, carefully balanced against her knees as she ate. *A good time to diet,* she had thought. While Josh was gone and she wasn't responsible for seeing that he had balanced meals, she could cut a few calories, maybe lose that stubborn ten pounds she'd put on while she'd carried him. She remembered her mom's chiding the last time she'd mentioned her weight, reminding her that she wasn't a teenager any longer and that she'd only make herself miserable if she tried to look like one.

She had put on her long Crimson Tide nightshirt, although it wasn't bedtime, only an hour or so after the fall of summer's late-arriving darkness. The TV was on, its volume deliberately low enough that she wouldn't be aware of words, simply background noise to defeat the loneliness.

She had seen them off, smiling as if she were enjoying the children's excitement, as if she were looking forward to the trip as much as the masculine contingent that had set out very early this morning on the first leg of the extended vacation. All day the silence of the empty house had echoed around her.

If he hadn't gone with his uncles and cousins, she had reasoned during those long afternoon hours, Josh wouldn't necessarily be with her. He might be at a friend's, or spending the night with his grandmother, or playing under the shade of the sweet gum tree at the back of the property, talking to imaginary villains as he climbed in its accessible branches and jumped out, the cloak she'd made from an old half sheet dyed black billowing behind. Batman, she thought, singing the staccato TV series theme in her head.

She sighed, glancing up at the program, some sitcom that the critics were wild about, but she had never been able to identify with the aimless lives of the characters. They were so different from the person she was, from her upbringing. She had finished college in three years, never changing majors or having seen the need to take a "break." To her, college had been a job, a task to be completed before she moved on to the next one—her first teaching job, so green and uncertain that an unthinking remark from some kid could make her cry, make her lose sleep. She had learned a lot in the ten years since she'd begun. Marriage and having Josh had helped. And then Tommy's cancer.

With his illness, the insecurities had shifted into place, her priorities automatically straightening themselves out in the agonizing reality of life and death. All those silly things she had once thought important were revealed in their proper significance. Or insignificance.

The noise that interrupted those memories was indistinct, like the brush of a branch against the side of the house. She had been so unaware of her surroundings as she'd let the fleeting images of the past invade her head that she wasn't really sure she had heard anything.

Maybe the TV, she thought, her gaze returning to the screen. There was a car commercial on, and as she watched it she knew that the noise—if there had even been a noise—hadn't been related to that. It hadn't come from that direction. Out back, she realized. On the deck, maybe.

She could feel her heart beginning to race a little. She was listening so hard that it seemed she could hear the increased flow of blood in her straining ears. She reached downward for the remote that was lying on the floor beside the couch and silenced the figures on the screen and the annoying laugh track.

The stillness that surrounded her was no better than the canned laughter had been. She waited a long time, the dinner in her lap slowly cooling, forgotten. She knew the sliding door was locked. She had checked it and the front door before she'd settled in for the night.

She wondered what she was afraid of. She couldn't remember when there had been a crime in this tiny rural community. Although the road was isolated by the surrounding woods, she had never been afraid out here before. Was she simply spooked because she hated the idea of being without Josh? It would be a very long three weeks if she reacted this way to every unidentified sound.

She turned the TV back on, deliberately pushing the button that controlled the volume until the words of the people on the screen were distinguishable. She closed the magazine, dropping it on the floor beside the remote and turning down the lamp behind her. She tried to concentrate on the show as she ate her lukewarm meal.

Gradually she lost the tension, relaxing into the world of the sitcom and into the tranquillity of the familiar night sounds outside. No monsters in the dark, she thought, smiling at her anxiety of a few minutes earlier. There was nothing in her safe, peaceful world to be afraid of.

She never remembered turning off the TV, but when she

awoke, having apparently drifted off to sleep, the house was silent and dark except for the small lamp on the table at the end of the couch. She did remember turning down its three-way bulb to the lowest intensity after she'd decided not to read, and evidently she had gone to sleep with the lamp on.

She was disoriented for a moment, the contours of the den furnishings unfamiliar in the middle of the night. She didn't know what had awakened her, discomfort from sleeping in the cramped position the couch demanded perhaps, but she sat up, pushing her hair out of her face, trying to work up the energy to make the trek to bed. Almost subliminally she became aware of the figure standing in the hallway leading to the front of the house. A man, was her first bewildered thought. There was a man inside her house.

"We're not gonna hurt you," he said, his voice deep and richly Southern.

It was what John Evans had said to her. That strange comment he'd made before he'd kissed her.

"John?" she questioned softly. He shouldn't be here, not in the middle of the night, was the next thought that tumbled into her sleep-fogged mind.

The man, simply a blacker silhouette against the surrounding darkness, turned, and only then did she realize there must be more than one person standing silently in the dark hallway, watching her sleep.

"You were right," he said, the statement not addressed to her, but to someone who stood out of sight, someone near enough, however, to hear that low assurance. And then the speaker turned back to face her, his features still hidden by the darkness. "You expectin' him?" he asked.

"No," she denied. "I'm not expecting anyone. It's the middle of the night. I just..." She wondered why she was explaining her unthinking question. The important one was why they were in her house. Stunned by the unexpectedness of it all, unaccustomed to worrying about the dangers others might live with daily, she was still struggling to understand what was going on.

"Who are you?" she asked.

"Don't you be scared, Ms. Travers. Nobody's gonna to hurt you. You just got yourself mixed up in somethin' that..." The deep voice hesitated, and Becki waited, digesting the information that he knew who she was, that he knew her name. This, then, was not a break-in on some random victim. "You got yourself mixed up in somethin' that don't concern you," the man continued. "Somethin' that's got nothin' to do with you."

"Then why are you—"

Her question was cut off by his order, "You just be real quiet and cooperative, and I promise nothin's gonna happen to you. You just do like you're told, and this will all be over soon."

"What do you want?" she asked.

"We just want to talk to the man next door," he said, his voice still a near whisper, but there was some shading to his tone that didn't fit the banal explanation.

"With John Evans?" she asked. *Had they gotten the houses confused in the darkness?* she wondered. But he'd said "the man next door," and he'd known her name.

"That's what he's callin' hisself," the man agreed. He turned his head again and said something into the darkness surrounding him. As silently as the shifting shadows they resembled, the shapes that she hadn't even realized were men began to move from behind him and through the doorway into the room where she was sitting. As they came into the light, they became more distinct but not any less frightening.

The men moving into her den were dressed in dark clothing, their faces covered by blacking, making the whites of their eyes gleam in the dimness like those of some feral animal. They were wearing boots, she realized, from the noise of their passage over the wooden floors, and they were all carrying guns. Rifles or some kind of automatic weapons. She sat on her own couch and watched her den fill with armed men who stood in a semicircle before her, their continued silence far more menacing than the soft, familiar cadence of their commander's speech had been.

The realization of who they must be was sudden, but immensely reassuring. Not robbers. These highly disciplined men must be some sort of law enforcement, maybe even the military. She couldn't imagine what John Evans had done that required this display of force, but she knew that she had done nothing; therefore, she had nothing to fear from these men. These were the good guys.

"You're the police," she said, still addressing the man who stood hidden in the dark doorway, the one who seemed to be in charge. "Some kind of SWAT team?"

She heard his soft laughter and was aware of the answering amusement in the relaxed shifting of a few of the men around her.

"Somethin' like that," the leader agreed, his tone indulgent now with her confusion, patronizing. "Some folks might call us a SWAT team. We might prefer some other term."

"But you are law enforcement? Or the army?"

"Ms. Travers, you can be sure of one thing. We ain't the *authorities*." He spat out the word, his voice filled with contempt. "We ain't gonna rush into your home in jackboots and flak jackets and start shootin' up the place. We ain't here to hurt law-abidin' citizens. We just need you to take a little trip with us. A short little visit next door. You just relax and cooperate, and this'll all be over before you know it."

"What do you want me for?" she asked. Nothing made sense, especially his disclaimer of authority. Who the hell were these people? Her initial panic subsiding, her brain was beginning to function again, but nothing tied together, nothing he'd said.

"What we got here, Ms. Travers, is a hostage situation."

"Hostage?" She repeated the word, examining it. John Evans was holding someone hostage? "But that doesn't explain why you need me," she offered, still trying to piece it together.

Again his laughter drifted out of the darkness of the adjoining room. "Why, ma'am, I'd have thought you'd figured that out by now. We need you to *be* the hostage. You're gonna be the bait that'll lure that ole boy right out of his hidey-hole. We've been lookin' for him for a long time. Lots of folks have. And with your help, we're finally gonna have us a capture. Yes, siree, we're finally gonna do the right thing for that boy."

"For Mr. Evans?" she asked carefully, making sure she understood who they were after. She knew she sounded like an idiot, but she still didn't have any idea what they were talking about. How did they think they could use her to get John Evans to do anything? She barely knew the man, but suddenly in the back of her mind stirred the realization that she knew far more about him than anyone else in this town. Things like how his mouth tasted against hers, about the strength of his body holding her. Could they somehow know that? *My God,* she realized, *they know about Sunday morning. That's why they think—*

"That's what he's callin' hisself," the leader interrupted her frightening realization, "but that ain't his name. That man livin' next door to you is Deke Summers. You ever hear that name, Ms. Travers?"

"No," she whispered, shaking her head. She had always known there was something hidden about John Evans, something mysterious and dangerous. *Summers,* she corrected herself, implanting the name he had said into her memory. *Deke Summers.*

"I just thought maybe somebody might 'a mentioned him to you. Your menfolks or somebody."

"No," she said again.

"Well, it don't really matter if *you've* never heard of him, 'cause there's more than enough people who have, and those people won't ever forget. They got long memories," he added softly. "Especially for men who kill little babies. You got a boy, don't you, Ms. Travers?"

She shivered at the threat in his cold voice. *Josh,* she thought, automatically afraid for her son, and then she remembered that he wasn't here. *Thank God, Josh is safe. Away with Mike.* Even she couldn't find him if she wanted to—no set itinerary, the men had said again this morning, bragging about their freedom of movement, freedom from schedules.

"Yes," she said. Nothing else. She didn't intend to give them any other information.

"I know he ain't here. Don't you worry about your son, Ms. Travers. Don't you worry about anything. You just ease up from there now…" He paused, waiting for her to obey, and on trembling knees she did, shivering slightly with reaction. The voice from the doorway went on when she was standing, clearly directing the operation, "And you stay real close to Richard there. Richard, you speak to Ms. Travers so she'll know who you are."

"Ma'am," said the nearest man, standing almost at her elbow.

The voice was younger, more like the adolescent timbre of her students' voices, and more than a little nervous. Surely too young, she thought, to be involved in all this, to be carrying guns and threatening people.

"Now, the rest of us are gonna go next door and wake up Summers and tell him about your…situation," the commander went on. "You and Richard are gonna wait real quiet out in the backyard. It won't be long, I promise you. He ain't gonna take no chances with you. That ole boy don't make the same mistake twice. You even look like her, you know. Same hair and eyes. He tell you 'bout his wife?"

"No," Becki said, feeling as if she were in the middle of a nightmare. Surely she'd wake up and this would all be over. Things like this didn't happen to real people. Things like this were the stuff of movies, not reality. At least not her reality. "I don't even know Mr. Evans—Summers—whoever he is. He built my deck. He lives next door. I don't know anything about him. He hasn't told me anything. I don't know what you're talking about."

"Well, I don't want to seem to be doubtin' the word of a lady, but that ain't what we've been told. No siree, that ain't the story we got about you and Summers.'' The sarcasm was heavy now. He was laughing at her, enjoying making her afraid, and that made her furious.

"I don't know who told you what, but you've made some kind of mistake. I don't know anything about him. I told you—"

"That ole boy's been on the run a long time," he said, breaking into her denial. "I don't know that I blame him for gettin' him a little whenever he can. And it's a mighty convenient setup he's got hisself here. Gettin' it from the widow lady next door. I told y'all that boy was smart." It was obvious by the pronoun that he was directing his observation to his followers and not to her.

"That's a lie," she said hotly, but she sensed their amusement at her vehemence. There had been a couple of responding titters from the men in the den. They were just playing with her, she realized suddenly, and panic rose in her throat so strongly that she was almost sick. She couldn't allow herself to believe anything they said. None of their assurances about her safety. She was as certain now of their enmity to her as she had ever been of anything in her life. Despite those promises veiled in politeness, these were not nice men. And they didn't like her one damn bit, because they thought she and Summers…

Her mind hesitated at putting that suggestion into words. It was so far from the reality of the cold distance Summers had maintained between them. This, of course, was why—because he knew these men were out there, looking for him. And now that they'd found him, they intended to use her to get to him.

The knowledge of what they believed and of their dislike of her was terrifying, but at least it clarified her course of action. Pretend to cooperate until the opportunity presented itself to get away. Despite what they had promised, they wouldn't care if she got hurt. Their only concern was taking John Evans—Deke Summers, she corrected herself again— and they believed, with what they had been told about her relationship to him, that having her as their hostage would finally allow them to do that.

At the commander's instruction, the men moved out the sliding door and across the new deck, their passage as carefully noiseless now as that into her house apparently had been. It was very dark outside, and unwillingly she remembered the moon-washed night she had stood in the safety of her kitchen and watched John Evans. *You even look like her,* the man had said. Like Deke Summers's wife. And she wondered what role that woman had played in the events leading up to tonight's.

Under the directions of the man named Richard, made voicelessly with a movement of the weapon he held trained on her with casual efficiency, she walked to the back of the yard to stand under the low branches of Josh's favorite tree. There were reminders of her son all over this small area—like the crudely lettered sign he'd nailed so carefully to the trunk. She couldn't read its inscription in the darkness, but she knew it by heart. BAT CAVE—the red letters painstakingly painted with a jar of her craft paints and her best brush, taken and used without permission.

She blocked thoughts of Josh from her mind and forced herself to concentrate on the here and now, on her situation. She watched the men who had invaded her house creep across the lawn toward the shadowy bulk of the one next door. She was still trembling, her reaction a combination of fear and the effects of the night's slight chill after being forced to leave so abruptly the warmth of sleep and safety.

When the last of the men had disappeared, she waited, ears straining against the silence that surrounded her. All the night creatures were aware of the unusual activity, their familiar noises hushed. It was as quiet out here as a tomb. As she thought that, she shivered again.

The one they had called Richard made a convulsive movement and some sound, guttural and quickly cut off. She glanced into the darkness beside her to watch the man who had been standing there rise, like magic, off the ground. Looking up to follow his body's ascent, she found Deke Summers

carefully balanced in the low vee of the branching trunk of
the tree, holding her captor off the ground by the forearm he
had fastened around his throat. She watched the man's eyes
bulge at the pressure Deke was exerting, their terror-stricken
whites vivid against the black paint that surrounded them. The
man fought to relieve the implacable pressure, the combat
boots kicking fiercely, rocking his hanging body, and desper-
ate fingers tearing at the corded arm that held him relentlessly.
Eventually the struggling figure stilled, his legs straightening
again to hang limply, booted toes barely touching the damp
grass. As she watched, the body was lowered silently to the
ground beside her, and she had to move her bare feet out of
the way of its boneless drop.

He's dead, Becki thought. She had just witnessed a murder.
She looked up from the body sprawled at her feet and into the
eyes of Deke Summers. Like the men who were hunting him,
he was dressed in clothing that blended with the surrounding
night, but his face had not been blackened. Its strong planes
and sculpted features were clearly visible, even the color of
his eyes. Grasping a branch with one hand, he swung down
from his perch, landing beside her with a small thud. His hand
found her elbow and gave a small reassuring squeeze.

"You killed him," she whispered, her eyes, dilated with
shock, locked on his.

"That's not likely," he said softly.

"But I *saw* you," she whispered, jerking her arm from his
hold.

"It takes a more than that to kill a man," he said. "And I
figure we've got maybe thirty seconds before he comes to."

Bending, he quickly looped silver duct tape he had taken
from the side pocket of the camouflage pants he was wearing
around the man's head, securely covering the mouth he'd first
closed with pressure from his hand under the slack chin. He
then taped the limp wrists together and dragged the body further back into the shadowed depths under the tree.

When he'd finished, he looked up into her strained face.
She was shivering uncontrollably. He knew he couldn't afford

to let her go into shock. There was still too much that had to be done.

"Josh?" Deke asked, trying to make her think about something besides what she'd just watched him do.

She blinked, but she answered him immediately, despite whatever she believed was going on here. *Good girl*, he thought. *Just keep functioning until I can get you out of this. Just hold on.*

"He's not here," she whispered. "He's with Mike."

"Mike?"

"My brother. They're on a camping trip."

Which explained why he hadn't seen Josh today, Deke thought. Relieved that he wouldn't have to go back into the house to bring out the child, he nodded. "Then let's go," he said, taking her elbow again and pulling her toward the woods.

"Go?" she said. "Go where?"

"Anywhere but here. They're going to figure out pretty soon that I'm not inside that house, and then they're going to come looking for us. You want to be here when that happens?" he asked calmly, hiding his impatience.

"No," she admitted.

"Then let's go," he said again. Still holding her elbow, he eased into the woods that bordered the back of her yard, guiding her through the thick undergrowth. With his grip on her arm, she had no choice but to follow. He released her when they broke onto more open ground, but they had only gone a few yards when she realized how handicapped she was without shoes. Every twig, rock and pinecone was agonizing to her tender feet as she trailed behind his steadily moving figure. When her toes connected sharply with an exposed root she hadn't seen in the darkness, she stumbled and almost fell. She gasped aloud with the unexpected pain.

"What's wrong?" he asked.

"My feet. I don't have any shoes."

From behind them came the first sounds, voices, the words as yet indistinct, though they both knew what those noises meant. The men had discovered Deke Summers had once more evaded the capture they had seemed so sure of. They would realize, however, that he hadn't had time to go far. When they discovered that she, too, was missing and when they found the body of the man they had left to watch her—then would begin the pursuit, following them through the tangling vines and punishing branches of the forest.

Deke Summers took a step closer to her, and suddenly she was afraid. His action was unexpected and again she gasped a little with shock as he bent, locking his arm around her hips and lifting to throw her unceremoniously onto his shoulder in a classic fireman's carry, her head and shoulders dangling over his back. Turning, he began to move again through the darkness of the woods, ignoring her almost voiceless protest.

She tried to raise her upper body, but his furious growl convinced her. "Be still, dammit, or you're going to get us both killed," he ordered.

Despite the questions she had about what was going on, Becki decided she was better off with a man who would slow his own escape to carry her away from his pursuers than with the strangers who had invaded her home tonight. She might know little about Deke Summers, but what she did know was far more reassuring than the nothing she understood about the men who were following them. *Bullies,* she decided, thinking how apt the old school-yard term was for the group who had come in the middle of the night to take, sleeping and unaware, the man who was now carrying her.

And then she didn't think about them any more. Deke Summers had broken into a jog as soon as they'd reached the relative openness in the heart of the forest. Despite her weight, which he seemingly carried without effort, he was moving at a steady pace between the dark trunks of the tall pines, carrying her always farther away from the familiar security of home.

Chapter Four

Becki could not have estimated how long Deke Summers kept up his distance-eating pace. Gradually she felt the thin cotton of the black long-sleeve knit shirt he wore grow wet with sweat, clammy and uncomfortable under her body, chafing the softness of her breasts and stomach.

As the first streaks of dawn were starting to bleed through the night sky, she wanted to suggest that he put her down, that she could walk, but her feet were still burning from the short distance she had managed on her own when they'd begun, and she knew that would only slow them down. However, despite his strength and obviously excellent physical condition, she also knew there had to be a limit to how far he could carry her.

Still, she was not prepared when he stopped. Since she had only been able to catch occasional bouncing glimpses through the woods behind them, she was suddenly afraid he'd encountered some danger, some menace blocking the path of their retreat.

He eased her down, bending his knees to allow her feet to touch the ground before he released her. He even kept his hand under her elbow until he knew she'd found her balance. He looked back in the direction they'd come, listening for any sound of pursuit. There was nothing in the forest behind them, no sign even that they were being followed. The only noise was his own harsh breathing, panting with the exertion he'd made.

Deke turned back to find her looking at him.

"Everything's okay," he reassured. "I just needed a breather."

"Are they back there?" she asked. "I can't hear anything."

"They're there. But I think we've managed to put a little distance between, and they don't know the direction we're heading."

"*Are* we heading somewhere?" she asked. She hadn't thought about where he might be carrying her. Just away. Away from the pursuit.

"Always have a destination," Deke advised softly, gentling her fear with his confidence, exactly as he would have done with a frightened animal, with a spooked and terrified horse.

"And we do?"

"Just a few miles away."

Becki tried to think, more familiar with the area than he was, she believed, but she was so disoriented by their passage through the woods that she really had no idea where he might mean.

"The highway," he said, reading the questions moving behind her transparent features. Deke was surprised at how clearly he'd been able to follow what she was thinking. But, then, that was what had gotten them into this situation to begin with. His awareness of what she was thinking.

"But…?"

"There's a car. And some equipment. No shoes, I'm afraid. I didn't know I was going to have to take you with me."

He waited patiently for the impact of that information to reach her brain. He knew everything was happening too fast for her to assimilate it all. She had had no warning, although he had considered, after he'd been stupid enough—drunk enough, he amended—to kiss her, whether or not he should prepare her for this possibility. And then he had decided that he'd been wrong—too edgy and suspicious. Living the way he had for so long would do that to a man, he knew, so he had seen no need to frighten her with his bogeymen. No need until they had shown up tonight. And by then it was far too late to explain to her what was going on.

"Go with you?" she repeated, her voice rising slightly at the end of the phrase.

"You can't stay here," he said, glancing back into the midnight forest behind them.

"Why not?" she asked. "I live here. I don't have anything to do with this. With you."

His gaze came back to her face, studying it, evaluating how much he should tell her.

"*They* think you do," he said softly.

"They think we're…" She paused, searching for words to describe what they'd suggested, words less offensive than the crude phrase the leader had used.

"I know," he said, saving her the trouble.

"But that's not true. I…" She paused again. The truth had little value here. What was important, and dangerous, was *their* perception of the truth. "They said you killed babies," she accused, suddenly remembering what she'd been told, but at the flinch of pain in his eyes, quickly controlled, she was sorry she'd repeated it.

"No," he denied. Nothing else. No explanation.

"No?" she said, still a question, thinking of his treatment of Josh, his aversion to allowing the child to get too close. Could it be… She blocked that thought because instinctively she knew it wasn't true. This man didn't kill children. No matter what the voice from the darkness had suggested.

Deke didn't answer her. He was tired of defending himself against their version of events, which it had never done him any good to deny.

"I'm sorry I said that," she whispered. "I know it's not true."

"Do you?" he asked, the quiet bitterness in his voice unexpected after its calmness. "And how do you know?"

"Because…" she said and then paused. *Because of the way I feel. Because I couldn't feel about someone, be attracted to someone who would do that.* "I just don't think you could do that."

He turned his head again to the almost impenetrable darkness behind, hiding his eyes, she realized. Not allowing her to read his reaction to the disclaimer she'd just made.

"Why did they say that?" she asked.

Head still averted, he answered, his voice carefully emotionless again. "Because..." He hesitated, wondering why he was bothering. *Because it matters,* he admitted to himself. *Because for some reason it matters what she believes.* "Something went wrong. A long time ago. Something I was part of."

"Did *you* do something wrong?" she asked.

Right and wrong, he thought. Black and white. Good and evil. All the easy divisions people make every day. *Did you do something wrong?* It was the question he lived with. Was there anything he could have done differently? Anything that would have made a difference in the outcome? And still, after all this time, he didn't have an answer.

He turned back to meet her eyes, wide and dark, searching his face for the truth. He let her look at whatever was there, wondering what she saw. Too often when he looked into the mirror now, he no longer knew the man who was reflected there. A stranger, after so many years on the run, years of living someone else's life.

"We have to go," he ordered, putting an end to the discussion. Bending, he put his arm under her hips, lifting her slight weight with the muscles in his thighs. This time she made no protest as he picked her up. Sighting on the stars he could still see through the branches that spread darkly above their heads, he moved off again in the direction of the car he'd left at the other side of the huge woods that backed the two houses, always ready for a situation such as the one he'd been confronted with tonight.

Only, as he'd confessed to Becki Travers, this was a journey he had never expected to make with a woman. That possibility had not entered into his careful planning of an escape route, planning that was as automatic to him now as buying groceries for the upcoming week was to normal people. This was his life. Not one he had chosen, but one that had been forced on him. And one that now included a responsibility he had never wanted. The responsibility for the woman he carried, and for the dark-eyed little boy he knew he had to find.

WHEN THEY STOPPED AGAIN, it was full light and the heat was beginning to build even in the shaded depths of the woods. It had taken him far longer than he had hoped to reach the automobile, but he had been hampered, of course, by the burden he carried.

He eased her down by the old black Trans Am he'd bought two months ago and hidden here. He had fixed the mechanical problems he'd found, working on the car on his way to and from the carpentry jobs he'd taken. An hour stolen here and there, not enough discrepancy to cause comment. Nothing in his careful existence was allowed to draw attention to himself or to seem out of the ordinary. That was the key to hiding successfully—becoming invisible to the people who surrounded him, people who were exactly like whatever role he'd undertaken.

He allowed himself to lean against the car for a moment, a brief respite to catch his breath. His clothing was wet with sweat, but the unpleasant sensation was something he unconsciously ignored, his long-ago military training standing him in good stead. It had taught him to disregard pain and tiredness, setting his mind on the goal ahead rather than on the trivialities of the present. He glanced up finally at the woman he had carried for miles through the dark woods, standing silently just where he'd put her down. Watching him.

Becki had been vaguely aware that her cotton nightshirt was wet with her rescuer's perspiration, but she hadn't realized exactly how revealing that dampness was until Deke Summers's gaze skimmed over her body, touching on the small peaks of her breasts, clearly outlined against the material. She put her right hand on her left shoulder, massaging as if trying to relax a cramped muscle. At that protective movement, his eyes lifted, finding a focus beyond her, examining the woods behind them.

"Now what?" she asked.

His eyes came back to her face at the question. He had felt the responses to her small body in his, hard and suddenly aching. And he fought them. Denying, as he had denied all along. He was too near the edge, too close to losing control—and that really scared him. Control was how he kept functioning. He had known he was in trouble here. First, the pull of the little boy, seeking his attention. And then his physical response to the woman.

He had gotten drunk and then he'd kissed her—despite the fact that caring about another person was the most forbidden luxury in his carefully emotionless existence. And the sight of Becki Travers standing before him in the light of morning, her thin shirt wet with sweat from his body, clinging to her softness in all the wrong places—wrong at least for his peace of mind—reinforced the fears that he was losing this particular battle.

She had had enough to accept in the past few hours without having to worry about his obvious sexual attraction. He turned away, opening the passenger door he'd been leaning against, trying to control not only his breathing, still unnaturally heavy, but his other involuntary response. Heavy, he thought, described both pretty well.

He was about to have to tell this woman that she had to get into the car with him and leave behind all she had ever known. It wouldn't help that situation if she were aware of the effect she had on him. The same effect she had had since he'd first seen her. His body's reaction would not be a convincing argument that he intended to do nothing but take care of her and Josh until he could figure out who he could trust enough to arrange some kind of protection for them. But that had been what he had tried to do before, he remembered. Arrange protection.

For an instant, the images Deke Summers never allowed to invade his mind were there, sneaking in against his constant vigilance. That way lay madness, he had recognized long ago. Just thinking about the heat and the color of the flames. And the noise. The smell. Suddenly it was all there in his head, fighting against his sanity, against his ability to function.

He closed his eyes, and when he opened them again he was still standing before the passenger door, looking blindly down into the interior of the Pontiac. He could feel the metal of the door frame biting into his palm from the force of his grip. And her hand on his other arm, which rested against the top of the low car.

"Mr. Summers?" she said hesitantly, her voice full of unease, fearful.

Who the hell wouldn't be frightened, Deke thought. He was. Afraid of what happened when he lost control. A control he had imposed on his consciousness for four years. A refusal to remember.

"Are you all right?" she asked.

Deliberately, he turned to her, aligning his mouth in the contour that his brain told him was a smile. It felt forced and unnatural, but hell, he thought, it *was* forced. And pretty damned unnatural for the man he had become.

"I'm just thinking about the best thing to do."

"And?" she questioned, her hand still on his arm. Against his will, he could feel his body responding again. It had been so long since a woman had touched him. Such an achingly long time since *anyone* had touched him.

"I think you're going to have to come with me. Given what they think."

"I can't. This is my home. My family—" She stopped, realizing that her argument was having no effect on the surety in the blue eyes, and with what had happened during the night, she even understood. "We can go to the sheriff. He can arrange protection. Something."

"For the rest of your life?" he asked softly.

"That's ridiculous. No one—" she began, intending to assure him that no one would want to harm her when he was gone.

"You think he can hide you? For how long? And where? They'll find you, Ms. Travers. They won't give up until they find you. Or Josh."

It was his strongest inducement, Deke knew. Reminding her of the danger to her son.

"Please let me call Sheriff Tate."

"Look," he said patiently, trying to make her understand. "You don't know these people. You can't ever know who's involved with them. A lot of law-enforcement guys get caught up in the Movement because of their frustration. They see themselves as vigilantes, shoring up a system that doesn't work any more."

"I don't know what you're talking about. I don't understand who those people back there are or what they want, but I've known Jim Tate all my life. He's a good man. A family man. He wouldn't be mixed up in anything—"

"He doesn't have to be involved," he said. "He just has to be…connected." It was so hard to explain, the tenuous ties that bound them. Sometimes they consisted of only a conversation with a faceless, nameless entity, information shared without thought of its consequences, of the dark reality of those consequences. The computers somehow allowed that distance, that disassociation from normal constraints. "Just a connection. And a lot of those men who were in your house last night see *themselves* as good men."

She remembered that that had been her first assessment. She didn't know how she could argue against his reasoning when she didn't understand what it was based on.

"Who are they?" she asked.

"Those particular men? I have no idea," he told her truthfully. Then against her puzzled rejection of that, expressed by the negative movement of her head, he went on. "They're part of a network that stretches across this country. Bound together by ideology. By frustration. Fear."

"I don't think—" she began, denying the ridiculous scenario that the two of them were being chased by some nation-wide group of conspirators.

"The militia movements. Paramilitary. Patriot groups. Tentacles spread out in all directions like an octopus, all the way to the extremities of the hate groups, the real crazies. They're out there, all shades of the rainbow."

"That's what those men were? Militia?"

"I honestly don't know where on the spectrum they fall. It's a pretty wide range."

"And they're after you? Because of something you did?" Again seeing reaction in the tightening of the muscles around his mouth, she amended, "Something they think you did?"

He nodded.

"How did they find you?"

"My picture's posted on a couple of bulletin boards."

"Wanted posters?" she asked, thinking about the black-and-white pictures in the post office, which she never really looked at.

"Something like that. Only mine are on electronic bulletin boards sent out all over the country. One way the Movement communicates is through the Internet. There's a lot of information shared that way. My whereabouts have sometimes been part of that information."

"But I don't have anything to do with that. I don't even *know* you. Why do I need to come with you? Surely—"

"Ms. Travers, I'm truly sorry, but I don't think you have a choice."

That stopped her, her eyes widening as she tried to decide if the threat he'd implied came from him or from the men who were following him.

"They're not going to stop and listen to explanations," he went on. "Not yours. Not mine. They've made up their minds that…"

"That we're involved," she finished when he hesitated and watched the tight nod of response. "And they think you'll give yourself up if they have me?"

Again he nodded, his eyes gauging her reaction.

"And if you do? What do they want from you? What will they do if they catch you?"

He hesitated again, and in the waiting stillness was aware of the morning sounds and the sunlight filtering through the pine needles over their heads. He watched a flicker of light gleam blue-black in the richness of her hair. He looked down at her hand, slender fingers still spread against the darker brown of his forearm. Her nails were short and unpolished. He closed his eyes, allowing himself to savor, just for a moment, the softness of her palm against the bare, hair-roughened skin of his arm.

"Deke?" she asked.

It was the first time she'd used his name, and the sound of it was unfamiliar. It had been a long time since anyone had called him by his given name. And even longer since he'd heard the softness of a woman's voice wrapped around that single syllable.

He knew that he had to tell her. It was the only way he could make her do the one thing that might keep her safe— to get into the car with him and run, to trust herself to a stranger. The only possibility was to tell her the truth. No matter how brutal.

"They'll put the muzzle of a rifle to the back of my head and pull the trigger," he said. He looked up in time to watch shock invade her eyes.

The picture he had suggested developed in Becki's head like some documentary of wartime atrocities. Black and white and more horrifying for the lack of response in the faces of those watching, those silent figures in the background of the newsreel. That same lack of response was in the eyes of the man who leaned against the opened doorway of the car.

She took a breath, breaking the spell of horror he'd created. He didn't mean that. He was only trying to make her do what he wanted. He was just trying to frighten her. But even as she offered those softening explanations, the truth was in his eyes, calmly meeting hers.

Unable to speak, she simply nodded. He moved aside and allowed her to climb into the passenger seat of the car, closing the door with as little noise as possible. He walked around to the other side, and through the dusty windshield she watched that short journey. He never looked at her again, but he glanced once over his shoulder into the forest. When he opened the driver's side door and slipped into the bucket seat, she didn't look up, didn't make eye contact. Instead she focused on his hand, turning the single key he'd dug out of his pocket. The engine caught the first time, smoothly purring, almost noiseless. He eased the stick into reverse and began to back the car out of its hiding place, then down the rutted dirt road, and eventually out onto the smooth black asphalt of the Alabama highway.

They traveled a few miles in silence. Deke knew she needed time to think through everything he'd told her. Time to accept before they had to move on to what came next. To the next realization.

"I have to have some clothes," she said finally.

He cut his eyes toward the passenger seat. She was looking out the windshield rather than at him. He wondered if he should be reassured by the prosaic quality of that comment.

"And I have to call my mother."

That wasn't on his agenda. He had learned to break all contact to whatever life he had been leading and move on. But then he never allowed himself to form any ties, emotional or physical. Those were his rules and they had served him well; however, he knew they would have to be adjusted for the woman sitting beside him—a woman who came with a lot of ties.

"We can't afford to give anyone a clue as to—"

"Do you want the police looking for us, too?" she interrupted calmly, turning her head to meet his eyes.

He returned his attention to the road, trying to think.

"Because if I just disappear," she went on, "my family will certainly notify them, and my picture will be on every television newscast."

He was forced to acknowledge the probability of that and the fact that it would only make it easier for their pursuers to track them. "What will you tell her?"

"That I've decided to get away for a few days. While Josh is gone. Go to the Gulf, maybe."

"Will she believe it?"

"For a few days, I think. Maybe a week. Unless she decides to go to the house."

"Your house?"

"She's got a key. If it's even locked now," she said, remembering how she had left things—the den light on and the lock on the front door probably forced to allow the invaders' entry. "My purse is there. And Wimsey. My God," she said, realizing that she'd never even thought about the stray cat she'd tried to adopt, "what about Wimsey?"

There was a slight sound of amusement from the man behind the wheel. *Laughter?* Becki wondered, trying to identify the noise. If it was, it seemed, like his smile, to be rusty from lack of use.

"I think...Wimsey can take care of himself. I think he's had experience."

She knew he was right. The cat had a bowl of dry food on the deck and when that was gone he'd slip back into his old ways, procuring his own supper from the woods. She knew from the frequent trophies he left at her back door how capable a hunter he was.

"What do *you* call him?" she asked, recognizing his obvious amusement with the name she had given the tom.

Again his eyes flicked toward her.

"Butch," he said, and then he redirected his attention to the road ahead. Fascinated, she watched the small movement at the one corner of his mouth she could see. Almost a smile. Unlike the other time he'd smiled at her—in the forest—this appeared to be less a grimace and more a relaxation, a true expression of amusement.

"Butch?" she repeated, and then she laughed. It was such a contrast to the aristocratic Lord Peter Wimsey she'd bestowed and, of course, far more appropriate. "Butch," she said again, still smiling.

Deke didn't look at her, but he was relieved by her laughter.

Despite all that had been thrown at her, including the horrors he'd suggested, she was still hanging in there. Still holding it together. *Good girl,* he found himself thinking again. He wondered how many people confronted with this situation, something so sudden and terrifyingly alien to their way of life, would cope as well as she seemed to be.

They were going to make it, he thought. If he could just shake the pursuit and then locate Josh. He knew he'd have to work his way around to that, finding out where her brother was camping. That would decide which direction they'd go when they reached the interstate. She was probably right. It would be better to get some clothes for her and to let her make her phone call before they left. Surface one last time in an area the Movement knew they were in, do the necessary things here and then disappear. Get to Josh and disappear again.

And then he would keep them both safe until he could figure out what to do next. Who to trust. He knew that would be the hardest thing he would have to do. Convince himself that there was someone out there he could trust to keep them safe. Someone who would be willing to die to keep the two of them safe. Someone besides Deke Summers.

He let her make her phone call at the small filling station he'd used before. He had chosen the place because the outdoor phone was a safe distance from the building itself. It was almost out of sight of any passing cars, and he parked the Trans Am as close to the old-fashioned enclosed booth as he could get it. She slipped out of the car, barefoot and still in the nightshirt. He eased out to stand behind her, his back to hers, as she made the call.

It was a little more dangerous this way—not to be in the car, ready to go if anyone pulled in, but he felt safer when he considered the woods that surrounded the building. He didn't really believe they were that close, and he didn't understand how they could already know the car he was in, but he'd learned not to underestimate the quality of their information.

Just a sighting was all it took, and then the hounds would be in full bay.

Deke listened with only half his mind to the one-sided conversation behind him. They had discussed what could be said and what shouldn't be, and he trusted her to do what she was told. She wouldn't want anything to happen to Josh. She wouldn't take any chances.

The stop was uneventful. He didn't even ask about her mother's reaction. It didn't make any difference to his plans even if she didn't buy the story.

He chose a Wal-Mart store not far from the juncture with the interstate. He waited a minute after he'd pulled the car into the closest parking place he could find, his eyes tracking the movements of the cars that came into the lot behind him. There was nothing out of the ordinary. Nothing that sparked that prescience of danger that he took for granted now.

He had always been a man who trusted his instincts, and years on the run had done nothing to change that. Most of the time when he was being stalked, he knew. The slight rising of the hair on the back of his neck. A coldness. Something intangible, but he always knew.

He had felt it that morning in the dawn stillness when he'd kissed her, but he'd denied his instincts, put them down to drunken overreaction. He should have run then, but it was getting harder each time to destroy whatever identity he'd created. It felt as if he were destroying little pieces of himself until one day, he knew, there would be nothing left to destroy. And he hadn't wanted to run this time because of her.

When he had wakened during the hot summer nights, it had not been the familiar nightmares that had pulled him out of sleep. Her skin had been under his mouth, the fragrance and the smoothness, its texture tantalizing. His body had responded to those dreams. A hard, painful response. And in the silent darkness of his lonely existence, it had taken him a long time to go back to sleep. Although he had denied himself any other physical contact with her, knowing the dangers, he still remembered the kiss and the images of the dream.

He shattered those memories by opening the car door. He had already stepped out when her voice stopped him.

"A bra," she said.

He hadn't asked about sizes other than for the shoes, intending to grab knit shorts and a T-shirt, mediums, shapeless and formless, and some athletic shoes. Whatever he found first. Automatically, over the top of the low-slung car his eyes scanned the people entering the store, deliberately not looking at her.

"32-C," she said, her voice disembodied, coming from below his range of vision.

He closed the car door and walked toward the front entrance, the electric-eye doors sliding smoothly open before him. He refused the buggy the elderly man offered, but returned his greeting.

He made his selections, and then waited for the girl to ring them up. She was being very careful with her long artificial nails, and he felt his impatience building. He knew they'd been here too long. Not in the store, but in the area. First the journey across the woods and then the phone call. And now this. Too long, his instincts screamed, but he allowed no outward indication of his unease.

The girl, whose name tag read Joy, smiled at him, fingering the lace bra.

"Buyin' your wife a present?" she asked coyly, glancing down to find the bare ring finger of his left hand. He fought the urge to remove his hand from the counter between them. "Or maybe your girlfriend?" she asked, raising green eyes, their lashes heavily darkened with mascara. Flirting with him. His eyes didn't respond, but he answered her. If he didn't, that would call attention to himself. Make her remember him more than she would otherwise.

"My daughter," he said.

She evaluated the answer, her eyes tracing over his features, and then she smiled, deliberately hiding her teeth which were not her best feature. The smile was probably supposed to be provocative, but the effect was not quite what she intended.

"My, my," she said, shaking her head, the too-red hair brushing her shoulders. "You must've got started *real* early."

Although she hadn't finished ringing up the transaction, he took a fifty out of the pocket of his pants and put it on the unmoving belt of the counter. He met her eyes, no response to her suggestion in his.

She glanced down at the bill and then turned back to the register. She carefully pushed buttons, never endangering her nails, until the total appeared.

"That'll be $29.47," she said, her hand reaching for the fifty. She made change, placing it on his outstretched palm, and then turned to put his purchases in a big bag that seemed to take her forever to shake open.

Again Deke deliberately reined in his impatience, his eyes moving to the glass front of the store. He watched a small red pickup drive slowly up the central lane of the parking lot, turn left at the entrance and then head down the row in which he'd parked the car. *Looking for a parking place,* he thought, but as he watched the driver move past two empty spaces something triggered warning signals.

"Here you go," the girl said, handing him the bag into which she'd stuffed the shoes and clothing. "You have a nice day, now."

Deke ignored the brush of her hand against his as he took the sack. "Thanks," he said, turning his attention back to the circling truck. It was headed up the adjoining row, still obviously in no hurry.

He walked past the lady checking packages at the exit. He moved out into the morning sunlight, his eyes narrowing against its glare as they searched the lot. The pickup was still there, stopped, or almost stopped, a couple of rows over.

He felt the adrenaline kick in, his mind automatically sifting through the possibilities. They probably wouldn't shoot at him here in the lot. There were too many people around. Too many people who could get hurt and too many witnesses. Neither of those was what they wanted. Only him.

He walked down the front of the row where he'd parked

the Pontiac. When he reached it, he kept going, never glancing toward the car and the waiting woman, hoping Becki Travers was watching, that she'd realize something was going on, although he didn't have anything to base that hope on.

A horn blew behind him, one time, a quick, short signal. She must think he'd lost the car. He walked on, almost down the end of the row now. Moving toward the last of the parked cars. Before him lay the outer section of the parking lot, deserted this early. Too much empty space, he thought. Too wide an area to cross without anything to offer protection. There was nothing to hide behind.

He dove between the last two cars in the row, inching carefully to the front bumper of the next to the last to look back in the direction he'd come. The red truck turned the corner in front of the store, moving slowly again down the central avenue of the parking lot—in the opposite direction it had taken when entering. There were two men in the cab, close enough now that he could see the one on the passenger side point to the end of the row where he'd disappeared. The driver gunned the engine a little, picking up speed.

Deke heard again the soft beep of the horn, but this time it came from behind him. Glancing over his right shoulder, he found the Trans Am, positioned exactly between the cars he was hiding behind, motor idling, driver's side door opened invitingly. He felt an urge to motion her to drive on, to try to make her leave him here, but then, he realized, if he did manage to get away from the two who had found them, she'd have no idea what to do next, how to protect herself. This wasn't her life.

And he acknowledged that he wasn't ready to surrender himself to the men who were hunting him. Maybe it was only an instinct for self-preservation, but he'd been in worse fixes than this and escaped. There was always a chance, and as long as there was, he knew he'd take it. Especially...

He stopped the thought before it could form. He couldn't allow himself to think about the possibility of being with this woman other than to make sure she was safe, to protect her from his enemies.

The decision he reached took maybe a second. He didn't check the progress of the pickup again. He had tried to lead them away from her, but she had taken a hand in the game. He slid into the driver's seat through the open doorway, throwing the sack into her lap, and fought the urge to put his foot down on the accelerator and just get them the hell out of here. Instead he eased into the center road that divided the two sides of the massive parking lot and out into the main road, all the time watching the red pickup gather speed also, until finally it was directly behind him, so close that if he slammed on the brakes, a rear-end collision would be inevitable.

Now what, hotshot, he thought, disgusted with himself for allowing the delay that had put them in this situation. *What the hell was he going to do now?*

Chapter Five

"They're following us, aren't they?" Becki asked.

He didn't look at her, his eyes traveling instead back and forth between the image in his rearview mirror and the road ahead.

"It looks that way," he acknowledged. He could see them clearly now, as closely as they were following. Kids, he realized. Teenagers. He wondered for a moment if their motivation might be something else, harassment or car-jacking, but as he thought it, he remembered what he was driving. The beat-up old sports car might run like a scalded dog, but wasn't going to attract anybody's interest in stealing it.

He was relieved that it appeared they had no mobile phone. They wouldn't be able to alert anyone else to help in the chase, and apparently they didn't care. He could almost feel their excitement, like a couple of coonhound puppies scenting a quarry they'd never hunted before. *The most dangerous game*, he thought ironically, remembering the old short story.

He slowed down to turn onto the entrance to the interstate, and then pressed the accelerator, the car smoothly climbing the concrete ramp to sail out onto the highway, already pushing seventy. He was pleased by the Trans Am's responsiveness. Ready to run, he thought, like a horse that had been pastured too long. It had been built for the exercise he was about to put it through, designed purely for speed, long before the regulations on horsepower demanded by the need for fuel conservation.

He held the car steady at around eighty, looking for some combination of events that would allow him to evade his pursuers. This was what he was best at. Improvising. Taking advantage of whatever the situation offered. Always ready to take a chance because he had nothing else to lose. And so far he had been remarkably lucky. *Which probably meant that some day soon his luck was going to run out,* he acknowledged ruefully. Just not today, he thought, automatically studying the traffic patterns ahead. *Just not today.* He wasn't sure if that was a plan or a prayer.

"Hold on," he said softly to the woman beside him, when the opportunity he'd been looking for appeared. He didn't take his eyes off the road, but he was aware that she had reacted, turning toward him at the command.

He pushed the gas pedal all the way to the floor, accelerating suddenly, and the pickup faded behind for an instant. The kid driving reacted just as he'd anticipated, quickly increasing speed. The huge truck Deke had targeted loomed ahead of him, and he guided the Pontiac into the passing lane to go around it. Only then did he realize there were *two* eighteen-wheelers traveling closely together in the right-hand lane.

Even better, he thought, adjusting what he had intended. The pickup eased over into the passing lane behind him, flying now, pushed to its limits and far less stable at this speed than the car he was driving. The exit warning sign flashed by, barely visible on his right before his front bumper was parallel with the rear of the second truck.

Timing, he thought, holding his breath. *All a matter of timing.* Hoping his was on the money, he swerved the Trans Am in between the trucks which had been running in tandem and worked the brakes. A angry blast on the horn of the rearward truck was an indication of how close he had come to kissing its front end.

He had left it too late, he thought as the exit appeared immediately on his right, but even as he thought that, he swerved

again, out onto the ramp. The rear end fishtailed as he fought
for control against the push of his own acceleration and the
rush of wind from the eighteen-wheeler that blew by behind
him. He righted the car, the frame rocking precariously as he
tried not to overcorrect, but the rear flared out again, to the
opposite side, tires squealing. He eased into the skid, not fighting it, and allowed the car to rocket sideways down the ramp
for several seconds. Finally he regained control, straightening
out and picking up speed, but his heart was in his throat and
his stomach somewhere directly underneath it.

Breathing room. He knew that was all he'd accomplished.
Unless the kids in the small truck were crazy enough to attempt a U-turn on the interstate and a return against oncoming
traffic, they would be forced to travel to the next exit before
coming back to pick up the trail. They might find a place
where they could cross the median, but the division between
the lanes had been deep, wide and wooded for miles. If he
was lucky, it would continue that way for a few more, following the natural topography of the land.

"You better get dressed," he ordered. "We'll have to ditch
the car."

Her mouth dry and her heart still hammering in her throat,
Becki began to obey, taking the gray knit athletic-style shorts
he'd bought out of the bag. Her hands were trembling enough
that the operation was pretty noisy.

"You okay?" he asked, for the first time glancing at her
features, blanched and strained.

"Yes," she said. She was embarrassed that her voice was
so shaky. Low and uncertain. She swallowed and finally took
a breath, deep enough to allow her to ask.

"How did they find us?"

Deke shrugged. "Somebody put out the word."

"But how would they know what to look for? It was obvious back there in the lot that they were looking for something. If they didn't know the car—"

"Maybe they did. Or maybe they'd been given a description
of me. Or of you." He let her think about that, about who

would furnish them with her description. "It doesn't matter how they knew. It never does any good to speculate on how they found you. What matters is getting out of this area before someone else spots us. And getting another car. If they didn't know what we're driving before, they certainly do now."

She nodded. She laid the shorts in her lap and released the buckle of her seat belt. She bent down to slip the garment over her bare feet, pulling it up under the knee-length nightshirt.

When she lifted her bottom to ease the shorts the rest of the way on, Deke caught a flash of white panties covering a nicely rounded hip before he deliberately turned his attention back to the scene through the windshield. They were barreling down some county road, two-lane, not yet crowded with traffic. He needed a paved turnoff, one that led somewhere other than to a dead end. He glanced again at the woman beside him.

Becki had picked up the white lace bra, holding it a moment, trying to decide the best way to put it on without removing the nightshirt. She took her arms out of the sleeves, leaving the shirt draped loosely over her body from her shoulders. She leaned forward to slip the bra around her waist, and bringing the two ends together in the front, she fastened the hooks and eyes by feel, her hands hidden by the fall of the nightshirt. Then she turned the bra around, so that the fasteners were in the back and lifted the straps up over her arms.

"You know this road?" Deke asked. His eyes were carefully back on the windshield, and he hoped she wasn't aware that they hadn't been before.

Unthinkingly, Becki adjusted the fit of the bra over her breasts as she glanced up to study the scenery that was flying by.

"It goes to Coalridge."

"Any turnoff that goes somewhere."

She tried to think. "You can get back to the interstate if you turn right just past the traffic light. Pretty twisting roads, several cutoffs, but I can get you back to the highway from there."

"Which traffic light?" he asked.

"There's only one," she said, her lips tilting. She didn't look at him as she picked up the dark green tee he'd bought, but before she removed the nightshirt, she stole a quick glance. The only thing visible was his profile, its strength limned against the light of the window behind, outlining the nearly Roman nose and strong chin. The high cheekbones. Eyes resolutely on the two-lane ahead.

"I'm not looking," he promised softly.

She felt the blood suffuse her cheeks because he'd felt compelled to offer that assurance. She was a grown woman. They were being chased by madmen. What the hell did it matter if he caught a glimpse of her bra? Why did she have to act like some sex-starved old maid, terrified of the first attractive man she encountered?

When the answer to that rhetorical question suggested itself, she suppressed it, turning her attention instead to completing the act of changing clothes so she could give him the directions he'd asked for. And that was *all* he'd asked for, she reminded herself. All that Deke Summers had indicated he had any interest in—at least when he was sober.

The road was as winding as she'd promised, and conveniently isolated. There were actually too few houses for his purposes, so Deke decided to let her help him look. It would be easier if they each took a side of the road, especially since his attention was needed for driving, considering the speed he was maintaining over the tight curves.

"We need to find somebody who's gone on vacation," he said.

Becki had been thinking about her mother's reaction to her phone call. Disbelief would be too mild a word for what had been in her voice. It was so out of character for Becki to just take off. She had tried to reassure her mom that nothing was wrong, but she had heard the worry underlying the hesitant admonition to have a good time.

She couldn't be sure how long it would be before her mother decided to check on things. If she went to the house and found Becki's purse still there and the lights on... She had been wondering how to break the news to Deke Summers that her vacation story had probably only bought them a couple of days at best before her family put out the alarm.

"What?" she asked, her thoughts forced back to the present. He'd said something about a vacation.

"We need to find a house where they've taken off for a few days and left a car at home."

"How are we going to know they've gone on vacation?"

"Newspapers piling up. Outside lights on in the daytime. Unmowed grass. The signs are there, if you know what to look for. Burglars do it all the time."

"And car thieves?" she suggested. She could never remember stealing anything in her life, and now she was going to help him steal a car. She believed that was called grand theft auto.

"We're going to leave one in its place," he said. "Not really a theft. Just an exchange."

There was a trace of humor in his assurance. Apparently he knew exactly what she was worrying about, and this was not the first time he'd seemed to know what she was thinking.

"Oh, of course," she said, allowing a touch of sarcasm, "that makes it all right. And what if they didn't want to exchange cars with us?"

"Then they should have stayed home and guarded what's theirs. Everybody knows it's a cold, cruel world."

Surprisingly, it was she who found what they were looking for. The signs were all there, from the unmowed lawn to the newspapers yellowing in the summer heat. They had driven by before the evidence registered, but Deke turned the car around in the next side road they came to, more than a mile past the house.

The vehicle parked in the attached carport was an ancient truck, several years older even than the Trans Am they were driving. Becki's lips lifted involuntarily as she remembered all the jokes about Southern rednecks and their car-strewn yards.

"You might be a redneck…" she said very softly, climbing

out of the car. Her remark had not been intended for Deke, and she was surprised when he completed the statement.

"If you're even *thinking* about stealing a pickup that's older than you are," he said. His eyes were on the battered vehicle and not on her, but he was aware of her surprised laughter. And when he found himself watching her bend over to examine the tread on the rear tires, he again deliberately pulled his eyes away.

"Not too bald," she said, straightening and pushing a strand of hair behind her ear. "As long as you don't try maneuvering between trucks at a hundred miles an hour, it ought to make it."

"At least it won't be any trouble to wire," he agreed. "Too old to have any antitheft features." He climbed into the cab, but he didn't shut the door, and she found that she was aware again of the curve of his shoulder and upper arm, the muscles strongly defined under the black cotton. Whatever he was doing underneath the dash, he was managing by feel alone. Suddenly his body shifted, his feet aligning themselves on the pedals as the engine came to life, deep throated and noisy, but as he let it idle, reassuringly steady.

He stepped down out of the truck, leaving it running. He walked to the trunk of the Pontiac and removed a canvas bag which he threw over the tailgate into the back of the truck. He closed the trunk and walked around to the passenger-side door, which she'd left open, and bent to remove something from the glove compartment. When he closed the door and came toward her, he was holding a gun, a big, extremely efficient-looking handgun, and her nightshirt.

"You might like to take this with you," he said, offering the shirt.

She took the wad of crimson material and watched without comment as he slipped the gun into the pocket of the camouflage pants he was wearing. Hands again free, he pulled the black shirt out of his waistband and then quickly over his head. The white T-shirt he wore beneath lifted slightly with the rise of the outer shirt, revealing a glimpse of flat brown stomach, ridged with muscle and not an ounce of flab. And somewhere inside, Becki again felt the heat of reaction.

Deke folded up the black shirt and stuffed it into the canvas bag he'd thrown into the bed of the truck. When he turned back to face her, he was running his fingers through the disordered blond hair, pushing it away from his forehead.

"I'm going to park the car around back. It may give us a couple of extra days if nobody connects us right away with the truck's disappearance. You can go ahead and get in."

When he returned, she was ready to go. She wasn't prepared, however, for the question he asked as soon as he'd climbed in.

"Where's Josh?"

"Josh? I told you. He's with my brothers. Camping."

"Where?" he asked, beginning to back the pickup out of the driveway.

"I have no idea," she said truthfully.

The truck's backward progress stopped, and the blue eyes turned from the rearview mirror to focus intently on her face.

"What does that mean?" he asked.

She shook her head. "Nothing. I don't know where they are. They didn't..." She stopped, confused by the change in his expression. It was like watching a metamorphosis. The unsmiling stranger who had lived next door to her for three months was back, the ice suddenly returning to the blue eyes that were locked on her face.

"What do you mean you don't know where they are?" he asked, his voice very calm.

"They just took off. They didn't want a set itinerary. They just wanted freedom to go wherever..." Still puzzled by whatever had happened to produce the sudden change, her explanation faded and she shook her head. "What does it matter where they are? Wherever they are, I promise you Josh is okay. Mike and Bill aren't going to let anyone bother Josh."

"Damn," he said, his eyes finally releasing hers. He turned to look out the windshield, but she knew that his mind wasn't on the clutter of the carport he had just backed out of, the only view in that direction. "Damn," he said again, crossing his wrists over the top of the steering wheel. He put his forehead down on the crossed wrists a moment and then lifted his head to look back through the windshield. She watched his mouth tighten, the movement obvious even in profile.

"What's wrong?" she asked, feeling fear climb into her throat. She didn't understand why she was suddenly so afraid. Mike would take care of Josh. She knew that. Nothing could happen to her son while he was with his uncles. Even as she tried to convince herself, she remembered the small army that had invaded her home. If not military, at least pseudomilitary. As macho as Mike believed himself to be, she knew he'd never been confronted by anything like those armed men or the dangers they represented. Then she thought about her bespectacled older brother, Bill, who was noted for his intellect, but definitely not for his combat readiness.

"Deke? What's wrong?" she asked, but already she knew. He believed they would go after Josh, that they would try to find Josh in order to use him to capture their quarry.

"Tell me everything you *do* know. Everything they said before they left. Even if you think it's insignificant."

She swallowed against the fear crowding her throat so she could obey. "They just decided to take off. To see the West. The parks and tourist sights. Camping out."

"*Just* decided?" he asked.

"A couple of days before they left. Or at least that's when Mike told me. When he asked me if Josh could go."

"A sudden decision to travel?" he asked. There was something in that question she couldn't quite read, but she began to explain all the reasons Mike had given her.

"They've talked about doing it for years. Something always came up. And then this year, it didn't. Everything just seemed to...fall into place."

She watched again the corner of his mouth lift, the movement slight. She wondered how there could be so much difference in that small lift she had seen before, which she had known was a smile, and this reaction. How she could be so certain that the same movement this time didn't signify amusement?

"And you let him go. Without knowing where they'd be."

She waited a moment before she answered, feeling as if he were accusing her of something—only she wasn't sure of what. Josh was her son. Deke Summers had no right to try to make her feel that she'd done something wrong in letting him go.

"He's with his *uncles*. Two very dependable men."

"And you don't see anything coincidental about the timing of this *camping* trip?"

"Coincidental?" she repeated.

"With your brothers' sudden decision to take a trip, given what happened last night."

It took her a moment to realize what he was suggesting.

"Are you saying there is some connection between my brothers taking the kids camping and those men last night?"

He didn't answer, but he turned his head to meet her questioning eyes.

"That's crazy," she said. "If you're implying that my brothers had anything to do with what happened last night, you're out of your mind."

He didn't attempt to argue against her anger, but he held her eyes a long time, maybe to read the depth of her conviction.

Finally he turned to look out the rear window and began to back down the driveway. He didn't speak again until they were on the road, the deserted house behind which he'd parked the Trans Am several miles behind them.

"What attractions?"

"They didn't say," she answered, tight-lipped. He believed those men were going to go after Josh. And that scared her, no matter how much she trusted her brothers. But surely, if *she* couldn't find Josh, then the men who were following them couldn't either.

"And in the past? When they talked about the trip before?"

Unconsciously, she shrugged, trying to remember. "The

usual places. The Grand Canyon. Yellowstone. Yosemite. The Alamo. I don't know. They just wanted to go wherever they felt like going. That was the whole point.''

"No provisions for an emergency? No arrangements in case anyone needed to get in touch with them?''

She thought about that. They would call home periodically. Louise, Bill's wife, would hear from them. And Mary. And they'd call her empty house, the answering machine assuring them that she couldn't come to the phone right now. Probably they'd wait until they'd been on the road a few days, but eventually they'd call, just to let the waiting mothers know that everything was all right.

"They'll call," she said, sure now of the information she was providing.

"When?''

"In a couple of days.''

"Who will they call?''

"Bill's wife. And Mary, my sister. Her son's with them, too. And they'll try to call me.''

She waited, letting him digest what she'd told him, but when the silence lengthened, she knew she had to ask.

"You think those men will try to find Josh?''

"If they don't already know where Josh is.''

"You're still implying that my brothers took him for that purpose? That they're part of whatever is going on? That they set me up for what happened last night?''

"You didn't think it was odd that your brother left Josh with me that afternoon?''

Because she *had* been surprised at that, she hesitated, not willing to condemn Mike and yet bothered by that reminder of his uncharacteristic behavior.

"What was odd about it? He had an emergency, a hurt kid he was responsible for. You were at the house, and he knew I'd be home soon.''

"Or maybe he just wanted to check me out. To take a good look. To verify the identification he'd made.'' The cold bitterness in his voice matched the transformation she had watched before.

"Mike has nothing to do with what's going on. Whoever your enemies are, Mr. Summers, you had them before you met me and Josh."

"You don't understand how—"

"I *understand* that you're accusing my brother of kidnapping his own nephew," she interrupted angrily. "Of putting Josh and me into danger. I understand that pretty well. Only I don't buy it. This is all a coincidence. The trip and what happened last night. If you'll wait a few days, I can find out where they are. As soon as they call. My family is *not* part of some kind of giant conspiracy to capture you. My brothers have got better things to do than to play cowboys and Indians or G.I. Joe or whatever the hell y'all are playing with your guns and your midnight raids. You just keep us away from whoever is chasing you until I can find out where Josh and my brothers are. And then, if you'll take me there, you can be on your way, footloose and fancy free again."

Her voice had risen as she'd talked. She was a little embarrassed by her outburst, but the fact that he wanted to blame Mike for what had happened the previous night infuriated her. They had nothing to do with what was happening to Deke Summers. He had gotten drunk and pulled her into the center of whatever was going on in his life, and he had no right to blame anyone but himself for the result.

"Then until we find out exactly where they are, we drive. West, I think you said."

"That's what I said," she agreed, the hostility still in her voice.

He turned his complete attention back to the road and she did the same, resolutely not looking at him. Deke Summers could think whatever the hell he wanted to, she decided, just as long as he carried her to Josh and her brothers.

THEY DROVE MOST OF the day, stopping only to fill up the gas tank. She didn't go inside the store part of the service station where they stopped, only to the outside rest room. Deke took time to fish a pair of sunglasses out of the canvas bag in the truck bed before he filled the tank. He didn't remove them when he went in to pay for the gas, snack crackers and canned sodas he bought for lunch. He continued to wear them as he drove west, heading now into the afternoon sun, carefully observing the speed limit, nursing the old truck. The heat built in the cab, although they had the windows down. The humid Mississippi air disturbed by their passage wasn't the least bit cooling.

In the late afternoon, he turned off the interstate again somewhere deep in Louisiana. Becki assumed he was planning another quick stop, but instead he continued down the two-lane he'd exited onto, moving past a couple of conveniently placed service stations and out among the rural communities that lined the county road.

He gassed the truck in one town, and then turned north, driving on about twenty miles to the next community before pulling into a fast-food restaurant's drive-through, stopping before the menu board. He studied the offerings a moment and then, having apparently made his own choices, turned questioningly to her.

"This is going to be supper," he warned. "We won't go out again after we find a place for the night."

She thought about the implications of that. She wondered how much sleep he'd had in the past thirty-six hours. Not much, she knew, which meant, of course, that he was probably ready to find a bed and do some catching up. Except...

"I can drive," she offered, thinking about accommodations for spending the night. She didn't think he would opt for two rooms, and the possibility of sharing quarters with Deke Summers was more than a little disturbing.

"Drive where?" he asked. "We don't even know if we're heading in the right direction. We may have to backtrack when you find out their location. We don't want to get too far ahead of them."

"Then you plan to stay here?"

"If we find something that looks promising. We've come far enough that we should have lost any pursuit. We just need to crawl into a hole and stay put until we can find out where Josh is. Or at least find out the direction they're heading."

The distorted question from the metal box saved her from having to reply. Deke placed his order and then turned back to her. She couldn't see his eyes behind the dark glasses, which he hadn't removed, despite the fact that it was almost sundown.

"Just a couple of burgers," she said, thinking again about the coming night. About spending it with him. And suddenly, despite all that had happened, despite worrying about Josh, she felt the same sensation deep in her stomach that she had felt when his mouth had lowered to hers that Sunday morning. Anticipating.

SHE COULDN'T BELIEVE the motel he eventually chose, wondering now about his use of the word *promising*. The place was several more miles down the narrow northbound county road he'd detoured onto. *Most of its business was probably done by the hour,* she had thought when he'd cruised slowly by, taking a good look. The tiny units were designed like log cabins, and each was carefully isolated from its neighbors.

Deke made her get down on the floorboard when he stopped at the office, and she waited, cramped, folded into the narrow space, even as he climbed back in and cranked the truck. He stopped the vehicle, engine left idling and stepped out. When he finally opened the passenger door, she could see the dark lenses scanning the area around the most isolated of the units, whose door now stood slightly ajar.

"Okay," he said.

She darted from the truck into the room and was surprised when he didn't come in behind her. She turned around in time to watch the door close, and then she followed by sound the truck's passage to the back of the cabin, its engine distinct in the silence of the gathering twilight. Deke entered after a few minutes, putting the canvas bag on the floor and the food on the bedside table before turning back to lock the door and prop the room's single chair under the knob, a primitive but effective deterrent to anyone attempting to force entry.

He examined the window not occupied by the chugging air conditioner, checking the ease with which it functioned by raising, then closing and locking it again. He also devoted careful attention to the bathroom window over the toilet, seeming to be assessing whether or not the width of his shoulders would go through. When he came back into the bedroom, Becki was still standing, watching the practiced routine.

He didn't look at her, instead opening the sack containing the food and beginning to set out the items they'd ordered. For the first time, she wondered about money, how much he had and how long it would last. He had paid cash, untraceable, for everything he'd bought, of course. *Just have enough money to get me to Josh,* she found herself thinking. *That's all I ask.*

"You might as well eat," he advised. "Going without food isn't going to get back at me for what I suggested."

He sat down on the edge of the lumpy bed, unwrapping an unappetizing-looking cheeseburger and then, one-handed, pouring a container of fries onto the wrapping paper, which he had spread out on the bedspread.

"I'm not trying to get back at you," she said, walking to the nightstand and picking up one of the burgers. "I just think you're paranoid. I suppose it's understandable, living the way you do, but—"

"Paranoid?" he repeated, speaking around the bite he'd just taken. "Hell, lady, if you think I'm..." he began, and then apparently decided it wasn't worth the effort to deny the accusation. "Paranoid," he said again, almost to himself, his tone clearly derisive, and he shook his head in disbelief.

"I meant about Mike. About my brothers."

"Yeah," he said. "I know what you meant."

She watched his steady consumption of the food. There appeared to be no pleasure, no satisfaction taken in eating, although she knew he must be hungrier than she was—and smelling the rich, salt-encrusted fattiness of his french fries, she was beginning to realize just how empty her stomach was. Deke Summers ate like a stoker fueling an engine, out of necessity, eating because he needed the food's nourishment to keep running. As she thought that, she was sorry for what she'd said. You certainly weren't suffering from paranoia if men carrying automatic weapons were trying to kill you.

"I'm sorry," she offered.

He glanced up, but made no comment.

"Do we have to be enemies?" she asked when the silence grew again between them. *Why did she say that?* she wondered. Because he hadn't treated her this way the previous night. Or even this morning. Like she was the enemy.

"We're not enemies," he acknowledged.

"All of a sudden it feels like we are."

"What we are..." he began, and then he paused, his eyes still on hers. "What we are," he said again, "are two people put together in a bad situation by mistake."

"Mistake?" she questioned.

"My mistake," he acknowledged. "And I take full responsibility."

"Because you kissed me that morning?"

"Because I got drunk," he said flatly.

"Why?"

"For a lot of good reasons," he said, but his expression indicated he didn't intend to share any of them.

"Because I look like your wife?" she asked, wanting to see his reaction. Something happened in his eyes, all the life disappearing suddenly.

"What the hell do you know about my wife?"

She hesitated, but she had gone too far to back away from what she'd said, especially as suspicious as he already was.

"*They* said I looked like her. Those men. And that you wouldn't make the same mistake again."

His face didn't change. There was no further shift in the hard alignment of his features. Nothing moved behind the cold, dead eyes.

"At least they were right about something," he said finally.

He gathered up the remains of the meal he'd eaten, and she realized only then that she was still holding, unwrapped, the sandwich she'd picked up from the night table. She knew that she couldn't manage to get any of it down now.

She had done something she didn't think she'd ever intentionally done before in her life. At least, not in her adult life. She had deliberately caused another person pain. She might want to know what had happened to forge the man Deke Summers was now, but that gave her no right to probe the scars his past had inflicted.

"I'm going to take a shower," he said, throwing the trash he'd collected into the battered metal wastebasket and heading for the bathroom, slamming its door behind him.

Conversation definitely over, Becki thought, dropping the burger she held on top of the other garbage. She still felt like the enemy.

AFTER SHE'D TAKEN HER own shower, she washed out the white nylon panties, hanging them over the towel rack to dry, a little embarrassed by that intimacy in the small room they were forced to share. She dreaded reentering the adjoining room, which contained the bed. Maybe he'd offer to sleep on the floor. She wasn't afraid of him, just embarrassed at the situation—sharing space with a stranger.

She finally pulled the chain that cut off the bulb above the rust-stained lavatory. She stood in the darkness a moment, delaying the inevitable. When she opened the bathroom door, she was surprised to find the outer room dark as well. She allowed her eyes to adjust and gradually the furnishings began to take shape out of the dimness.

Deke Summers was stretched out on the side of the bed nearest the door. His hands were crossed behind his head. He was wearing jeans, but no shirt, his tanned chest a contrast to the dingy whiteness of the sheets.

She hesitated a minute, wondering what she should do. Somehow, she couldn't imagine calmly crawling into bed beside him. Someone else, perhaps, but not her. Despite how he made her feel, despite her reactions to his masculinity, she had never reached the point of envisioning herself sharing a bed with him.

"We both need sleep." His voice was low pitched, and it contained none of its earlier coldness.

Still she waited, unsure.

"I'm not going to touch you," he said. "You have my word."

Most people nowadays jumped in and out of bed at the drop of a hat. And here she was wondering whether to sleep beside a man who was only interested in saving her life. And his. Nothing else. He had made that abundantly clear. She was only embarrassing them both by her hesitation.

Her bare feet made no sound as she crossed the coolness of the vinyl tile. There was far more light filtering around and through the thin shades that covered the double windows than she would have thought possible. She could see his face clearly, eyes directed toward the water stains on the Celotex ceiling above the bed.

She lifted the top sheet and slipped under it, the bed sagging, the springs groaning with her weight. She lay perfectly still, and in the silence she could hear the occasional truck rumbling past on the highway. And from the woods that surrounded the cabin's isolation, the normal rural night noises. And the quiet breathing of the man who lay, unsleeping, beside her. The cold hard-eyed stranger on whom her life—and the life of her son—now depended.

Chapter Six

When Becki drifted out of the shadowed images of sleep, she wasn't sure what had awakened her. She wasn't frightened, but aware that something was wrong. Something was different. She opened her eyes. The moonlight was stronger now, silvering into the small room around the torn edges of the shades that covered the windows.

She turned her face toward its light, as remembrance of the man who slept beside her swam into her consciousness. She wasn't awake enough yet to feel uneasy about his presence in the narrow bed as she had been the previous night. And even then, his breathing had gradually become comforting, lulling her into a relaxation that was eventually deep enough to become sleep.

The sound that had pulled her from that sleep was protest. Anguish. Creeping out of the darkness. Horror. It had no words, but its message had been unmistakable. As harsh and painful as the sounds he had made once before, when, standing behind the sanctuary of her kitchen door, she had listened to Deke Summers's agony, unaware and undefended.

Nightmare, she realized. Even his legs were moving, the brush of denim audible as they strained convulsively against the sheets. Running. A man who spent his days fleeing the vengeance of relentless pursuers. *And* his nights.

She wondered if what she had said to him had precipitated

this. Because she had reminded him of the woman who haunted his eyes?

The violence of the dream was increasing, its intensity obvious in his movements, in the volume of the wordless sounds he was making. Unable to bear it any longer, motivated by her guilt and by a natural aversion to intruding on anyone's suffering, she sat up slowly. She could see him now, panting, his hands clutching the sheet that was tangling under his twisting body, their gripping fingers like talons.

She whispered his name. Too softly. The single syllable lost in whatever he was reliving, hidden by the gasping efforts he was making to get air into his lungs. So she said it again, louder, and tentatively she put her hand on his chest, comforting, as she would have tried to protect her son against night's demons.

Only, the man beside her was not a child. And he was unaccustomed to the caress of fingers against his naked skin. Suddenly she was flat on her back, his forearm across her throat as she looked up into his eyes. Their pupils were too wide, attempting to react to the lack of light and still lost in the throes of the nightmare. Even as she watched, they began to clear, to come back from the web of horror that had entangled him.

"Lila," Deke whispered, as he took his arm away from the slender pulsing column of her throat. His mouth lowered to hers. His tongue eased inside, caressing, savoring the reality of her response against the remembered terror. He lifted his lips a fraction away from hers to explain. He had probably frightened her to death.

"I thought..." he said, remembering the dream. He had dreamed he'd lost her. The explosion had been too real, flames shooting into the night sky, even the sounds embedded like splinters of broken glass into his consciousness. But he knew now it had been only a dream, because she was here with him. Safe. "I had a terrible dream," he whispered, lowering his mouth again to hers, nuzzling gently against the softness of her lips.

He could feel her body beneath his, familiar and reassuring. Cool as always under the hot need of his skin. Her breasts pushing upward into his chest. Wanting him. Letting him know that she wanted him. That she never tired of making love, of touching him as she was touching him now, her palm flattened against his shoulder, her mouth opened under his, tongue sweet and somehow hesitant.

She had been asleep, he thought. Slightly unresponsive because she had been sleep. But he needed her. He needed to move inside her, to feel her body, hot and wet, opening to surround him. Waiting for his touch. Welcoming. He needed her to destroy the sight and sound and smell of the dream, because he could bear anything but that—losing her. Anything else but that.

He eased his tongue deeper into her mouth, his hand drifting downward, trying to find the hem of the gown she wore. She loved silk, and so he bought it for her, delicate lace decorating the necks and hemlines of the gowns he chose. He wanted the sleek, so-achingly-well-known slip of that fabric over his skin, but what his searching fingers encountered was unfamiliar. Something was wrong. Something...

And suddenly he remembered. Everything. All of it. No barrier between his charred soul and that memory. No protection.

He had been hard and aching, ready for her. Anticipating release. So long. Such a long, agonizing denial. A denial that his body had been aware of even as his mind had briefly escaped the reality of it. He put his hands against the mattress, one on either side of the trembling woman who lay beneath him. He pushed himself up, away from her softness and back into the cold darkness. Awake now. Aware of what he had done. Aware of everything again.

"I'm sorry," he said softly. He could see her face, eyes dark and too wide, afraid of him. "It was a dream."

"I know," she whispered. She touched him, her fingers gentle against his cheek. "It's all right," she said. "I understand."

They stayed unmoving for an eternity. Finally he could feel his arms begin to tremble with reaction. He had to get out of here. Just for a little while. Just away. Because... He tried to banish the realization, to deny it, but he knew. And he would always know.

Even after he had realized his mistake, he had still wanted her. He wanted to make love to the woman who lay beneath him—even after he'd known she was not his wife. And that frightened him far more than anything else that had happened. The realization that he wanted so badly to make love to Becki Travers. Even after he had remembered it all.

He pushed away from the bed with one strong surge of motion. And then he was across the width of the small room, as far as he could manage within the confines of the space they were forced to share. The quietness drifted back gradually, the creaking springs beneath the mattress finally silenced, no traffic on the highway in the near dawn. Only the hum of the air conditioner, background, already unheard.

"Sometimes..." she said, the sound touching him out of the darkness. He could no longer make out her features. She was simply a shape in the dim, eerie illumination of filtered moonlight. "Sometimes," she said again, her voice stronger, wanting him to hear and to know that she understood, "after my husband died, I'd wake up and think I could hear him breathing. Just beside me. It would seem so real that I'd reach out my hand and touch the emptiness." It was a long time before she finished. "Just to be sure," she whispered.

He felt his eyes fill, suddenly wet with the tears he could not allow. Had to control. He felt one slip downward and stop beside his mouth, blocked by the tightness of the ridged muscle there. He licked it off, tasting salt. When the second followed, it trickled unhindered to his chin, hanging a moment before spilling onto his bare chest. It was hot. Burning his skin. He clenched his eyes to prevent the escape of another. Not his right, he thought. He had no right to cry. And no right to her sympathy.

And so he spoke, his voice cold and dark from the shadows.

"Did you kill your husband, Ms. Travers?" he asked.

"No," she answered finally, after he had waited a long time. Her voice was now only a whisper.

"Then you can't *really* understand, can you?"

There was no answer from the woman whose body had lain acquiescent under his. He picked up his boots and shirt from the floor beside the bed. He pulled the chair from beneath the knob of the door and set it aside. He stepped out into the sticky heat of the Louisiana night, welcoming its warmth on his shivering skin.

And now she knows, he thought, and closed the door behind him.

BECKI LAY A LONG TIME in the darkness after the sound of that closing door. Her thoughts touched on and then skittered away from what he had said, like birds that wanted to feed but were frightened by the wind-driven movements of the scarecrow. She wanted to think about what those words meant, but her mind wouldn't allow her to.

They had said he killed babies, and she had seen him strangle a man. Or thought she had. He had claimed the man they called Richard had only been unconscious, but how could she know? She was in the hands of a man about whom she knew nothing. A man who admitted that he had... Again her mind fled from the memory of what he'd said.

She had no idea what to do. Trust him to take her to Mike and Bill? Let him find and protect Josh? Or run as far and as fast as she could from a man who just might be insane? How did she know that the men who followed him, who had appeared out of the darkness, were what he had said? How could she possibly know what was really going on? She felt panic beginning to build, and she fought it, knowing that she couldn't figure out the right thing to do if she were afraid. Afraid of him. Afraid for Josh. Fear would only interfere in her ability to function, to make the wise decision.

Suddenly, she threw the sheet off and began to hurry into her clothes. He might come back at any minute, and she hadn't decided what to do. At least his absence made it possible to have an option. Unless he was waiting just outside the door.

She finished dressing, almost throwing on the garments, hands trembling, and then she sat down on the edge of the bed to put on her socks and shoes. She froze, afraid he might hear the movement of the springs. She listened for any reaction, waiting, but when she heard nothing, she completed the task. Then steeling herself, she tiptoed to the windows and pulled the shade back a fraction to look out.

In the early morning stillness the small cabins scattered under the moss-draped oaks were absolutely silent. The landscape was unpeopled, and there were no cars before any of the units. Apparently, they were the only ones who had taken advantage of the motel's unwelcoming hospitality the night before. There was no sign of Deke Summers, and she wondered if he had simply left her here. Then she remembered that she hadn't heard the truck. If he *had* gone, it had been on foot.

Her eyes continued to examine the area, moving past the entrance with its neon vacancy sign, to the office where he'd gotten out to rent the room, and over the distinctive blue-and-white stand by its door. Her eyes, skimming past, came back suddenly to the telephone, her mind racing. Contact with the outside world. Except, she remembered, she had no money.

She walked over to his canvas bag. She stood a moment, her natural inhibitions about invading his privacy strong. Finally, she knelt, and unzipping the bag, rummaged through, finding nothing but a few items of clothing and clips for the gun she had seen.

Still on her knees, she glanced toward the door and remembered the soft clink of the sack when he'd put it down on the bedside table the previous night. Her mind had automatically registered the sound. He had dropped the change from the transaction into the sack with the food instead of putting it back into his pocket, an action almost impossible for a man seated behind the wheel of a car.

She stood up and walked over to the grease-stained paper

bag. The second burger she'd ordered was still there, the paper-wrapped bun cold and hard under her searching fingers, and in the bottom, on top of the napkins, were the coins.

When she slipped out the door of the cabin a few minutes later, she held her breath, waiting for someone to question her right to leave, but nothing happened. Everything was as deserted as it had been when she'd taken her survey from the window.

She walked quickly toward the phone, head down, letting the fall of her hair screen her face. Expecting at any moment a challenge to what she was doing, she lifted the receiver. She raised her hand, the quarter she'd found poised before the slot, and then she hesitated.

Who could she call? The local authorities, about whom she knew nothing? Despite what had happened the previous night, in the back of her mind were the warnings Deke Summers had given. You never knew who might be involved, he had said. Overlying the words was the image of the filmed execution she had watched so long ago, carried out exactly as he'd described. *They'll put the muzzle of a rifle to the back of my head...*

What if he had been telling the truth about the men following him? Suddenly she remembered the words of the commander whose face she had never seen. *That ole boy don't make the same mistake twice.* Which implied his wife's death had been the result of a mistake. Not deliberate. Some kind of tragic mistake. And if that were true...

Her family, she decided finally. She could at least call to see if they'd heard from the boys yet, if they had any information. She couldn't call her mother. Mike would have been the one she would normally have turned to. Or maybe Bill. Not her oldest brother, Don, because of her run-in with Charlotte. Which left...Mary.

She slipped the coin in and dialed the code for a collect call. She told the operator her first name and then waited, listening to the distant ringing, wondering what time it was. Surely it was early enough that Mary hadn't left the house.

"Hello." The reassuringly familiar texture of her sister's voice, still half asleep, came over the line, and Becki smiled, listening to the operator's question.

"Mary," she said, when her sister had agreed to take the call.

"What's wrong?" came the automatic response.

"Nothing's wrong. What makes you think something's wrong?"

"It's the crack of dawn, and you're calling me long-distance. Why wouldn't I think something's wrong?"

"No," Becki said, forcing a reassuring laugh, and then she wondered why she wasn't explaining that there were lots of things wrong. *Wasn't that why she'd called? To get help?* "I just wondered if you'd heard from the boys."

"From the kids?"

"If Mike or Bill had called you."

"They just left day before yesterday," Mary said, her tone rejecting the question as ridiculous. "You okay?"

"Just missing Josh. I just wondered if you'd heard."

She was aware that her sister had put her hand over the phone. She heard some sound, muffled.

"Mary?" Becki questioned.

After a small pause, the familiar voice came back.

"Sorry," Mary said, "I thought I heard something. Mom on one of her 'I thought you'd be awake by now' visits, but I guess not."

Becki smiled, relaxing at the complaint, the remembrance comforting. Their mother often just walked into their houses. If it was early enough, she didn't knock or call out a warning because she was afraid she might wake someone. That was part of the familiar normality of the life she had left behind.

"Give me your number at the beach, and I'll call you when I hear. Or I'll have Mike call you down there," Mary offered.

It wouldn't do any good to give the number, Becki realized. She couldn't stand out by this phone, waiting. She wasn't registered at the motel, so Mary couldn't ask for her or leave a message. She didn't even know if she'd be here another night.

"The place I'm staying doesn't have a phone," she lied. "I guess they're afraid somebody will run up a bill. I had to find a pay phone. That's why I called collect. I'll have to call you back. Unless you think they might have called Louise last night?"

"No, I talked to her. It was after nine and she hadn't heard. They might call tonight, but I'm thinking Saturday. Friday at the earliest. They'll probably eat out somewhere, maybe get a couple of rooms and make the calls."

"Friday?" Becki repeated, thinking. This was Thursday morning. It was a long time to wait, especially now that she was unsure about the man who had taken her from her home. Unsure about everything because of what Deke Summers had said. "Okay," she said, finally. "But I may call you back tonight. Just in case."

"Is something wrong?" Mary asked again, her voice concerned, more awake now, more conscious that *something* wasn't right about the conversation.

"I'm just missing Josh. And feeling homesick."

"I was a little surprised when Mom told me you were going to the beach, but then I thought it was great. You need a break."

"Yeah," Becki agreed. "I guess."

"Call me tomorrow night. They might be in touch by then."

"Okay."

"Love you, Bec."

"Love you, too."

The connection was broken, too soon, and she stood, holding the phone, listening to the slight hum of the dial tone.

She finally put the receiver into the metal hanger and turned to look back toward the cabin where she'd spent the night. There was a light mist over the dirt between, drifting upward from the warmth of the ground into the cooler morning air. Nothing moving, no sounds to disturb the peace. She took a breath and realized that she had to go back to the cabin and wait. Unless she wanted to set out on her own and try to find her brothers with the eighteen cents that remained of the change she'd found. Hitchhike, maybe? Suddenly, the known danger seemed highly preferable. *The known danger,* her mind repeated the phrase. Deke Summers. Only, there was so little that was *known* about him. And maybe, she decided, it was time to find out more.

SHE HADN'T BEEN BACK inside the room thirty minutes when Deke returned. She had locked the door behind her, but she hadn't put the chair under the knob. She hadn't even thought about it until she heard the key turning and then realized in quick panic that it was too late.

Deke pushed open the door, his big body outlined quickly against the light outside, and Becki took a breath in relief. Despite everything, she was glad it was Deke and not someone else. Instinctively, she trusted him more than the men who were looking for him.

Deke closed the door and again put the sack he was carrying down on the bedside table. Because he'd had to get away from what had happened, he'd convinced himself that going for food was a necessary risk. They had to eat. Based on his long experience, he figured they should be safe here for a few days. He had done everything right. There was no reason for the uneasiness he'd felt the entire time he'd been in the small café a few hundred yards down the highway.

Despite the early hour, there had already been a couple of people eating breakfast, their eyes sliding over him as he stood by the counter to order. In this rural environment, he'd told himself, strangers were probably rare enough to seem interesting. No one had followed him out. No one had seemed suspicious. He had no valid reason to feel the apprehension that had tightened his gut when he'd walked out. No reason other than his dread of having to return to the motel and face Becki Travers's reaction to what he'd told her.

"I brought you some breakfast," Deke said, carefully controlling his voice and his expression. No nuance of the dawn intimacy was allowed in either. Nothing would change in their relationship. Nothing *could* change, despite the fact that he had admitted to himself how close to the edge he was, how badly he wanted to make love to her. "I thought you'd be hungry. Since you didn't eat last night."

"Thanks."

Becki made no move toward him, held back by what had happened between them less than an hour ago. She couldn't tell what he was thinking, his features arranged in the expressionless mask she'd grown accustomed to when he'd lived next door.

When she said nothing else, Deke walked into the bathroom and returned with the single glass that comprised the amenities the management had provided. He opened the sack and took out a large container of coffee, and taking off the plastic cover, poured half of it into the glass which he set down on the table. He stepped toward her, the disposable white container held out.

"I've got cream and sugar," he offered. "I wasn't sure how you took your coffee."

"Black, hot and by the gallon." She had forced her mouth to form the words, but when she reached for the container, her hand was shaking.

His mouth tightened, aware that she was afraid of him. "Sausage and biscuits?" he asked, forcing himself to move back to the table, acting as if he hadn't seen that telltale reaction. "Or just a biscuit? I picked up some jelly."

When he turned back to face her, a wrapped biscuit in each hand, she was still holding the untasted coffee, the cup vibrating visibly with the trembling of her hand, her dark eyes held by force of will on his face.

"I think you have to tell me what you meant," she said.

He didn't pretend not to understand. After a few seconds he tossed the food on the unmade bed and walked to the windows. As she had earlier, he lifted the tattered edge of the shade and looked out. A muscle moved in his jaw, and she waited, wondering what she would do if he refused.

"You want to know how I killed my wife," he said finally. "*They* said it was a mistake."

"And you prefer their version?"

"I prefer that you tell me the truth. I need to know. The truth about everything that's happened."

"The less you know, Ms. Travers, the better. *That's* the truth," he said.

"It's not my fault I'm here," she said, trying to be reasonable. "I don't have anything to do with what's happening. Josh and I are involved in all this just because we lived next door to you."

"And because you couldn't leave it alone," he said with a trace of bitterness. *Because I always knew what you were thinking.*

"What the hell is that supposed to mean? That I didn't leave *you* alone? I tried to be neighborly, so I deserve those men breaking into my house? Is that what you're saying?"

"No," he admitted softly, his eyes still directed outside. He regretted the accusation. It wasn't her fault that her reaction had been...obvious. He had known she was attracted. Interested. And he had known from the first she was special. Except there was no place in his life for any of that. It was *his* life that was unnatural, not her reactions.

"Then what? Don't you think you owe me some explanation for all this? For what's going on?"

"I owe you protection. You and Josh."

"And I'm just supposed to accept that you're the good guys and they're the bad? Because you say so. And then at the same time you tell me you killed your wife. What kind of sense does this make to you?"

"None of it has made any sense to me from the beginning," he said. "None of it's ever made sense."

"Look," Becki said, still trying for calmness, but knowing she was losing the battle. This was too important—her need to know what was going on so she could decide how best to protect Josh. "You can be cryptic as all get out some other time. When this is over, when I've found Josh, and when we're safely back home. But right now, you've put me and my six-year-old son in the middle of... God, I don't even *know* what," she said, despairing. "Men with guns. Being chased down the interstate. Being dragged through the woods in my nightgown. I think you owe me *some* explanation besides somebody's trying to put a bullet in your head. I'm beginning to believe you're playing me for the world's biggest sucker. Conspirators connected by the Internet? I think Hollywood did that. Only I didn't buy the premise then, and I don't buy it now. Not without some proof. Some explanation."

Despite her rising voice, Deke hadn't turned back to face her. He was still leaning against the wall beside the window, one hand lifting the shade, and for some reason his lack of reaction made her angrier.

"I think that's all a bunch of crap, Mr. Summers," she finished, slowly and distinctly.

He turned toward her at that, assessing, the blue eyes calmly examining her face.

"You tell me the truth or I'm gone," she threatened.

"Gone where?" he asked, and his gaze shifted back to the scene outside.

"First, to the office to call the local sheriff."

The silence lasted a long time, while she wondered what she would do if he refused to answer her—if he called her bluff. Would she really make that call? Despite her angry ultimatum, she was surprised when Deke Summers began to talk, his voice very soft, his eyes still directed outside the window.

"I was working undercover. Inside one of the patriot groups. We'd been told they were stockpiling arms and explosives. Getting ready for Armageddon." She watched as the corner of his mouth flicked upward and then returned to its original tight line, not really amused by their fears. "There were several families living together in this compound they'd built. It was up in the Smokies, the country around it really beautiful. Spectacular."

His voice stopped, and she waited a long time for him to go on.

"And?" she prodded finally.

"And something went wrong. I'd found out what I'd been sent there to find out. I reported the information and then…" Again he hesitated, and this time she waited through the pause. "There was a raid by the authorities. It was supposed to be a simple operation to recover the weapons, the explosives. Something happened."

"What happened?" she asked when his voice faded.

"Somebody screwed up. For some reason…they rushed the place, shooting. The people inside returned the fire and…all hell broke loose." Again the thread of the narrative was broken, the quiet voice silent for a long time.

She waited, thinking about everything she knew, trying to put it together.

"Some of those people were killed? Some of the people in the compound?" she asked.

There was no answer from the man by the window.

"And some of them were children," she finished. It wasn't a question. It was obvious from what she'd been told by the man in the shadows that night. "And they blamed you?" she asked.

He said nothing, his eyes still focused outside.

"Why was your wife there?"

"My wife was five hundred miles away."

"Then…"

Suddenly, she knew she was going to have a hard time formulating that question. This was all too hard. What she was doing. She forced herself to remember that this man had endangered *her* child. And she had to know why. She had to understand if she was going to be able to trust him to take care of Josh.

"I wasn't going to work undercover again. We'd agreed. But I had to do that one because I was…perfect. I could get in. I'd grown up with people like that. Everyone knew I had to do that one, but we'd agreed it was the last time. Lila wanted a baby, and she thought what I was doing was too dangerous."

Becki waited because she didn't know what else to ask, what question would restart the halting flow of information.

"I knew those kids. I'd lived with them. I thought it was important, before we started a family, to get to know something about kids, to…" Again his voice faded and she saw him take a breath. "I'd never been around children before. And those were just…normal kids. Kids like Josh. I liked them. Liked being with them…a lot. And then they were dead."

She wanted to cry. Or maybe she wanted him to cry. Given the depth of pain in that carefully controlled voice, she honestly didn't know if she could listen to the rest.

"I've tried to tell myself that I'd given the authorities all the information they'd needed. They came too early. The kids were supposed to be away, already at school. They didn't have to start firing. Some idiot issued a shoot-to-kill. It wasn't necessary. Those people wouldn't have resisted. None of it should have happened."

He breathed again, his jawline rigid, the muscle pulsing once, its small movement exposed by the light from the window.

"I was the one they blamed. I was the one whose picture was put out on the bulletin boards. I was the traitor, the one who had been inside, supplying the information that led to the raid. Everybody said it would blow over. That they'd forget. Just give it time. So Lila and I went into protection. Different state. Different names. She still wanted a baby. She said we had lots of time on our hands, lots of time to concentrate on making a baby."

Again there was a prolonged silence before he made the confession he hadn't made before, when it might have made a difference. "When we cut out the lights, all I could see were those kids. But I never told her that."

She looked down into the container of coffee he'd brought her, no longer steaming, growing cool as he told her what she had said she had to know. Despite the need, she wished she hadn't asked. These were secrets no one should know. She knew, too, that the worst was yet to come. Whatever it was, the ending of his story would be no better than what had gone before.

"We had a fight. She accused me of not really wanting a baby. And then of…not wanting her any more."

Something had happened to his voice. She looked up in time to watch his eyes close. There was a small negative movement of his head, light shimmering through the platinum. "She went storming out, because I didn't know how to explain it all to her. I couldn't tell her I was afraid. That life is so damn fragile. I understood that for the first time, but I thought if I told her that… Somehow, I thought…"

Again she waited, just wanting it over. Whatever had happened, just over.

"They'd put a bomb in the car. My car. When she turned the key in the ignition, it blew up."

She closed her eyes against the force of the soft words, beating against her view of the world. Her reality.

"Then *she* was dead, just like the kids. Then they all were dead."

"None of it was your fault," she whispered finally, knowing that she had to say something.

"And if I had left it alone? Left them alone? They weren't doing anything to anybody."

"But they would have. That's why you were sent there. Because they would have. Eventually. People who stockpile explosives use them. To blow up buildings where innocent people are killed. To derail trains. Those incidents are in the news every day. How could you know they'd never have used them?"

He didn't look at her.

"How can I ever know they would?" he said.

It was so quiet in the room that she became aware again of the hum of the air-conditioning. The traffic on the road. Somewhere outside a car door slammed. The sounds too ordinary against what had gone before. Against the calmness of his deep voice.

"No," he said. She thought he must be talking to her, but when she glanced up, his attention was focused on the narrow crack his fingers were creating by holding the shade away from the window. "Damn it, I knew..." Deke was no longer leaning against the wall, and the tension in his body was not that which had been there before. Something had happened. Was happening.

"Get into the bathroom," he ordered.

"What?"

"Bathroom. Open the window. Don't do anything else until I tell you."

"What's going—"

"Now, dammit. Now."

He let go of the shade and stepped away from the window. He ran his hand under the pillow on the side of the bed he'd slept on last night, pulling out the heavy handgun. When he turned around and found her still standing where she had been before, paralyzed by the unexpectedness of the threat, he pushed her toward the other room.

He didn't even wait to see if she kept moving. He picked up the chair, one-handed, and fitted it carefully under the knob and then he retrieved the extra clips from the canvas bag and slipped them into the front pocket of his jeans. He backed across the room to the bathroom, where she stood trembling, the window opened as he'd directed. He eased the door closed behind him.

"It's okay. We've got time. They've gone inside."

"Time for what?" she asked, licking lips that were suddenly too stiff to form words.

He didn't answer, but he slid the small window up a little more and then carefully stuck his head out and took a quick look. He stepped up on the toilet and bending, inserted the top half of his body through the frame. His legs followed, the movement a controlled somersault, absolutely noiseless except for the soft impact of his back hitting the ground.

She heard his voice from outside.

"Come on," he whispered.

Knees shaking, she climbed on the rim of the seat and stuck her head out. He was standing just below, braced to take her weight. Somehow she couldn't convince her body to move. She was terrified of whoever was out front that had necessitated this escape, but she was also, ridiculously, afraid to dive down into his arms.

"I'll catch you," he whispered, and the slow one-sided smile touched his mouth. "I promise I'm not going to let you fall. Trust me, Bec."

Whether it was the familiar diminutive or her common sense coming to the rescue, she didn't know, but suddenly she put her knee up on the top of the toilet and launched her body downward, diving awkwardly into his arms. He caught her without any visible effort.

"Good girl," he said, as he literally turned her body upright.

She took a deep breath, moved by the compliment, by the fact that he had taken time to verify her small courage.

"Get in the truck," he said, turning to open the driver's door for her. She climbed into the cab and slid over the coolness of the vinyl seat to the passenger's side. He stepped up, leaving the door standing open, and laid the heavy gun across his lap. He did whatever he had done before to the wiring under the dash and the engine caught—too loud in the morning quiet.

Suddenly here were sounds from the front of the motel. Voices. Someone shouting.

Deke's face reflected nothing of the fear that moved sickeningly in her empty stomach. He appeared perfectly calm as he pulled the door closed and then wheeled the truck backward in a semicircle, stopping when the rear bumper touched one of the trees.

"Get ready," he ordered, and remembering the terror of the interstate, she somehow found the two ends of her lap belt. Hands shaking, she forced one into the other as Deke accelerated past the small cabin where they'd spent the night.

As he rounded the front of that building she could see that

the open yard, which had been deserted in the faint light of
dawn as she'd made her phone call, seemed full of men, not
in uniform, no blackface. Their gear was no different than a
hundred hunting parties she'd seen set out through the years,
except the guns this time were beginning to lower, the dark
muzzles pointing toward the beat-up old truck that was rushing
through their midst, scattering people right and left as Deke
pushed it for all it was worth.

Tires squealing, dirt spraying behind in a wide arc, he an-
gled to the right across the open space, trying to reach the
road. So tantalizingly close, and yet, under the aim of the
lowering guns, so dangerously distant.

She heard the first shots as they bumped up on the edge of
the blacktop. The rear end skewed, tires leaving smoking
streaks as Deke pushed the accelerator to the floor. Something
had rushed by through the open windows, brushing against
her hair like a night beetle. Somewhere in her mind she
knew—but couldn't conceive of it—that what had touched her
was a bullet.

Deke's hand was on the top of her head, pushing her down.
Panicked, she fought a moment against the strength of it,
against his control, and then she realized what she was doing.
She threw herself flat onto the seat, her face resting against
his denim-covered thigh, her entire body shaking.

The glass from the small back window suddenly blew inward, into the truck, showering them both, stinging her back
and shoulders. She felt the truck swerve and then right itself.

"Son of a bitch," she heard the man beside her hiss softly,
and she tried to struggle upright.

"Be still," he ordered, his hand again spread out over her
head, holding her down against his body. "We're okay. Just
need a cutoff. A road. Just..." His voice faded and behind
them the fusillade diminished, the noise decreasing gradually
with the distance he was putting between them and the guns.

She finally remembered to take a breath, and she eased her
hand up to touch his. It was still resting protectively over her
hair, which was littered with broken glass, still holding her

face against the hard, secure warmth of his thigh. It took her a moment to realize why the back of his hand was sticky. Wet and hot. At about the same time she realized what that meant, the truck swerved again to the right, and she felt the wheels leave the smoothness of the asphalt.

Chapter Seven

Becki pushed upward against the pressure of his palm, and he released her. Just as she sat up, the truck straightened. Apparently, despite the fact that he'd been hit, Deke had not lost control. They were now flying down a paved side road, a turn-off from the main highway that ran in front of the motel. She glanced through the shattered rear window and was relieved that there was no one there, none of the men who had been swarming over the motel grounds.

"Any sign of them?" Deke asked.

She turned back, and her stomach lurched. A gash ran across his neck, blood streaming. She had nothing to press against the wound, nothing to stop the bleeding. Too much blood, it seemed, for the thin cut.

"Deke," she said, and because she had to do something, she put her fingers against the solid warmth of his neck, now streaked with crimson.

Despite the speed he was maintaining, he glanced at her face. After a quick look at the road ahead, his eyes moved back to hers, and he smiled.

"It's okay," he said, returning his attention to the narrow, twisting ribbon he was following. "Somebody had a shotgun. A lot of sound and fury. I caught a few pellets that came through the back. Not straight on."

A few? More than the shallow furrow on his neck? They would be in his shoulder and back, she realized, but it was hard to tell because of the concealing darkness of the black knit shirt he was wearing.

"It's okay," he said again, concerned about her. Her eyes were glazed, almost shell-shocked by the sudden unexpected violence. Unprepared.

"Have we lost them?" she asked. She couldn't believe, given the number of men milling in the yard, that they'd gotten away.

"I don't know, but we don't have a chance of outrunning them. All we can do is try to hide."

"That's why we turned off?"

He didn't answer, allowing the truck to lose speed as he noticed that the woods to their right had begun to thin, probably as a result of a wildfire. The undergrowth had flourished, the saplings and brush shooting up rapidly since the removal of the taller trees that normally deprived them of light and moisture.

Deke continued to slow the truck, and Becki glanced behind them, apprehensive about their pursuers. She just wanted him to drive on, to put miles between them and those men with guns they didn't mind firing, even though they had to have seen Deke Summers wasn't alone. She had nothing to do with whatever they thought Deke had done, but a shotgun blast was pretty undiscriminating. She could just as easily have been the one who'd been hit.

Suddenly Deke turned the wheel, directing the pickup off the edge of the narrow road and out into the dense undergrowth. Becki was forced to put her hands against the dashboard as they bounced over bushes and rocks. Despite that precaution, her head bumped once, hard, against the top of the truck, and she was aware of the small grunt of pain, quickly stifled, from the man beside her. He was driving through the nearly impossible terrain one-handed, his injured right arm held protectively against his body, trying to direct the plunging truck between stumps and around obstacles that appeared too rapidly in their path.

He continued into the heart of the emerging growth, its density becoming greater with each foot they traveled. Suddenly the truck didn't clear, and with the resulting scraping jolt and loss of momentum, it was obvious it was going no farther. The engine died, and they sat in the stalled vehicle while the world surrounding them, which had been visible only in glimpses caught out of the bouncing windshield, settled into silence.

Becki took a breath and turned to look again out the back window—what used to be the window. She was surprised to find that the damage their passage had done to the flora was hardly visible. The small trees and undergrowth stretched behind them, appearing undisturbed except for those they'd struck, which were moving slightly, and even as she watched, that movement stilled.

"Let's go," Deke ordered, opening his door and climbing down. As she watched his descent, she was aware that he moved carefully. The graceful surety of motion she'd always admired was suddenly missing. Despite his reassurance, Deke Summers was really hurt.

She opened her door and saw that the ground was farther away than it should have been. The truck was being held up by whatever they'd hit. She jumped out, and was about to automatically close the door behind her when Deke's hand caught the edge, preventing the action. A slamming door, she realized belatedly, which would have revealed their location if the men following them *had* realized they'd turned off the main road.

"Sorry," she said softly, trying not to think about what could have resulted from that unthinking error.

Deke's one-sided smile touched upward in acknowledgment of her apology, and then he began to move away from the truck. He kept the gun in his left hand, his right arm again held tightly against his stomach, his body hunched forward. Although she hated to leave the battered old truck, feeling less secure to be fleeing on foot, she had no option but to follow him.

She was surprised by the difficulty of their progress. The

ground was uneven, cluttered with fallen trees, stumps and rotting debris. They hadn't gone a quarter of a mile before her legs and arms were scratched, stinging and burning. The man ahead of her seemed indefatigable, but she was tiring rapidly with the effort required to push through the undergrowth, climb over broken branches and struggle over the unevenness of the ground they were crossing.

She almost bumped into Deke, her eyes downturned, trying to pick the easiest route. She had been following him by the slight sounds of his progress, but she hadn't been aware when he had stopped. She looked up and he was there, facing the way they had come, head lifted, listening. When she realized that, she, too, became perfectly still, almost afraid to identify whatever he was straining so intently to hear.

What she heard, still very distantly, was frightening beyond her terrified expectation. Dogs. The excited yelping of some- body's hunting dogs.

"Is that..." she began, but all the slave-hunting stories, the movie images of prison guards and fleeing convicts crowded into her memory, blocking the completion of her question.

"They must have found the truck, and somebody decided to invite Lassie to the party," Deke said, his voice amused. He glanced down at her, blue eyes no longer intent on the distance behind them.

"Lassie?" she echoed, a little shocked by his humor in the face of this disaster. "Cujo," she breathed, fighting her terror because she was ashamed to be this terrified when he was so calm. Only, he had a lot more experience at this than she. "Or maybe the damn hounds of the Baskervilles, salivating down the trail of blood you're leaving."

"It's okay," he said again.

"The hell it is," she said, suddenly angry at him for the calmness she'd just admired. Maybe he *was* crazy. "They've got *dogs* after us, Deke. The hell it's *okay*." The last word was mocking, her tone furious. How dare he try to make her believe everything was all right? Deke had been shot, they had a pack of howling dogs after them, and no vehicle. "Don't you dare tell me that it's okay," she repeated.

His smile expanded slightly and then he made an effort to control it, but his amusement with her anger was still in his eyes, more alive than she'd ever seen them. There is some part of this he enjoys, she realized. Something that destroys that constant cold control.

"Somebody's brought his coonhounds. That's all it is, Becki. Listen," he ordered, the blond head rising again in answer to his own command.

She obeyed, hearing the faraway yelping, and she was calmer now because of his calmness. Even if he was lying, it was reassuring that he seemed unworried about the dogs.

"Those aren't bloodhounds. And unless somebody's got a bloodhound trained for manhunting, we're probably okay." The blue eyes dropped downward to hers. "Sorry," he said, apologizing for his choice of words.

She wanted that reassurance, and so she nodded, ridiculously giving him permission to go on. To convince her they were, indeed, okay.

"*Those* dogs are trained to trail coons, to tree possums and squirrels. There are too many scents in these woods that will be more interesting to them than ours."

"Not bloodhounds?" she asked, hoping he was telling her the truth.

"They don't make noise while they're trailing. They just concentrate on the scent they've been given, to the exclusion of anything else. That's why they're so valuable. Those dogs aren't going to find us, Becki. I promise you."

Again she nodded. "Then we better—" she began.

"But I'm not sure you were wrong about the blood," he said. "Help me get this off?" His left hand, hampered by the gun he carried, touched the black shirt, his fingers creating a small fold in the material that stretched over his flat stomach.

"Yes," she whispered. She held out her hand to take the gun, but he shook his head. He pulled the shirt out of the front of his trousers, and then pushed the barrel of the gun into his waistband. He put his left hand behind his body, tugging the shirt free all the way around. He bent forward, and Becki caught the tail of the shirt and drew the garment over his head. He jerked his left arm out of the sleeve as the shirt came free, but he let her help him ease the right off his hand.

From the sodden condition of the cloth she was now holding, she knew the damage was far worse than she'd imagined. Again, he'd been so casual about it all. There was no injury visible on the front of his body, other than the gash on his neck which had already clotted over. *Only a scratch*, she thought again.

"Turn around," she ordered, injecting her voice with schoolteacher authority, with the assurance of being in charge, but she was surprised when he obeyed.

Dark holes had been punched in the smooth brown skin of his back, clustered heaviest across his right shoulder and upper arm and extending in a scattered pattern almost to his spine, far more of them than she would have believed possible from the angle of the guns behind them, and all still sluggishly oozing blood.

"I don't think they're deep," he said.

"Probably not," she whispered, reaching up to touch his back, carefully avoiding the bluing holes.

"Can you tie the shirt around my shoulder somehow to stop the blood? Just to keep it off the ground?"

Maybe, she thought silently, but considering the condition of that soaked cloth, she would need something dry to put over the wounds first. A pad of some kind that could be tied on with the long sleeves of his knit shirt. Without giving herself time to think about what she was doing, she laid his bloody shirt over the sound left shoulder and began to pull off her tee. He made no comment as she undressed behind him. And he didn't turn around. She folded the soft cotton into a big square and laid it gently over his right shoulder, so that it covered most of the damage.

"Hold that," she ordered, and his left hand crossed over the front of his chest to hold the pad she'd made in place. She took his shirt, and using its sleeves, fashioned a rough sling that gave some support for the injured arm while keeping the pad in place over his back and shoulder. She moved around to the front to tie the ends of the sleeves tightly under his bent arm, hoping the whole thing would stay put.

When she looked up, his eyes were focused beyond her shoulder.

"It's okay," she said softly, realizing what he was doing. "I don't imagine I've got anything you haven't seen before."

She saw a corner of his mouth inch upward and she turned away, embarrassed despite what she'd said, despite the truth of it.

"We'd better go," she suggested.

He nodded, his eyes meeting hers.

"Do we have a destination?" she asked, remembering what he had told her before.

"Back where we started."

"The motel?" All she could remember was the crowd of men with guns. "Why? God, Deke, why go back there?"

"Because it's the last place they'll expect us," he explained, amusement again creeping into his voice. "And because as excited as those guys were, I'm willing to bet somebody left his keys in the car."

It made sense. All of it. If they could just get there.

She nodded. "Okay," she said, and watched his smile ease upward again. She was really beginning to like that movement far too much. Resolutely, she broke the connection between them and stepped aside, allowing him to take the lead as he had before. In the distance, the baying hysteria of the hounds was obviously closer than it had been before they'd stopped, and she hoped he had been telling her the truth. What he'd said about the hunting dogs had sounded plausible, but she didn't know. Again, all she could do was trust him. Trust Deke Summers to get them through.

They traveled for an incredible distance, far farther than it seemed they had in the truck, but thankfully the sound of the dogs gradually faded behind them. With the heat and humidity, she was fighting now just to pull enough air into her burning lungs. Her legs were heavy and her head was beginning to swim, because, like a fool, she hadn't eaten when she'd had the opportunity. Finally she realized she had to stop. Just long enough to get her breath. She was ashamed to ask, since she wasn't the one carrying around a load of buckshot, but she knew she had to rest.

"Deke," she called, no louder, she hoped than the sound of their passage had been. He stopped immediately, turning back to her.

"I have to rest," she gasped.

It was worse, somehow, now that they had stopped. She put her hands on her knees, bending forward, trying to draw in more air for her aching lungs. She watched the sweat drip off her forehead onto the black loam of the forest floor. Finally, when her breathing had eased a little, she lifted her head, hands still resting on her knees, to look at him.

Deke was waiting, his left shoulder propped against a small tree, watching her. His expression revealed no trace of impatience.

"Sorry," she said, still panting.

"For what?" he asked.

It was almost a sacrilege to treat her like this, he had been thinking, tracing with his eyes the scratches that marred the smooth skin of her bare arms and shoulders. He had been surprised at her stamina, her determination not to slow them down. She was far tougher than that delicate Southern-lady demeanor had indicated. The other wasn't a front, he knew. She hadn't had any idea she was this tough because she'd never been tested this way before.

There was a red slash across the top of her left breast, too clearly revealed by the low cut of the lace bra he'd bought. Sacrilege. When he realized the direction of his thoughts, he pulled his eyes away from the contemplation of Becki Travers's body. Not his right, he thought again, fighting against the pleasure of looking at her. Of allowing his eyes to drift where his mouth had once touched. Where his hands ached to caress. Just once to look openly at her, to have that right.

"You still *okay?*" she asked, her breathing beginning to ease. His eyes had been focused on the distance behind them, but at her question they came back to hers.

Suddenly, from the direction they had been heading, came the sound of voices. Men's voices. Much too close.

Deke put the barrel of the gun he carried across his mouth like a finger, urging quietness. She nodded to indicate that she'd heard what he had.

He pointed behind her, still using the gun, two quick forward motions, and she turned to see if she could figure out what he was telling her to do. There was an enormous overturned stump, the roots, which had been pulled out of the ground on one side, pointing skyward like fingers. Deke motioned again, and careful not to make any noise, she crept toward the stump, hoping that was what he'd intended.

When she turned around for further instructions, she was surprised to find him right behind her, his movement noiseless. He pointed down into the hole in the ground on the far side of the stump, and nodding again, she stepped around it to lie down in the depression. She thought he'd hide nearby, so she wasn't prepared when he eased down on top of her, his body covering hers. There was absolute silence now in the woods. She held her breath, listening for a repetition of the sounds that had sent them into hiding. Listening for any sound.

When the voices came again, only after she'd waited a long time, they were much nearer. Perhaps as close as where she and Deke had stood while she caught her breath.

"I swear I heard somethin'," one of the disembodied voices claimed.

"They ain't still gonna be around here. They've had too much time. You're imaginin' things."

"I tell you I heard somebody talkin'."

"Well, there ain't nobody here now. You probably scared off whatever you heard. Some kind of animal, maybe, but not the kind we're after."

As soon as the voices had begun, Deke had lowered his head, his cheek, warm and rough, pleasantly masculine, resting against hers. She could feel his right arm, tied to his body by the sling she'd fashioned, just under her breasts. Despite the voices—too close, too frightening, too unreal—she realized that, incredibly, she was enjoying the weight, the feel of his big, solid body lying protectively over hers.

She remembered when he'd kissed her, the almost irresistible urge she had had to step into his embrace, to welcome the strength of his arms around her. And how afraid she had been. Afraid of what he'd think.

She could smell the earth around them, slightly acrid with rotting vegetation. And the warm scent of his body. As compelling as it had been before. She turned her head slightly, feeling the dirt shift beneath her hair.

If they were going to die, she thought, there were a couple of things she wanted to do first. Had wanted to do for months. Her mouth opened, her tongue touching the stubbled softness at the corner of Deke Summers's lips.

Touched. Caressed. Traced along the line of his upper lip. Enjoying the feel and the taste of his skin. A long, endless stroke of her tongue, moving slowly, as far as she could reach without turning her head again, and then back to the point where she'd begun.

The voices eventually faded away into the distance, the small clearing once more deserted. Finally, after an eternity, Deke moved. His head lifted, the blue eyes looking down into her face. She couldn't read whatever emotion they contained—beyond the obvious question.

She hesitated, trying to find again the courage that had allowed her to put her mouth against his. "I've been wanting to do that for a long time," she whispered her confession, the sound of the words only a breath. "Longer than you can possibly imagine."

He made no verbal response, but the blue eyes continued to study her face. He was so close she could see the dew of perspiration at his temples and along his upper lip. Had known it with her tongue. Tasted its salt-sweetness. His whiskers were as fair as his hair, glinting gold against the darkness of his tan. Her gaze traced the pattern of lines around his eyes, small and white, caused by the automatic narrowing, seeking protection from the constant glare of the Southern sun. She realized for the first time that there were darker flecks in the pale irises, surrounded by the unmoving sweep of impossibly thick lashes.

"And I decided if I was going to die, I was going to do that first," she finished softly. She had no regrets—no matter what he thought. She had spent too much of her life worrying about what people might think. *Life is so fragile,* he had said. She had thought that was a lesson she'd learned from Tommy's death. But if not, apparently she was being given another chance to get it right.

Deke didn't answer, the tautness of his mouth unmoving, unsmiling. But his response was there, strong, clear and undeniable, given the proximity of their bodies.

She smiled at him, the corners of her lips moving slowly upward as, after another eternity, his head began to lower. She opened her mouth, welcoming. She wanted his kiss. And when life and death were as closely balanced on the scale as they had been a few minutes earlier, it had seemed hypocritical not to tell him.

She had wanted Deke Summers to kiss her, but she was surprised by how thoroughly he did. Tongue cherishing. Endless ravishment of emotions. Until her body reacted to its awareness of his. Again, something moving, deep inside, shifting. Pulling upward from the bottom of her belly. Aching this time with the intensity of the sensation, of her need. Her hips arched into his, and he reacted, pushing down strongly. Letting her feel his strength, the force of his desire.

His head lifted, his mouth moving only fractionally away from hers. So reluctant to let her go. Despite what he knew. Had known from the beginning.

"This is crazy," he whispered.

It was what he had said before, she remembered. Only this

time she didn't care what he said. Why was this crazy, when nothing made sense any more? There was no order in the world they shared, no normality. Why was this crazy, when they both wanted to do just what they were doing?

"Why?" she asked, touching her tongue again to his mouth, tracing the outline. "Why?"

"I can't do this," he said. He couldn't allow himself to care about anyone because—

"Because I'm not her?" she asked, bitter that he couldn't let go of the past.

"Because they'll come after anyone..."

I love. He had stopped the words, but they were there in his consciousness. It wasn't allowed. Lila was dead. He'd been responsible for her death. And this wasn't allowed.

"But they already think that...that we're involved. What can it matter if..." Becki hesitated. She had never before suggested that to a man. And this one was, still, almost a stranger.

The blue eyes rested on her face a long time, examining not her features, she knew, but what she had said. At least he was thinking about what she had said. Not an outright rejection.

But when he turned his head, it felt like rejection. He used his left hand, which still held the gun, to push himself away from her until he was on his knees, straddling her body. She could feel the rough fabric of his jeans against her bare calves, and her eyes lowered to find the reassurance that he, too, had wanted what she'd asked him for. The soft denim concealed nothing of what he wanted.

"Why not?" she asked, looking up again into his eyes, crystal as a mountain stream.

She was so beautiful, he thought. Leaves tangled in her hair. Dirt on the perfect curve of her cheekbone. And garish against the soft purity of her skin, a smear of blood on her chin from where it had rested against his neck.

Already marked with blood. And at the image, he finally found the strength to turn away from what she offered. There would be no other sacrifice for his failures. No more broken and bloodied bodies.

"Because I can't," he said simply.

He pushed up off his knees, the movement awkward. He staggered, the effects of blood loss, exertion and a too-sudden change of position. He stumbled backward into the roots of the stump they'd hidden behind. Using the thickest of those for balance, he stepped upward, out of the depression.

She felt naked without the warmth of his body. Aware for the first time that she was wearing her bra. Had lain beneath his arousal. Had asked him to make love to her. She closed her eyes against the hot rush of embarrassment. He had made it clear that he wasn't interested, had made it clear from the first. And now, of course, she understood why. He was still in love with the woman his enemies had destroyed. A woman whose death he felt responsible for. A woman named Lila.

"We have to go," he said, his voice coming from above her. Ridiculously, she nodded, feeling the debris caught in her hair moving against the dirt. She had not even thought about what she must look like. Dirty. Sweaty. Unappealing. Especially unappealing, coming on like a sex-starved spinster to a man like Deke Summers.

She put her hands on the ground under her body and sat up. Deke had already turned back to the direction they'd been heading, ready to move on. *Always have a destination.*

She stood up, feeling the trembling exhaustion in her thighs. She brushed the earth from the back of her shorts and legs and made some attempt to pick the junk out of her hair and then wondered what it mattered.

She used the root he'd touched to pull herself up out of the hole, the dirt shifting and falling back into the shallow depression that had briefly sheltered their bodies. She didn't meet his eyes again, hers focused somewhere around his knees, but when he finally turned and moved again into the tangled undergrowth, she was following.

EXCITED OR NOT, none of those men had thoughtfully left his keys. The three cars that lined the road in front of the motel were all locked. There was another parked by the office, but the exposed position made it impossible to check. She and Deke had edged carefully along the highway, hidden by the thickness of the woods. When they got to the parked vehicles, he had eased down into the ditch, crouching low, hidden by the cars themselves, until he'd checked all three.

Watching him from the relative safety of the undergrowth, she could read the expletive he mouthed in frustration when he'd reached the last. She was almost too bruised by what had happened in the woods to worry about what came next. She had made her attempt to have some direction over events and had been quickly reminded that she was not in control. This was not her game. She was only along for the ride. An unwanted passenger. A burden. No more in control of whatever was happening than Josh. Wherever he was.

God, she prayed, closing her eyes tight to prevent the sudden weakening rush of tears. *Please dear God, keep him safe. He's just a baby. Only a baby.* There was nothing she could do. Nothing to protect him. Except hope that Deke Summers knew what he was doing.

When she opened her eyes, Deke was almost beside her again, still moving in a deep crouch until his body was swallowed up by the thick brush in which she was hiding.

"Nothing," he said. "Locked up tight."

He had somehow found the calmness once more during the return journey, and if she hadn't been watching his reaction to the frustration of this denied avenue of escape, she would have thought the setback no more than he had expected.

"Now what?" she asked, the first words she'd spoken to him since her invitation. Too embarrassed to speak. Shamed by the realization of what she had done. And by his response.

"There's a café a little way down the road. It's where I bought breakfast. We check out the cars parked there."

She nodded, aware that he was again examining her features. She forced her eyes up and hoped that the humiliation she was feeling wasn't reflected there.

"I'm going to get you out of this," he promised. "And Josh. Just hang on, Becki. Just trust me."

She held his eyes a moment, reading in them, she knew, only what he intended her to read. Confidence. That damned calm surety that he had control.

"Since you got us into it, that seems fair," she said, fighting for her own control.

The corner of his lips began to tilt and then he stopped the movement. "That's what *I* thought," he said, agreeing with her accusation.

Except she had admitted now, to herself at least, that she'd been as responsible for what had happened that Sunday morning as he. Inviting what had happened. Welcoming his kiss. Because, she had been forced to acknowledge as they had lain together in the dirt today, she wanted him to make love to her.

"You ready?" he asked.

He wanted to touch her. To put his fingers under her chin, against her cheek. To bring back the woman who had followed, bravely and uncomplainingly, since he'd snatched her from her own safe backyard. He was aware of what he'd done. A rejection of something that he wanted more than she could imagine. Something that was too far beyond his reach. But that didn't stop the desire to reach out for it.

Forbidden, he reminded himself again. *All of it. Forever forbidden, because never again would he watch someone he loved die in his place.*

THEY FOUND WHAT THEY needed behind the café. Probably one of the workers' cars, keys and cigarettes left in the central console. Easier than unlocking the car each time he wanted a quick smoke, maybe. Or perhaps forgotten, just this once.

Neither of them examined the permutation of chance that had given them this gift. They simply climbed in, holding the unclosed doors, although the air conditioner jutting from the window above the parked car was loudly furnishing cold air to the restaurant. She held her breath as Deke started the engine. He drove out of the lot and back onto the same road that fronted the motel. There was no outcry behind them, no guns, no movement.

Because she had expected him to head back toward the interstate they'd turned off the day before, she was surprised when he continued to head away from it, still traveling north.

"Where are you going?" she finally asked. She might be only a passenger on this odyssey, but they had another person to consider, and this road wasn't taking them nearer to Josh.

"This direction until I find some kind of highway back east." His eyes remained on the two-lane ahead, although he was driving slowly, obeying the speed limit.

"East?" she repeated. "But I told you—"

"And somebody told them," Deke said.

"Told them what?"

"Where we're going. Where Josh is."

"Nobody told them anything. Nobody *knows* where Josh is. We don't even know. Why would you think—"

"They've picked us up too quickly. All along. They have to be getting information about where we're heading. They have to."

"You said not to worry about how they found you. That anyone could spot you, recognize you, and put out the word. What makes you think they know where Josh is?"

"Instinct, maybe," he said softly.

She thought about that. Instinct hadn't led him to that conclusion.

"No, damn it, you still think somebody's helping them. Somebody in my family."

"I didn't say that."

"Then who else? There are maybe five people, all related to me, who knew about Mike and Bill's plans to head west."

"You can't be sure of that. They could have told anybody."

That was true, of course. The community was small enough that people would be interested in the unusual vacation. Who knew how many people her mom, Louise and Mary had talked to in the meantime? At the beauty shop, the grocery store, the dentist's office. A hundred people might know by now. Maybe Deke was right. Maybe the people who were following them

did know that they would traveling on one of the major highways west.

"And this morning?" she asked. "How did they find us
this morning?"

"Someone estimated the distance we'd cover in a day and
then alerted the members in that broad area? A few phone
calls. My picture and updated information posted on the electronic bulletin boards I told you about. It could have been
recognition by the motel owner. Another guest. The people in
the café where I got breakfast."

Becki realized that he hadn't mentioned as a possibility that
someone had recognized *her*. She hadn't told him that she'd
gone outside. Maybe someone had seen her make her phone
call. Maybe someone looking out the window of the office.
She had been so close to those windows. So stupid because
she had been afraid. Afraid, at that time, of Deke himself.
Stupid, she thought again, trying to decide if she should tell
him about leaving the cabin. It would necessitate an explanation of whom she'd called. And why. The *why* would be
the hardest part, but also, she knew it would make him again
suspect a member of her family.

Mary hadn't betrayed her. There had been nothing out of
place in her sister's responses this morning, nothing suspicious. Mary didn't have any clue what was going on, and if
she didn't, then there was no way she could have been responsible for their having been discovered.

Deke himself had told her: *It doesn't do any good to worry
about how they found you.* Even if someone had seen her
making her phone call, which she knew now she shouldn't
have placed, it didn't matter. *Let it go,* she commanded her
mind. *Worry about something that matters.* Like how they
were going to find Josh before anyone else did. Getting to
Josh, she told herself, was the only thing that was important
now.

Chapter Eight

"I think you'd better drive," Deke said.

They had been traveling almost an hour on the eastbound state road he'd turned onto. Becki had been fighting the despair that had grown with each mile they traveled in the opposite direction to the one in which her brothers were headed. She couldn't help feeling that she was deserting her son, leaving him unprotected, Mike and Bill unaware of the danger they faced.

"All right," she agreed, realizing that Deke was as exhausted as she. As hungry. And injured. She had lost her previous concerns about him in his strength and confidence, in her worry about Josh. Deke Summers could take care of himself, she knew, but suddenly, seeing the grayish cast to his skin, apparent even beneath the tan, she knew she had again been stupid.

With her agreement, he had already begun to slow the car, preparing to pull off the two-lane highway in order to make the exchange. She watched his eyelids drift downward and then lift, the effort he made to keep his gaze focused on the road obvious.

"Deke?" she questioned. "You okay?"

The corner of his mouth ticked upward at her use of that word, and he took a deep breath. The car was still moving, but very slowly now, beginning to edge off the blacktop. His eyelids lowered almost in slow motion, like a sleepy owl's, and then opened again to right the path of the car, to hold it on the shoulder.

"Brakes," she ordered calmly, not wanting to startle him. Just ease them off the road. As long as he didn't run the car into a ditch, they'd be all right. She should have seen this coming.

Finally the car stopped, outside wheels still safely on the apron. Deke put his left hand on the top of the steering wheel, and then rested his face against his forearm a moment. He was working up the energy to climb out, knowing it wasn't going to be pretty. He should have let Becki drive from the café, but somehow the uncertainty that had been in her eyes had made him feel he couldn't demand anything more of her. Nothing more than what he had asked from the beginning. *Follow me. Trust me.*

He had offered her protection and with what was happening now, he knew he was not in a position to make good on that promise. All they could do was go to ground. Hide again. Somewhere where they wouldn't have to come in contact with anyone. Somewhere they could stay put until he could once more carry out the promise he'd made.

"We need a house," he said, fighting the debilitating weakness that had grown with each mile he'd put between them and the Louisiana town where they'd spent the night, with each drop of blood that had seeped out onto her makeshift bandage.

"A house?"

"Vacation. A house where the people are gone." He made his brain create the words and push them out of his mouth. It was too hard to think, to plan. "And will be gone for a few days," he finally remembered to add, to warn her.

"How can we know how long they'll be gone?" she asked. She could find a deserted house. He'd told her before how to do that. But as for knowing how long the owners would be gone... How were they going to find out how long someone would be away? And why did that matter? Surely he wasn't planning to spend any length of time in one place. They had to get to Josh.

Instead of trying to formulate an answer, Deke opened the door. He put his left foot on the pavement and began to pull himself out. He gasped a little with the cost of that movement. He put his left hand over the top of the door to help lift his unresponsive body out of the car.

When he finally was standing outside the sedan, Becki watched him lean against the car's frame. And then she wondered why she was still sitting inside watching. She opened her door and hurried around the car. She lifted his left arm over her shoulders and guided him around the front end to the other side. He eased carefully into the passenger seat.

Once they'd accomplished the maneuver, she glanced up at his face. Despite the efficiency of the air-conditioning, his forehead was beaded with sweat. Of their own accord, her fingers touched his cheek, her thumb under his chin, directing his face upward. The blue eyes, slightly out of focus, rose to meet hers.

"I'll find somewhere. I promise you, Deke. I'll get us somewhere safe. I promise."

He nodded, trusting her because he had no choice. His gaze held a moment, and then giving in, the eyelids fell downward, like the closing eyes of a doll.

And the blue had been exactly like that. Like the glass eyes of a doll. Unaware.

The heavy swish of a passing truck brought Becki out of the sudden, useless indulgence in fear. She pulled the shoulder belt she'd been using across Deke's body. Although he made no protest, she knew she was probably hurting him, pushing the injured shoulder against the seat, but she slipped the metal connections together anyway. If nothing else, the belt would help to hold him upright, prevent the chafing of his shoulder against the seat, the movement that had elicited that gasp of pain, which he would never have allowed had he been more in control.

In control, she thought, closing her eyes. Deke Summers

was no longer able to control this situation, but she had made him a promise to keep them safe until he could.

A COUPLE OF NEWSPAPERS at the end of the concrete drive. The grass a little long. There were no outside lights burning and no car in the driveway. But maybe, she thought. *Maybe.*

Deke's eyes were closed, his head against the headrest. She wondered in quick panic if he might be unconscious. He had made no response when she'd turned north again, unable to bear driving any farther away from where she thought Josh might be. She needed a map, but when she had opened the glove compartment of the stolen car and one-handed, eyes on the road, rummaged through the contents, she hadn't found one. She could only hope that the highway they were following would lead back to a major east/west artery, would lead somewhere.

She had almost missed the house in worrying about all she needed to consider. After she'd cruised past, she turned the car around, as they had done before, to get a better look. On the third pass before the two-story white colonial, a little way outside the town they'd just driven through, she stopped at the mailbox. She opened it and found that it was reassuringly full of what was obviously more than one day's mail. Mail that no helpful relative had been sent to pick up. Nobody was checking on things here, keeping the papers gathered up and the letters brought inside.

It seemed almost too perfect. Since there were no other cars on the road, she backed up and into the driveway, brazenly driving all the way to the two-car garage. Through the car windows she took a quick survey of the property and the road in front. Nothing. Nobody. She left the motor running, walked to the garage door and shading her eyes with her hand peered in through the row of small windows that stretched, uncurtained, across the front. A dark green convertible, some kind of vintage sports car, up on blocks, occupied one half. No one had come to the front door, which she could see from where she was standing, to investigate the strange car in the drive.

Without giving herself time to back out, she pushed up the heavy garage door, surprised to find it unlocked, and then got back into the idling sedan, driving it into the empty half. She sat a second in the car, again waiting for someone to challenge her right to be here.

Finally, hands trembling, she turned off the key and got out to retrace her steps and pull the double door down, effectively hiding the car from the road. She believed that no one had driven by after she'd pulled into the driveway. She didn't know if traffic would have convinced her to move on, to find somewhere else, but it was reassuring to think that she wouldn't have to make that decision. Instead, all she had to worry about was how to get them inside.

She glanced again at Deke and found his head turned toward her, eyes open, but he was making no attempt to get out of the car.

"I need to get us inside," she explained softly, wondering how much he understood. "I'm going to find a way to get in."

He nodded, and then let his lids close again.

She got out and climbed the three wooden steps from the garage to a door that she knew would lead into the house. A steel door, she realized. Maybe that was why they hadn't bothered to lock the garage—because even if someone got in here, they still couldn't get into the house. She knocked on the door and waited, trying to think of a reasonable story to explain their presence if someone did answer. There was only silence. No response, but she knocked again, just to make sure, pounding with more confidence this time.

Nothing. All she had to do now was get inside. There was probably a key hidden somewhere convenient. Everybody did that, provided an emergency key for when you were careless enough to lock yourself out of your own house. She just had to find it.

She searched on top of the door moldings, under the plastic-grass mat and everywhere else she could imagine hiding a key. She had to get Deke inside, to look at whatever was happening under the pad and sling she had designed this morning. Feed him. Get him into bed. Maybe even find some medicine. Their chances were certainly better inside the house than out here in the afternoon heat. It must be over a hundred in the enclosed garage. "Damn," she said, as her searching fingers ran futilely under the edge of the workbench, thinking maybe they'd taped a key there.

She stepped back from the precisely arranged workbench, trying to think. Where else? Where hadn't she searched? The neat row of baby-food jars that stretched across the back of the work surface caught her eye. Each appeared to be filled with a different size screw or nail, some small object. She found the key in the third one she opened and wasn't even aware of her triumphant grin.

"Bingo," she said under her breath.

She ran back up the stairs and inserted the key into the lock of the steel door, which now turned smoothly under her fingers. She hesitated, and then decided that Deke was better off where he was until she'd verified there was no one home.

The house was empty, everything clean and orderly, the same kind of preparation she herself would make before any trip, not wanting to return to a disordered house. The refrigerator was, disappointingly, as thoroughly prepared for the vacation as the rest of the house. No milk, meat or fruit. Nothing perishable. The freezer was a little better and the pantry was well stocked. She could at least fix them a meal.

With that thought, she realized Deke was still sitting in the heat of the garage while she explored. She had started across the kitchen when she looked up to find him standing in the doorway, leaning against the frame, watching her.

"I think it's safe. At least for the moment," she said.

He nodded and stepped inside, moving slowly away from the support of the frame. He put his left hand on the counter, and holding on, began to walk across the white tile.

"You better sit down," she said. She pulled one of the bentwood chairs from under the round wicker table and put it almost in front of him. He eased down into it, that careful movement accompanied by a soft grunt of effort.

She began to untie the sleeves of the sling. She held his right wrist as she slipped the black knit shirt away from his body, and then she lowered his forearm carefully to rest across his lap. She threw the ruined shirt into the sink. She dreaded trying to remove the green tee. She had taken a first-aid course or two, but she didn't remember anything about treating gunshot wounds. Everybody assumed you'd rush a person who'd been shot to the hospital, not try to treat him yourself.

She began to pull the cotton away from Deke's back. It stuck in far too many places, and the scattered holes she was exposing began to bleed again with the shirt's removal. Deke made no sound while she worked.

Finally she managed to peel the discolored fabric completely away from the injury. Shocked by what she'd uncovered, she stood a moment just looking at the damage. It looked far worse than it had this morning. Swollen, the flesh bruised as well as torn, and still bleeding. She gently put her fingers against an undamaged spot.

"A couple of them may have struck bone," Deke said. Although his voice was very soft, she had jumped, not only hearing the sound, but feeling it through the sensitive tips of her fingers. "But you should be able to get the rest."

"*I* should be able..." Her voice faded as she realized what he meant. He thought she was going to remove the pellets that were embedded in his back and shoulder. Only, she didn't have any idea how to go about that and wouldn't have dared attempt it even if she had.

"Deke, we have to get you to a doctor," she said. Not intending to give him time to argue, she stepped toward the phone that rested on the counter, sure that the directory would be somewhere in its vicinity. Before she could get there, Deke had pushed up from the kitchen chair, his face contorted with pain, determined to block her path.

"No doctors," he ordered. His eyes, bloodshot and still almost glassy, held hers by sheer force of will.

"You don't know what your back is like," she said.

"I know," he said. "Believe me, I *know*." The crooked smile flickered briefly.

"I can't do anything about getting the shot out. You need a hospital. Surgery. A real doctor."

"And Josh?"

The question stopped her as no other argument would have. *And what about Josh?*

"You're not going to do Josh any good in this condition," she said practically. "You're not going to do *anybody* any good if you bleed to death."

The unthinking words hung between them. Something had happened to his eyes, the pain and exhaustion replaced by the familiar coldness.

When she saw what was in his face, the realization came that what she'd just said was the exact opposite of reality. She didn't want the thought, but it crept, unwelcomed, into her intellect. *The people following them wanted Deke Summers dead. And if he were, there would no longer be any threat to her son.*

"I didn't—" she began and then stopped, because there was nothing to explain, nothing she could explain.

"If I'm dead, Josh is safe. You're safe. Did you just figure that out?" he asked calmly.

"I don't want you dead," she whispered.

"Not even to protect Josh?"

She wanted to deny it outright, that the idea had even occurred to her. The idea of exchanging one human life for another was obscene. Unthinkable. At least to her.

She shook her head, not sure what she was denying. She would die to protect Josh. Kill to protect him. But accept the sacrifice of another person's life? Especially considering the circumstances Deke had described. His life, not given in an emergency to save a child's, but brutally taken from him— execution style. It was not something she had considered, not even in the two days they'd spent together. And she wanted it out of her mind. Her eyes fell away from the emptiness in his, and she shook her head, trying to sort through all the feelings that were suddenly in her heart.

The back of his left hand touched her cheek, the knuckles moving downward, pulling lightly against her skin, until he reached her chin.

"I'm not quite ready to give up, Bec. Not quite ready to believe I can't get us *all* out of this alive. Despite... everything," he said simply, refusing to give voice again to the demons she'd forced him to share, "I always find myself trying to survive. Some kind of personality defect, maybe."

"I don't think there's anything defective about wanting to live," she said. She touched his hand, and then let her fingers close around his. She was disconcerted to find that his were trembling.

"No matter what?" he asked.

Maybe he needed affirmation of the God-given instinct to survive—considering all that had happened to him, all that he'd lost. Although she had had Josh to give her a reason to keep going, there had been days after Tommy's death when it had been so hard to believe that any of the things she was expected to do really mattered. Getting up in the morning. Going to work. Making the effort. The temptation was always to give in, to take the easy way, to just follow the course of least resistance. And for Deke Summers that course would be...to finally allow this all to end. *They'll put the muzzle of a rifle...*

Obscene, she thought again, denying the image. Pushing it to the back of her mind. Especially now. Especially the way she felt. And she found herself wondering how he found the resolve to go on. *Despite everything.*

"No matter what," she agreed softly, wanting him to believe that. To do anything else was a desecration of life. *So fragile* echoed in her heart. So infinitely precious.

And slowly he nodded.

SHE HAD FOUND TWEEZERS. Alcohol. Peroxide. Even a tube of antibiotic salve. Some gauze pads. Most of those items came from a well-stocked first-aid kit that had even contained a threaded suture needle, but she couldn't bring herself to imagine using that. To sew torn human flesh. She shivered, although the house was still hot, the central air-conditioning unit she'd reset not having had time to defeat the heat that had built in the time the house had been empty.

After she'd finished searching through the cabinets under the lavatory in the downstairs master suite, she had taken her finds with her, laying them on the night table beside the king-size bed. She had pulled back the spread, folded it and was about to place it over the bedroom chair when she glanced up to find Deke standing in the doorway.

"You've got to stop sneaking up on me," she said, smiling at him. He looked like death warmed over.

"I need the bathroom," he said simply.

"Of course," she agreed.

She had slept in the same bed with this man. She didn't know why she was embarrassed by that simple confession. Feeling the blush climb into her throat, she laid down the comforter and tried to step around him.

"I think I'm going to need some help." The words were very soft. "Getting my clothes off," he clarified, again reading too accurately what had been in her eyes.

"Of course," she said. "What—"

"Boots," he suggested hesitantly.

It seemed he was almost as uncomfortable with the situation as she was. She nodded and helped him sit down on the edge of the bed she'd just turned back. She tugged off the work boots and then the heavy socks he'd been wearing inside them. She stood up, preparing to give him some privacy.

"Jeans," he said softly. And this time the word was more question than suggestion.

She swallowed, her mouth suddenly dry. This was ridiculous. *Come on,* she urged herself, *grow up. Florence Nightingale. Injured man.* There was nothing sexual about helping a wounded man out of his clothes so you could dig around with a pair of tweezers for the shotgun pellets lodged in his back.

Deke stood up and with his left hand unfastened the metal buttons of his fly. Hoping her face was giving away nothing of what she was feeling, she put her hands on either side of the loosened waistband and pulled the jeans down, stooping as she followed their descent down the long, muscled legs. Deke put his left hand on her shoulder for balance and then stepped out of them. She forced her eyes to remain fixed on the filthy denim she held in her lap while he walked around her. She didn't look up until the bathroom door closed behind him. Almost immediately came the sound of running water. Deke was taking a shower, she realized in surprise. Which probably wasn't a bad idea, she thought, as long as he didn't pass out.

In the meantime, she decided, deliberately banishing the images that had crept into her head, she could wash their clothes. She opened the drawers of the dresser until she found one that contained masculine clothing. She laid a pair of navy pajama bottoms on the bed. Turning to the walk-in closet, she considered the items there and finally selected a short cotton robe, pearl snap buttons up the front and appliquéd tulips around the hem. Her mother would have loved it, she thought with a trace of amusement, and she took the robe with her as she left the bedroom.

Thinking about the bloodstains, she threw everything into the washer in the garage on cold-water wash. She could put them through a warm cycle later. After she'd stripped off her own garments, she had pulled the robe on over her naked body, but she knew she would also feel better with a shower. There would be another bathroom upstairs. The thought of just being able to wash her hair was an incredible morale booster. All the simple pleasures she had always taken for granted—clean clothes, clean body, food, shelter, safety—were now luxuries to be cherished.

ALTHOUGH DEKE HAD allowed no sound to escape during the ordeal, his body had involuntarily reacted a few times, muscles clenching suddenly under the agonizing probe of the tweezers. They hadn't talked during the procedure. He knew she was doing the best she could, and he was determined not to make the job any more difficult.

Something else to be endured, he had thought, closing his mind to the pain. He had had a lot of experience at enduring. Maybe too much experience. But this required a different type of endurance. Easier, perhaps, because it was only physical. And limited. He could manage this, he had thought, locking his teeth into his bottom lip. He was sitting on the kitchen chair, straddling the seat, with his arm and shoulder bent forward over the top of the chair to give Becki better access.

The first pellets she had dug out had not been too bad. She had chosen those nearest the surface and that success had given her confidence. He knew she was probably no longer even aware of him as a person, of the agony she was causing. That was, of course, exactly what he intended. To become an inanimate object from which buckshot could be extracted. No longer a person. No longer a man with nerve endings that were screaming their reaction to her probing.

When the pain became worse, as he had known it would, he devised his own escape. Remembering. He remembered her tongue tracing over his lips in the woods. The soft, involuntary color of her blush spreading upward under the smooth skin. And the kiss. Savoring the memory of each movement of his mouth against the responses of hers. Not hesitant as she had been before in the motel. Today her tongue had been seeking. As urgent as his. As hungry. He had known that Sunday dawn that she wanted his kiss. There had always been some thread of desire between them. He had responded to it then as he had today in the woods. A stolen pleasure. *Forbidden,* he thought, reminding himself again of all the reasons, and so he forced himself to destroy the images in his head.

With their destruction, the reality of the present intruded. He gasped as the tweezers dug into damaged flesh, and then the sound was quickly cut off. Responses again controlled.

"Sorry," she said softly.

"It's okay," he whispered. *Get it over. Just do it.*

"That's the last one," she said. "I'm going to pour on some peroxide to try to clean out the holes and then put antibiotic salve on the gauze and cover them," she explained.

Then I'm just going to hope for the best, she added silently. He hadn't given her much choice, since he still refused medical care. She knew that all gunshot wounds were reported to the authorities, which was why he'd refused a doctor, but surely there had to be someone they could trust, somebody not corrupted by the faceless, nameless enemy he feared.

Paranoia, she thought again as she worked, but the memory of how his wife had died denied that easy judgment. The horror engendered by watching a car bomb destroy someone he loved was not neurotic. A small army storming his house in the dead of night was not imagined.

"There's got to be somebody we can call. Someone you trust," she said aloud, her hands still attending to the lacerated flesh as she talked.

"I *trusted* those people before," he said.

She worked a moment in silence. "And someone betrayed that trust?"

"There's no other way it could have been done," Deke said. "Not without cooperation from one of the *good* guys."

She didn't say anything else because she recognized argument on that issue was useless. When she spoke again, it was on a different subject.

"I saw arthritis-strength aspirin in the kitchen. Nothing stronger. Except a little Jack Daniels," she amended, remembering the whiskey bottle in the cabinet over the stove.

"Some of each," Deke said, closing his eyes. His shoulder hurt like hell, but the real problem was that it would be much worse tomorrow. Increased soreness, a lack of mobility—and the strong possibility of infection. With the hike through the woods this morning and the time lapse before even this primitive treatment, the injuries were certainly ripe for going septic.

His system was usually pretty good at fighting off sickness, but he wasn't sure in this case it stood much of a chance.

"Could you eat?" she asked, putting the final piece of tape across her handiwork.

"Yes," he said, although the thought of food was repulsive. That was something else he had learned through these last four years. He did what he had to do to keep going, to stay strong, and eating was a necessity.

She stuck one of the frozen dinners into the microwave and then brought him the aspirin and whiskey. Over her protests he downed three of the big white tablets followed by a generous chaser straight from the bottle. He worked his way stolidly through the food when it was ready, managing the fork with his left hand, acting as if this were something else to be gotten through, eating with determination and without enjoyment. By the time he'd finished, he was exhausted enough to allow her to help him back to the bedroom.

He lay down on his stomach, his throbbing shoulder propped against the extra pillows Becki stacked under it. When she cut off the overhead light, he realized it was already dark outside. He had meant to tell her to bring the gun to him, but the thought had slipped, unarticulated, out of his mind.

If they weren't safe, they were at least hidden. They had given it their best shot, and with luck they'd have a few hours to recoup today's losses. He had thought he wouldn't be able to sleep with the pain, but the combination of blood loss, whiskey and exhaustion edged him quickly into a state that was only slightly to the right side of unconsciousness.

BY NINE BECKI couldn't hold her eyes open any longer. The clothes were still in the dryer, but she decided to leave them. She didn't turn out the small light over the sink that had been on when she'd entered the kitchen this afternoon, but she checked to make sure all the outside doors were locked. She had locked the garage door and retrieved the gun from the car before nightfall. That Deke had left it there was, she knew, an indication of the seriousness of his condition.

She entered the dark bedroom, and putting the gun and the aspirin on the table beside the bed, she turned on the small bedside lamp.

"Deke," she said. There was no response. She put the back of her hand against his forehead and felt the dry heat. The fever was only what she had expected, but she had nothing to fight the infection. She had spent a good deal of time after her solitary supper searching the rest of the house, looking for anything she could give him. She had finally decided this family obeyed the rules, either finishing prescriptions or throwing out the leftovers. It fit with the perfect order of the rest of the house, but given their situation, it was frustrating as hell.

"Deke," she said again. The glazed eyes opened in response, but she wasn't sure he recognized her. "You need to take a couple more of these," she said. "Sit up."

He pushed up, resting on his left elbow, just far enough to down the aspirin with a swallow of water from the straw she held against his lips. As soon as the pills were down, he almost fell back against the supporting pillows. She had thought about asking him if there was anything else she should do, but decided against trying to talk to him. She had done everything she could think of. Let him rest.

She turned off the lamp and waited for her eyes to adjust. She had planned to go up to one of the bedrooms on the second floor, but as she stood in the darkness she knew that she didn't really want to be up there, not even with the protection of the gun. She hated to leave Deke alone down here. It was possible that he might need something during the night. Help to the bathroom, if nothing else.

She wondered how much of that was rationalizing what she really wanted to do, and then she thought again, as she had in the woods today, how foolish it was to spend time worrying about what someone else might think if they knew. She only wanted to crawl into the warmth on the other side of this big bed. Despite Deke's condition, she knew she'd feel far safer down here with him than upstairs alone.

Finally, giving in to temptation, she walked around the bed, pulled back the sheet and climbed in. She lay very still, but her movements didn't seem to have disturbed the man beside her. His breathing was again reassuringly steady in the darkness. Becoming familiar. It was her final thought before her eyes drifted closed, her tired mind slipping effortlessly into the comfort of sleep.

Chapter Nine

Sunlight was streaming into the bedroom, but Becki knew it hadn't been the sun that had awakened her. She closed her eyes again, lying very still, too comfortable to think about moving, about getting up.

There was something in the back of her mind, however, that was disturbing. Fighting the pleasant morning lethargy, she reopened her eyes. From the angle of the light, the windows were in the wrong place. Unfamiliar wallpaper covered the walls and the ceiling fan was different. She tried to think why she wasn't in her bedroom, and suddenly realization flooded back.

Her left cheek was resting against Deke Summers's spine, her body spooned tightly along the length of his. Her right arm was across his side, fingers limp against the mat of hair that covered his chest. Still relaxed by the warm intimacy of that position, she let her hand smooth downward, a small, caressing journey over the flatness of his stomach, and slowly up again. She turned her head slightly, so she could put her lips against the uniform column of vertebrae that centered his back. It was only then that she knew what had awakened her. Heat. Deke was so hot, his skin burning beneath the cool touch of her lips.

She had known this was inevitable, despite all the precautions she had taken yesterday. Along with the buckshot, she had picked bits of fabric from the holes in Deke's back, and the peroxide had boiled out more. But even then she had known she had not gotten out all the dirt and debris that had been introduced into the wounds.

She eased away from his body, examining what she could see of his back and shoulder around the edges of the bandaging. Far more swollen than last night, more discolored. Not better, but worse. Much worse.

"Deke," she whispered, leaning forward to put her mouth next to his ear. She was careful not to press against the damaged shoulder, although her arm was still lying across his body. "Deke," she said again, this time without much hope that he would respond.

When he did, it wasn't with words. His big hand closed over hers, flattening her palm on his chest, holding it there.

"How do you feel?" she asked, her lips moving against his neck, infinitely reassured by his simple response. She trailed her hand downward again, this time carrying his on top of it, enjoying under her palm the texture of his skin, the narrow band of hair that led into the waistband of the borrowed briefs.

"You don't want to know," he said simply.

Conscious of his unthinking gesture, Deke released the small fingers he'd captured. He could feel her body pressed along the length of his, fitted against him as if she had been made for him, to sleep beside him. As if she belonged there.

"More aspirin?" Becki asked, wishing there was something else she could give him.

"Yeah," he agreed, but he knew how little that was going to help the pain that would be inevitable when he moved. Moving was something he was in no hurry to do. For more than one reason.

He felt her ease away from him, the coolness of the surrounding air touching his overheated skin as soon as she removed the warm softness of hers. *So cold*, he thought, shivering in reaction to the air conditioner's efficiency. Becki pulled the sheet up over his shoulders, but that was not an acceptable replacement for the too-pleasant warmth of her body.

Deke closed his eyes because the light hurt them. They were burning, aching, just as the rest of his body ached. And he hadn't even tried to move his shoulder. He had enough experience to know that was going to hurt like hell, despite the aspirin she kept poking down him. *Take two aspirin and call me in the morning.* He wished he knew someone he could call. Someone who could get them out of this. Get Josh. He had to hold on to that thought—no matter what.

He knew Becki couldn't understand the urgency of finding her son. He was the one who knew the ruthlessness of the bastards who wanted him dead. *And this time,* he acknowledged, trying to find the strength to sit up and take the caplets she was holding out to him, *this time they might finally get what they wanted.*

"Can I help?" Becki said softly. The blue eyes lifted in response, bloodshot and fever bright.

Deke managed a small negative movement of his head. He closed his eyes again, trying to find the courage to sit up, dreading what was coming.

He tried to push up on his left elbow as he had the previous night—some night. The pain sliced through his control like a blowtorch. That was exactly what it felt like. As if his shoulder were on fire. He groaned aloud against its force, but at least he was up. Unsteady, body trembling, but erect enough to swallow the aspirin. The water.

"Maybe that will help," she said hopefully as he eased carefully back onto the pillows.

He didn't answer, couldn't find any words. He was waiting for the pain to recede, to fade again to some level that was manageable.

When he finally reopened his eyes she was still there, kneeling beside the bed, eyes, full of worry, fastened on his face. He knew that what she was seeing wouldn't be very reassuring. If he looked only half as bad as he felt...

"We have to stay put," he said.

She nodded.

"If anything happens..." he paused, hating to admit defeat.

Hating, after all this time, to give in and let them win. But he knew, given his condition, that he had to make her understand.

"Get out," he ordered. "Just get out. They'll let you go. It's me they want."

There was no reaction in the dark eyes.

"Do you understand?" he asked, the question harsh with his need to be reassured that she did, that she would do what he'd told her.

"I understand," she said.

He tried to search her eyes, to read the truth in them. Tried to decide if she had agreed only because she thought that was what he wanted to hear. To pacify him.

"For Josh," he said, still holding her eyes. "Promise me. For Josh. No more, Becki. No more..."

Broken and bloodied bodies. No more deaths. No one else dying in my place.

He didn't complete the thought. His eyes closed against the pain and the fever. He had told her, and he thought she'd agreed. Maybe, if they were lucky, they had bought a few days of safety by finding this house. A few days to recover, to get his strength back. Maybe...

DEKE'S FEVER BUILT during the day, despite the aspirin. Becki found a first-aid book, and trying to fight the swelling, she applied cold compresses. By afternoon, Deke was sleeping most of the time, and Becki knew he was not totally aware of what was going on. She sat beside him and listened to his incoherent ramblings as he slept, listened to him endure again the horrors he had told her about. And because he had told her, she understood most of it—the muttered phrases, the fever-induced nightmare images.

By late afternoon she knew she had to do something. The fever was still climbing, his skin on fire and his lips cracked with its heat. She had made him drink water throughout the day, hating to wake him, but knowing that the danger of dehydration was very real.

Something to fight the fever, she thought. She had to get her hands on some antibiotics. She wondered briefly if she could talk the local druggist into giving her the medication. That might have been possible at home, where she was known, but in a strange town? Unconsciously, she shook her head, knowing that idea would never work.

She needed a prescription, and even as she thought the word, she remembered. The last prescription for antibiotics she'd been given had been written more than three years ago, written by Nita Fisher's husband—for an abscessed tooth. Dentists could write prescriptions as well as doctors. But could they call a prescription to another state? She wasn't sure of that, but she was sure of Nita's friendship. And sure she could be trusted.

She left the bedroom, closing the door carefully behind her, although she thought that Deke was sleeping again. She didn't want him to overhear the call she was about to make because she knew he would never allow it. He would think it was too dangerous to give *anyone* information about where they were. Deke trusted no one, but she had no choice now but to trust.

There were only two pharmacies listed in the yellow pages of the thin phone book. She left the directory open on the counter and picked up the kitchen phone. She dialed the area code and the familiar number.

"'Lo," Nita said. Becki could hear the customary noises of kids and television in the background.

"Nita," she said, trying to decide how much she could explain. "It's me."

"Bec? I thought you were at the beach. Surely you're not back already. Not much of a vacation, girl."

"No, I'm... I'm not at home."

"What's wrong?" Nita asked immediately. Like Mary, she recognized that a long-distance phone call usually meant trouble.

"I need a favor," Becki said.

"From me? Shoot."

"From Warren really, but since you sleep with the man..."

Becki suggested, trying to duplicate the familiar teasing that had always been part of their relationship.

"Warren?" Nita repeated, her voice filled with disbelief. "What in the world do you need from Warren?"

"A prescription for an antibiotic."

There was a brief silence. She could imagine Nita sorting through all the possibilities and rejecting those that didn't fit with their years of friendship. And of course, she could never imagine the truth. Becki held her breath, hoping for no more questions.

"For you?" Nita asked finally.

"No."

"But your mom told me Josh had gone with Mike and Bill." There was another silence as Nita waited for her explanation. When Becki offered none, Nita said, "You want to tell me what's going on?"

"Not really. I just want you to get Warren to call me in a prescription. I'll give you the pharmacy's name and number. It's out of state. Can he do that?"

"Out of state?" Nita repeated. "Florida?"

"Arkansas. Can he do that? Call a prescription out of state."

"Arkansas? The last time I looked, Bec, Arkansas didn't have a beach."

"Will you do it?" Becki asked, ignoring the geography lesson, the automatic best-friend sarcasm. "Please, Nita. I can't tell you anything else, except it's important. You know I'd never ask unless—"

"Penicillin?" Nita interrupted.

She thought about that. So many people had reactions, which in this case...

"I don't know," Becki admitted. "Maybe...maybe something else. Something that's safe for anyone to take. And powerful."

"For an adult?"

"Yes," Becki acknowledged, finally knowing that this was going to work, that Nita was going to do it.

"Are you in trouble?"

"Yeah, but I can't tell you anything about it. Just do this, make Warren call, and I'll explain when I can. You know—"

"Okay," Nita broke in again. "You don't have to say anything else. Give me the name and number of the pharmacy. Warren's still at the office. It'll take me maybe half an hour to get everything done. Call me back."

"I'll try," Becki hedged, and gave her the information.

"Don't you let anything happen to you, Bec," Nita warned, after she'd taken down the name of the drugstore and the phone number. "Whatever the hell's going on, you take care of yourself. Are you sure I can't call some—"

"Don't tell *anybody* I called. That's the one thing you can't do. Make sure Warren understands that. Don't tell *anyone* about this. Promise me, Nita. It's so important."

Again she waited, hoping the bond between them was as strong as she believed. Strong enough to accomplish what she'd asked.

"I don't like this," Nita objected softly.

"Me either. Believe me. Promise me you'll do it."

"Yeah, okay, but you better let me know you're all right. As soon as you can. You understand me?"

"I will. I promise. Half an hour?"

"No more. I'll call right now."

"Thanks, Nita. I owe you."

"Big time, sweetie. Big time."

Becki smiled as she hung up the phone, somehow reassured by the brief contact with the world she had once inhabited. It was all still there: family and friends, safety. Just waiting for their return. For hers and Josh's return. *And Deke?* some part of her mind reminded. *What would happen to Deke?*

Like some exotic endangered species, Deke Summers would never fit into the peaceful world they had been driven out of less than a week ago. No matter what her subconscious kept imagining, her conscious mind had always known that whatever part of his existence she would be allowed to share was only the here and now.

As THE MINUTES of Nita's half hour dragged by, Becki debated the wisdom of taking Deke, as sick as he was, with her to the drugstore. But the alternative was even more frightening. If somehow her call had given away their location, if it could somehow be tracked back to this house...

She didn't believe that Nita would betray her, but Deke's lack of trust was rubbing off. She couldn't stand the thought of leaving him here alone, unable to protect himself. Or the thought that someone might be waiting for her at the pharmacy, waiting for her to lead them back to him. It seemed a better idea to load Deke in the car, pick up the prescription and then drive away. Get out of this town. She could find another house or get a motel room. Deke still had money. She had verified that when she'd emptied his pockets to wash the jeans.

She hadn't realized how difficult it would be to get him into some clothes—back into his own jeans and boots and then a borrowed button-up shirt from the closet. She helped him put his good arm through the left sleeve and then draped the other side over the injured shoulder. He never complained, never questioned her explanation that they had to move. Deke Summers was not a man who easily relinquished control. That he was letting her take charge was almost as frightening as the climbing fever and his obvious reluctance to move.

SHE LEFT DEKE, eyes closed and head against the headrest, in the locked car while she went inside to pick up the prescription. She had parked in the lot at the side, away from the lights that cast pools of illumination along the sidewalk fronting the old-fashioned drugstore. She looked back at the sedan, reassured by how well hidden it was in the shadows between the two buildings, and then she walked toward the door of the pharmacy, keeping close to its wall and away from those revealing circles of light.

Once inside, in the brightness of the fluorescents, she wondered why she had bothered. If anyone was looking for her, they would have little trouble recognizing the woman walking to the back of the store where the pharmacist was talking to a customer. She was still wearing the clothes Deke had bought at the Wal-Mart back home. She hadn't wanted to take anything else from the people whose house they'd invaded, but now she realized that missing the opportunity to change her clothing had been foolish.

Not as foolish, however, as not remembering to give Nita a fake name to leave the prescription under. That thought surfaced only when the druggist turned, smiling, to question her.

"Yes, ma'am," he said, "What can I do for you?"

"I had a prescription called in. Becki Travers?"

"Yes, ma'am, it's ready," he said, turning to sort through a couple of small white sacks before he located hers.

When she had paid, the medication safely in her possession, she turned to walk out of the store, finally taking a deep breath. Despite her mistake in not thinking up an alias, it seemed that nothing was going to go wrong. Nobody was going to ask questions. She just had to walk out to the car and drive away. She knew that in spite of what Deke had said about their pursuers, she would head west this time, nearer to where she believed they would find Josh.

She was on the sidewalk, almost to the side of the building where she had left the sedan, before she realized Deke would need something to help wash down the pills. She walked back to the drink machines lined up in front of the drugstore on the far side of the entrance. She inserted the coins, punched a selection and then bent over to retrieve the can as it fell into the slot at the bottom.

"Mighty fine," a deep voice drawled behind her. "Yes, sir, that's *mighty* fine."

Turning, she found a man leaning against the metal pole of one of the streetlights she'd avoided on her way in. He was dressed in jeans and a black T-shirt, the picture of some cowboy-hatted country singer she didn't recognize on its front. The shirt's fit was designed to show off his physique, heavy muscles almost certainly created by lifting weights.

"Weather we've been havin'," he added innocently when she looked at him, and then he smiled at her.

He wasn't unattractive, probably a few years younger than she. And what he had said didn't seem threatening, but her heart had stopped and the hand holding the soda had begun to tremble. She didn't know why she was surprised. Deke had tried to warn her.

Hoping she was wrong, she ignored the comment, turning to continue her journey toward the lot at the side of the building where she'd parked the car. She realized then there was a second man, standing almost in the center of the sidewalk, almost but not quite blocking her path. He was much larger than the one who had spoken and not as good-looking. His lank brown hair was too long, starting to recede, and he had the beginnings of a belly.

She tried to step around him, but he moved to the side, once more directly in front of her. She moved the other way, and again he cut her off.

"What's your hurry?" the man behind her asked. "You got a date or somethin'?"

"Something," she agreed. "And I'm late." She raised her eyes challengingly to the man standing in front of her. "If you'll excuse me," she said, speaking very deliberately.

Instead of stepping out of her way, he put out his hand, reaching across to rest his fingers on the top of the parking meter at the curb. The outstretched arm was before her face, about eye level. Suddenly she could smell the sour odor of sweat, an unclean body in unclean clothing, and overlying that the sharp reek of alcohol.

She jumped when the man behind her spoke again, the words very close to her ear. He had abandoned his pose against the light post to move nearer. Suddenly they were both too close, her body sandwiched between them. They weren't touching her, not yet, but the beer-tainted breath of the one behind was overpowering. Her stomach reacted, coiling sickly with fear. *Flight or fight.* Only she couldn't fight two men. Like a fool, she had left Deke's gun in the car.

If she could get to the car, she thought, and then she discarded the idea. That would lead them to Deke. She wondered how much they knew. Did they know Deke was here? And helpless?

"It's not often we get such a pretty lady in town. All alone on a Friday night," the one behind her said. His fingers slipped under her hair, caressing upward along her neck to her earlobe. Involuntarily she shivered. "Pretty hair. Ain't she got pretty hair, Clarence. All black and soft and shiny."

He caught a curl, holding it out in an attempt to show his friend. When she looked down, she could see his fingers, rubbing the strands together. His nails were rimmed with grease and his hand smelled of tobacco. She closed her eyes briefly, fighting the terror that would rob her of the ability to think. She had to get away, but she couldn't lead them to Deke. If anything, she should try to lead them away.

She opened her eyes and jerked her head to the right. The hair he'd captured slipped from between his fingers, and she felt the breath of his laughter against her cheek.

"I said," she said again, more forcefully, "excuse me. I'm not really interested."

"Yeah, but we are," the man in front of her spoke. "Real interested," he added, smiling at her, enjoying the fact that he was making her afraid.

"What's a little girl like you doin' out all by herself?" the other said. The question was almost against her neck, his mouth closer, more daring. "Don't you have no man to take you places on a Friday night?"

They were not after Deke Summers, she realized suddenly. Only her. A woman alone. For some reason that was more reassuring that it should have been. The danger was real enough, but these men were offering a very different kind of threat.

She stepped to the right, to the side of the sidewalk not blocked by the outstretched arm. The man behind her caught her upper arm with a grip that was tight enough to bruise.

"You ain't goin' nowhere," he said. "At least not 'til I tell you you can."

"Let me go," she said, struggling in quick panic to pull away. Hating the feel of his hand against her flesh.

"I don't think you're big enough to make me, sweetheart. I don't think you better even try. Now, I like a little bit of fight in a woman. But I got to warn you," he said, moving his head slightly side to side, smiling again, "I am one *mean* son of a bitch. Don't you go and make me mad now. You hear?"

His voice was still amused, still playing with her, but there was nothing playful about the pressure of his fingers, biting into her arm.

"Look," she said, trying to reason with him. Reason with a drunk, she mocked herself, but she had no choice. She was outnumbered, outsized and alone. "I don't want any trouble. I just need to get home. I've got a sick little boy."

"That's what the medicine's for? A sick kid?" he asked, his thumb moving up and down over her bare skin. "You a married lady?"

"Yes," she said, fighting against the rebuilding fear. Different from what she'd expected, but still terrifying. A different terror clawing its way upward through her stomach and into her throat.

He moved closer to her, his chest against her shoulder, holding her to him with the grip he had on her arm.

"He treat you right?" he whispered.

"Yes," she said again. She turned her face away from his breath, from his nearness, and closed her eyes.

"I bet he don't treat you as nice as I would. I know how to pleasure a woman. You ask anybody in town. Anybody'll tell you. You ask Clarence."

He paused a moment, giving her the opportunity to follow his suggestion, but she couldn't speak, aware of his growing arousal pressed against her hip. The entire front of his body hard against her side.

"Ray's *real* good," Clarence said obligingly.

"I have to get home to my baby." She pushed the words past the tightness in her throat. "I've got a sick baby at home waiting for this medicine."

"Then you're most likely in a hurry," the man who held her suggested. "I don't mind. We'll just go over there into the alley, and we'll be done in no time. I'll make it good for you. I'm real good. You just asked Clarence."

Drunker than she'd thought. Maybe, just maybe, if she were smart...

"And then you'll let me go?" she whispered. "Let me go home and tend to my baby?"

"Word of honor," he vowed softly. "Cross my heart and hope to die if I don't."

"And me," Clarence said, reminding them of his presence. "Don't you go forgettin' about me."

"I ain't forgettin' you, Clarence," he said patiently. "You're my friend. My buddy. I don't forget my buddies."

He pulled her along the sidewalk, Clarence following. They reached the entrance to the parking lot, and she was infinitely relieved when they walked into the shadows there, relieved that she had not been mistaken about their destination.

There were only three cars in the small lot between the two stores. The sedan, where she'd left Deke, was the first one they would come to. The other two were parked at the back, nearest the alley. She had guessed they belonged to the pharmacy's employees. The man holding her arm began to urge her past the sedan, but she stopped, resisting for the first time since she'd seemingly agreed to go with him.

"Let me put my little boy's medicine in the car," she begged. "It won't take a minute. I don't want to drop it in the alley. It's so dark I might not find it again and it cost me a lot of money. I can't afford to buy any more. It won't take me a minute, I promise," she said again. She was talking too much, trying so hard to make him believe.

"Now, that sounds like a trick to me. Don't that sound like a trick to you, Clarence? She's gonna try to jump in that car and drive off or somethin'. You must think we're real stupid."

"I just don't want to lose this," she said. She took a breath. "And besides, if I put it in the car my hands will be free," she added softly, repulsed at her own invention.

His head tilted, drunkenly trying to read her voice. The shadows were deeper here, and she could only see half his face, the rest of his features hidden by the darkness. She held her breath, hoping. *Just let me get to the car.* And to the gun she'd left on the driver's seat.

"Now I *do* like the sound of that," he said, his voice low and intimate. Too close. Again drawing her toward his body by his grip on her arm, he bent his head to put his mouth against her throat. By the strongest force of will, she held her eyes open as his tongue, hot and wet, licked up her neck, the odors of stale sweat and beer revolting. She couldn't give in to her terror. She tried not to think about what he was doing. She focused her gaze on the sedan. So near. She swallowed her nausea as his mouth covered her ear, his tongue invading, caressing, whispering what he intended.

Finally, he moved back a few inches, staggering slightly, finding his balance only by his hold on her arm. "Don't you like the sound of that, Clarence? She's gonna put her kid's medicine in the car so her hands'll be free. Don't that sound nice."

"You watch her," Clarence warned.

"She ain't goin' nowhere," he jeered at the other's concern. "I got hold of her arm. She ain't goin' nowhere except into that alley. Then she can go home to her baby. I promised her that. Word of honor," he added solemnly, moving his left hand in an awkward, drunken X over his heart.

He allowed her to walk toward the parked car. The most dangerous moment would be when she opened the door. The dome light would come on, revealing both Deke and the gun. She would have only a few seconds at most, before he realized what was happening. Even with his reactions slowed by the alcohol, she would have only seconds.

"I have to get my keys," she said. "I can't do that if you're holding me." As proof of what she'd said, she held out her hands, the white sack containing the prescription in the left and the soda still clutched in the right.

"You figure it out," he instructed, smiling at his own cleverness, at having denied her freedom.

She waited a moment, and knowing that she couldn't afford to make him suspicious, she transferred the soda to her left hand and reached into the pocket of the knit shorts. She took out the ring and found the car key. He was still holding her left arm, but not as tightly as before. She inserted the key into the lock of the driver's side door, fumbling in the darkness. Hand trembling, she took a breath and then opened it.

There was no light. The interior remained as dark as the surrounding shadows. No light. It took her a few seconds to adjust to what hadn't happened.

"The medicine," she said, moving slowly, trying to ease her left arm out of his hold, careful not to jerk it away, not to startle him. And unbelievingly, she felt him release her.

She stepped nearer to the car, putting the door between her body and his. She laid the sack and the can on the front seat and groped in the darkness for the cool metal of the gun. Her hand closed around it, and she felt it slip into her palm, fitting smoothly there by design, her finger already automatically over the trigger.

When she straightened, she did it in one motion, her entire body turning, her right hand coming up over the top of the door to point the gun at the center of his chest. She moved her other hand to join it, to hold the gun steady, the classic shooter's stance her father had taught her, the frame of the door offering additional support.

"Move back," she ordered. "Get away from the car."

His eyes fell to the gun in her hand and then widened in disbelief. Even in the dimness she could see them jerk up to her face, the whites gleaming in the surrounding darkness, stretched with shock at what was happening. So different from his expectations. He took a couple of steps backward, automatic retreat from the threat of the weapon.

She was aware of another movement, something happening

at the back of the car. Clarence, she realized. Moving closer to them. She wondered if he could see the gun.

"Aw, hell, Ray, she ain't gonna shoot," Clarence assured drunkenly. "She ain't got the guts to pull that trigger."

"Whoa, man, this here is a *big* gun," the other one said softly. "A real big gun."

"Get away from the car," she ordered again. She wanted to include Clarence in the threat, but she was afraid to move the gun she had trained on the cowboy-hatted singer, a clear target at the center of the dark shirt. This one was closer, a greater danger, and he was the leader. She knew that. Clarence would do whatever he was told.

"She ain't gonna shoot," Clarence offered again, his voice full of disgust. "Just take the damn thing away from her. It prob'ly ain't even loaded."

"Don't you bet on that," she said. "It's loaded."

"And you're gonna shoot me with it?" Ray mocked, attempting to gather his courage despite the muzzle trained steadily on his body.

"If you don't get away from this car. I don't want to hurt you. I just want to go home. I've got a sick baby," she lied again. She *didn't* want to shoot them. She just wanted to get out of here, get into the car and get away.

"Okay," he agreed softly. "I'm movin' away. I'm goin'. Just don't you get anxious, sweetheart, and shoot that thing off by mistake."

His voice trembled slightly, despite the suggestion of coolness he was trying to inject, trying to save face before his friend and to insure that she wasn't going to blow the middle out of his chest at the same time. "You just stay real calm," he said, backing farther away from the door.

"I *told* you she ain't gonna shoot," Clarence said.

He began to move toward them again, coming far faster than she would have believed a man of his bulk and level of inebriation could have managed. She hesitated. A fatal second of hesitation before her mind made the decision to swing the gun toward the advancing figure.

Suddenly the rear door flew open, catching Clarence in the side. Deke Summers exploded from the car. His foot, kicking with as much force as his muscled thigh could put behind it, slammed into the back of the big man's knee. Clarence staggered, his chin cracking into the top of the open door. Deke's left shoulder came up into his midsection as he bounced back off the frame.

Using that shoulder, Deke pushed the man away from the car, throwing him onto the pavement. Then he kicked again, connecting this time with fat-covered ribs. Clarence doubled over sideways, writhing on the ground, the sounds he was making harsh and wheezing, as unpleasant as the noise of the thudding blows Deke had landed with his booted feet.

Deke staggered back against the car, his face ashen in the gloom, but the blue eyes were open, savage and deadly, still focused on the man he'd downed.

Becki became aware again of the other one, the leader, retreating farther into the darkness at the mouth of the alley. As she watched his retreat, Deke's hand close over hers, still holding his gun. She let him take it out of her grip, knowing that she'd screwed it all up. *Don't pull a gun on a man,* her daddy had always said, *unless you're ready to shoot him.* And she hadn't been. Nothing in her life had prepared her to shoot someone.

"*I've* got the guts," Deke threatened, holding the gun out before him, left arm stretched straight and steady, letting them see the weapon. Letting them get a good look at it. The metallic gleam in the shadows emphasized its size and its lethal power.

Clarence was sitting up now, the keening noises he'd been making softened, but they were still audible and apparently beyond his control, like a child trying desperately to stop his tantrum's hysteria.

"Get," Deke ordered, the command very soft. It was the kind of command you gave a stray dog that had wandered into your yard, threatening your pets and your children. A command that showed no respect. No fear. Just certain domination. Just *get*.

And they did. She watched the one who had done all the talking vanish into the blackness where they'd planned to take her. It took Clarence a little longer to stumble across the lot, holding his arms tightly around his stomach, protecting what were probably broken ribs. Then they were alone in the shadow of the drugstore.

"You're okay," Deke said.

It wasn't a question, she realized, but a promise, a reassurance. He had lowered the gun, but other than that he hadn't moved, his legs spread to maintain his faltering balance.

"I'm okay," she agreed, knowing that would probably never be true again. Nothing would ever really be *okay* again.

"Come here," Deke said, swaying a little, his elongated shadow on the pavement wavering.

As she walked toward him, he lifted his left arm away from his body, the gun still in his hand, relaxed and yet very professionally held. When she realized what he was doing, she moved into his embrace, finally invited to rest against the warmth and strength of his chest. She felt his arm come around her, pulling her tightly into his body. Safe and protected again.

His lips found and caressed her temple. She thought of the man who had touched her, his tongue wet and repulsive, and then she banished the image. She put her arms around Deke Summers's midsection, holding on to him. Holding on to him as long as she could. *So little time, and all of it infinitely precious.*

Chapter Ten

"We have to get out of here," Deke said finally.

She realized he was leaning most of his weight against her, upright only because she was supporting him.

"They weren't..." she began and then hesitated over what to call the men who followed him, who wanted him dead. "They weren't after you. They just wanted—"

"I know," he interrupted. His arm tightened around her body, reacting to the fear he could hear in her strained voice.

"I couldn't shoot him. God, Deke, I'm such a coward. I just couldn't decide to pull the trigger. I knew what would happen if I didn't, but—"

"Killing someone should always be the hardest thing you ever have to do."

"But they would have..." She paused, trying to block the remembrance of the crudely phrased promises the drunk had whispered.

"It's over," Deke said, his tones soothing, reassuring. "It's all over."

"I should have shot the bastards," she said suddenly, her voice full of hatred, bitterness replacing the fear, more of it directed at her own weakness than at the men who had vanished into the shadowed alley. "They were going to rape me, damn it. And I had a chance to make sure they would never do that to anyone else. That they wouldn't be capable of it."

She felt the small movement of his chest against hers.

Laughter? Was he amused with her threat? Condescending. Just like Clarence. *She ain't gonna shoot...*

"Next time, Annie Oakley," Deke said softly, his breath stirring her hair. *Even with all that had happened,* he realized, *the fear and the horror, her spirit was intact, her courage undaunted.* Admiring Becki Travers's ability to deal with whatever was thrown at her, as he had from the beginning, he repeated his reassurance, "You can get them next time."

Suddenly she was furious with Deke, with his mockery of her anger. Furious with her own failure. She pushed away from his body. She doubled up her fists and pounded them as hard as she could against his chest. Unreasonably furious with his soft comment.

"Don't you laugh at me, you son of a bitch. Don't you dare laugh at me."

She hit him again and again, surprised at how good it made her feel, her fists battering his strength, his hard masculinity. "Stop laughing at me, you son of a bitch," she said again, gasping, out of breath with the force of her rage. With the effort she was making to have some impact on his eternal calmness.

She was shocked, however, when his knees suddenly gave way, buckling so that he fell onto the pavement. Only the automatic drop of his left hand, the one which held the gun, touching against the ground, prevented him going down completely. He swayed drunkenly on his knees, his shadow again mocking.

"Sorry," he whispered, his voice only a thread, but the night was still and dark around them. A small country-town stillness. He pushed upward a little, his knuckles against the pavement, his right arm held tightly to his body. "Not laughing," he added.

To stop her from hitting him again? Or the apology he thought she wanted? Watching him, mesmerized by the slow sway of his torso, as fascinated as if she were watching the hypnotic movements of a snake charmer, it took her too long to react. When she did, she went down on her knees beside him, automatically lifting his left arm over her shoulders. She hadn't even been aware that she was crying, her nose running and the tears still wet on her cheeks. One traced down her throat, and she raised her hand, still clenched into a fist, wiping the moisture away with its heel. And remembered that the drunk had touched her there, had licked her skin.

"We have to get out of here," she said, shivering, unaware that she was repeating Deke's warning.

He nodded, his head hanging loosely. He didn't look at her, but with her help he finally staggered to his feet. They made it to the car before his strength evaporated. He fell into the passenger seat, and again Becki found herself securing the shoulder strap around his unresisting body.

It was only when she was climbing into the other side that she remembered the antibiotics. The dome light had not come on when she'd opened the door, and she realized only now that was because Deke had cut it off. He had been sitting in the dark car, waiting for an opportunity to rescue her, despite his condition. Or waiting for her to succeed once she had the gun in her hands. And instead…

Resolutely she denied the remembrance of her failure. She'd deal with that another time. When she had time for it.

Her fingers were struggling with the childproof cap of the bottle. Struggling because they were still shaking.

"Open, damn you," she said, feeling the unreasoning fury building again. Suddenly, thankfully, the white top released. She couldn't read the dosage in the darkness, and she didn't intend to turn on the light, knowing that would provide a clear target for anyone watching from the surrounding shadows.

She poured two of the capsules into her palm and then had to hold them awkwardly enclosed in her fist while she popped the tab on the soda. The resulting hiss was comforting, offering familiarity in a world where nothing else was familiar. Not even herself. She was no longer the woman she had always been. She banished that thought and the image of her fists driving an injured man to his knees. A man she loved. Cared about. What the hell was the matter with her?

"Deke," she said.

His head lifted, the darkness so intense she couldn't see his features. By some trick of the shadows, nothing was visible but the fevered eyes, again palely luminescent in the gloom.

"You have to take these. Open your mouth," she ordered. When he obeyed, she rolled the two capsules from her palm onto his tongue, and then held the soda up to his lips. His mouth closed over the opening and she tilted the can, following the small backward slant of his head.

"Get them down?" she asked when he straightened his head.

He nodded and put his head against the headrest. His eyes were closed. She watched him a moment, and then shivering once more against the memories, she stuck the key into the ignition and started the car. There were no headlights behind her, no one following as she left the small town behind in the darkness, and obeying the road signs, headed again to the west.

SHE DROVE THROUGH the night, carefully obeying the speed limits, just as Deke had done. When she finally knew she had to stop, that it was dangerous not to, given the level of her exhaustion, it was after three. She had reached the outskirts of Oklahoma City, and she pulled the car off the interstate and into the entrance of a brightly lighted chain motel, one that advertised nationally their clean rooms and reasonable prices. She paid cash for the room and signed the registration form with the name of an elementary-school friend who had moved away in the fourth grade. She made up the tag number the form requested.

She got back in the car and followed the clerk's directions to the room they'd been given. It was on the ground floor, as she'd requested.

She had a hard time waking Deke up enough to get him out of the car, and their journey to the room was little more than a stagger, her slender frame supporting most of his weight. She eased him down on the bed, on top of the quilted spread, returning to fasten every lock and chain on the door.

She coaxed him to take two more of the capsules, washing them down this time with water from the bathroom. She had to hold his head up while he drank it, but he obeyed her instructions and got the medicine down.

She found the extra blanket in the top of the closet and spread it over Deke before she turned out the bedside light. She crawled onto the bed, not even bothering to take off her shoes, and this time she didn't resist the desire to curl up beside the heat of his body. This was where she wanted to be. The only place she would ever feel safe again.

SHE KNEW WHAT HAD awakened her this time. Images from the darkness. The touch of the drunk's breath, hot and fetid, against her throat. The things he had whispered. Both threat and promise. She jerked her eyes open. The room was still dark, protected from the invasion of day by the thick plastic backing of the draperies, but strong sunlight was seeping around the edges of the flowered fabric. She took a shaky breath, pushing the memory of the dream away, back into the night shadows where it belonged.

She turned her head and found Deke watching her. She said nothing, simply meeting his gaze. Gradually she realized what was different. The blue eyes were no longer glassy. No longer unfocused. They were coherent, the mind behind them once more in control.

"I'm so sorry," she offered softly, wondering how much of the scene in the parking lot he remembered.

"For what?" he asked, a slight negative movement of his head against the pillow they shared.

"For hitting you," she confessed.

His eyes made no response, holding hers, and then the corners of his lips began to creep upward.

"You don't remember," she said.

"No, but I'm sure I deserved it."

"No," she admitted, "you didn't. That's why I said I was sorry."

"Okay," he said, accepting.

For some reason it struck her as funny. Apparently it was his favorite word. At least, his favorite reassurance. She laughed out loud, the sound of it destroying the pain of what had happened between them the night before. And of what had happened in the woods. The memory of his rejection. All of that disappeared while she looked at him, the echo of her laughter the only thing between them now.

She wondered when he'd last shaved. After his shower in the house in Arkansas? Whenever it had been, he needed another. His beard was lighter than his hair, glinting even in the artificial gloom created by the blackout drapes. She was close enough to see the lines around his eyes again. And the darker flecks in the irises. The whites surrounding them were clear once more. There was a tiny scar on the bridge of his nose. *Football, maybe,* she found herself thinking.

"What's wrong?" he asked.

Her eyes were tracing his features as if she were trying to memorize them. Her face was so near to his, he could see the dark down of hair at her temple. A faint dust of freckles across her nose. The curl of the long lashes shadowing her eyes. Her mouth was too wide, he thought, the small imperfection infinitely appealing.

"Nothing," she whispered. "Nothing's wrong."

She wanted him to make love to her. He knew that suddenly. It was there in her face. That desire somehow revealed as clearly as was the flawless bone structure underlying the smoothness of the olive skin. The laughter had disappeared from her eyes to be replaced by something he could read just as well. Something that his body was responding to. Had always responded to. The filament-thin strand of physical desire that had stretched between them from the first.

"I'm going to take a shower," he said, denying it again. Rejecting.

She said nothing in response. There was no change in the careful composure of her features. No movement of the generous mouth. Finally she nodded, breaking the spell, releasing him.

Despite the morning stiffness, the now-familiar pain in his shoulder, he sat up, resting a moment on the edge of the bed. He took another of the antibiotic capsules, washing it down with the glass of water she'd left on the bedside table. If she touched him, he found himself thinking. Her hand against the small of his back. Anything. He knew that he'd not be able to leave then. But he waited a long time, and there was nothing.

Pushing upward finally with his left hand on the table, he got to his feet and negotiated his way to the bathroom, closing the door behind him, a small protection against the emotions she'd evoked. He stood a moment in the darkness, feeling the aching aloneness. And the physical ache, hot and tight. He closed his eyes.

No more, he prayed. *Dear, sweet God, please, no more.*

WHEN SHE OPENED THE door, steam drifted out, curling around her bare feet and legs and then disappearing, feathering away into the artificial gloom of the bedroom. She stood a moment in the doorway, listening to the sound of the shower.

"Deke," she called softly.

The white plastic curtain was pushed aside, and she watched the water cascading over his dark body. She allowed her eyes to follow the path it took down to the swirling, soap-whitened pool in the bottom of the tub. And then allowed them to move back up. Slowly.

One of the teachers in her school had been criticized for showing her students Michelangelo's *David.* Too sexually explicit, the protester had argued. *This* was explicit, she realized. What was happening now to Deke's body.

Her eyes found his face. Nothing of what he must be feeling was revealed there. His features were still and set, as if they, too, had been carved from marble. His eyes were hooded, dark and remote. Watching her.

She put her hand flat on the tile of the shower enclosure. Using it for balance, she stepped over the side of the tub, moving between Deke and the spray of water. It was hot against her back, pulsing. Still he had not moved. Waiting. Watching her.

She took the bar of soap from his unresisting fingers. Hesitantly, not having planned her actions this far, she began to move it over the beaded moisture on his chest, almost in slow motion, looking only at the patterns she created in the thick, fair hair, now darkened with the water. The small nubs of his nipples tightened, and she could feel their response under the circling movements of her hand.

Lower. Over his stomach. The same deliberate pattern repeated, her thumb straying once, daringly, into the depression of his navel.

And then lower.

Suddenly Deke's fingers closed around her wrist. He took the soap out of her hand and placed it carefully on the edge of the tub. She was afraid to look up, braced for his anger, his rejection. He had never indicated that he wanted her. Just because she—

He picked her up, lifting her with both hands, turning her body to hold it against the sweating side of the enclosure. He moved against her, his chest slippery over the water-dewed softness of her breasts. Her legs automatically fastened around his hips as with one strong surge of motion, he entered her.

Her eyes closed and her head fell back against the tile, feeling the invasion in every part of her body. At some level she was still aware of the steam, of the water, pounding now against Deke's shoulder, its small splash hot on her skin where it was not sheltered by his.

She put her arms around his neck, holding tight, her throat next to his unshaven cheek, its roughness again pleasant. So strange and yet familiar. Achingly familiar. Beloved. She turned her face, feeling under her cheek the wetness of his hair. He lifted into her again, sure and powerful. Demanding response.

For a second she was frightened by the strength of his demand. There was nothing gentle about what he was doing. It was elemental. Whatever she had unleashed would have to be borne. Endured, she thought, gasping a little with the next upward thrust. Driving into her. There had been nothing like this in her marriage. Nothing like the force with which he invaded and possessed.

As she thought that, Deke's hand found her breast. Cupped under its fullness, hard fingers claiming ownership. His thumb flicked over her nipple, and she heard some sound, deep and wordless, and realized in sudden wonder that it had come from her own throat. In response to the noise she made, his hips pushed upward again.

Somehow his mouth found hers, his tongue echoing his body's movements. As demanding. But there was no more fear. Whatever was happening within her was not born of fear. Excitement. Satisfaction that he had wanted her this much, that her tentative invitation had elicited this response, the strength of it. His body in gasping bondage to hers. His power constrained by its need, by its desire to be enclosed in her fragility.

She was the one in control, and as she thought that, she used her thighs to raise her hips slightly and then to lower into his motion, meeting it. The sound of his reaction was harsh, breath caught, gasping, and then released in a groan.

Her lips tilted, delighting in her power. She had known he wanted her. Against his denial. Against the memories that blocked his response, that strangled the emotions he feared.

Fear, she thought again, wondering why she had never realized what lay between them. *Only fear.* His fear for her safety. His determination to protect her from the darkness of his existence, from the past. Only fear.

"It's all right," she comforted. Holding him, her body as involved now in what they were creating as his. As lost in the sensations that were building, pulsing upward from where he possessed her. As hot as the stream of water that flowed over them. As liquid. Seeping upward into every nerve and artery like rising floodwaters. Filling them. Overflowing. Overwhelming whatever control she had foolishly believed was hers. There was no control, and it didn't matter.

When she realized what was happening, she wanted to protest. Too soon. Too soon. She wasn't ready. Almost. Almost to the edge, but not yet. She said nothing, of course, realizing even as the thought formed that it was too late. She tightened her legs around his waist, her mouth caressing permission against his temple.

His movements were convulsive. There was no way he could have waited. *And no need,* she knew. This was enough. What could be more precious than his release into her body? His seed into her emptiness. So empty until Deke had filled her. Lost and alone.

Gradually the eruption quieted. As his breathing began to ease, he held her still against the wall of the shower enclosure, his legs trembling.

"Sorry," he said finally.

He released the pressure of his body against hers, and she allowed the grip of her legs to loosen from around his waist. He supported her until she was standing beside him. The water around her feet was warm, and she was suddenly so cold. Exposed. Blue-veined skin chill-bumped and shivering. Embarrassed. The aftermath of lovemaking with a stranger. No intimacy of long friendship to soften what had happened between them.

"My fault," she whispered, knowing that it had been.

"Yes," he said. His hand eased under her chin, lifting until her eyes met his again. "All your fault," he echoed. He was smiling at her, the hard lines of his face totally relaxed for the first time since she'd met him. The cold blue eyes filled with warmth.

"It's been a long time," he confessed softly.

Apologizing, she realized suddenly. Deke was apologizing to her. For...

She took a deep breath, wondering how to respond. There was nothing she wanted to criticize in what had happened. Maybe he hadn't given her time to join him, but it didn't matter. There had been something totally satisfying in the uncontrolled quickness of his release. In the strength of his passion. Satisfying that he had wanted her that much. At least that's what she had believed until he'd said...

"Is that *all* it was?" she questioned. "Because it's been a long time?"

She forced her eyes to hold his, but she was aware that he had smiled again. His hand fitted under her face, caressing, cherishing with his touch. And then the tips of his fingers floated down her throat, flattening against her breastbone as they moved downward. His palm settled finally over her breast, enclosing. Expressing the gentleness that had not been there before, that had been lost in need, in its hot fierceness.

"That's *not* all," he acknowledged. "You have to know that's not all."

Deke Summers wasn't a man who openly expressed his feelings. He might never say the things she wanted to hear, but they were in his face. And in his eyes. Like those ancient creatures who strayed too close and were captured forever in amber. Waiting there, to be found and examined, wondered over, a million years later.

She nodded.

"It's okay," she said, and watched his smile inch upward, escaping his control.

"It will be," he promised. "I promise you, Becki. The next time it will be."

AND FINALLY IT WAS. He had carried her to the bed in the other room, throwing the coverlet back with one strong sweep of motion. It slid unnoticed to the floor as he laid her wet body on the sheets. She was so cold, and she wanted to tell him to turn off the air conditioner, but before she could formulate the words, his mouth and his body were over hers. His tongue caressing. Seeking. Searching her. Beginning to know her responses.

His hands were very sure. Slow and painstakingly competent. She had never thought he would be patient. But this time he was in no hurry, his touch selective. He didn't intend to rush any of the detailed examination he was making of her body.

She was grateful at first for the dimness of the bedroom. Embarrassed by what he was doing. By the caress of his eyes, followed deliberately by the surprisingly feather-soft stroke of his fingertips. Drifting, examining every inch of her skin. Lingering over its small imperfections. The thin lines of pregnancy, clearly visible on the smoothness of her belly, traced like silver etchings over the darkness of her skin. Following them with his eyes and then echoing that examination with his hands.

He had lifted onto one elbow, easing away from her body to ask, his voice low in the shadowed isolation of the world they now shared. Only they.

"From Josh?" he asked, still touching the telltale marks.

Unable to speak, she nodded, wondering what he was thinking, if he found them ugly, disfiguring. Then his head lowered to her stomach, his tongue replacing the satin glide of his fingers. And, reassured by the worship of his lips, she knew that was *not* what he had thought.

They traveled, eventually, hot and demanding, to cover the aching nipples of her breasts. She was reminded again of when she had carried Josh, of their heavy fullness. Of the sweetly satisfying suckle of an infant. Mouth seeking. Unknowingly seductive. Her hips writhed against the dampness of the sheet. Arching. He was creating the same deeply erotic sensations within her belly. The same way. Yet stronger, and this time demanding release. Sexual. A different fulfillment, just as compelling.

His mouth examined her throat. Her ear. Slowly. Tongue probing. Soft whispers erasing the other so that finally she no longer remembered that the men the previous night had wanted to profane this act. Aware only of his voice.

As tender as his fingers, rolling the taut peaks of her nipples slowly between them. His lips had created their pearled hardness, and now his hands delighted in it. His mouth over hers. Making her forget to breathe. To be afraid. To think.

His breath silvered her skin with moisture, touching each rise and fall of bone with its mist. Gliding like fog over her ribs. Tantalizing with promise over the faint marks of her body's ripeness, which he had traced with his tongue. Floating across the small downward slope of her belly. Dropping words like hot incense on her skin, but she couldn't think what they meant. It was no longer important that he said anything. His touch communicated. Broke in waves over the center of her need. And he was as demanding there as he had been before, under the throbbing heat of the shower. Pulsing again, long, rolling waves of power pushing upward into her stomach. Into her consciousness.

Her fingers were locked into the gilt of his hair as he caressed her. Mouth moving. Tongue circling. So hot. She was on fire, tendrils of smoke from the sudden conflagration curling upward. Fluttering into her belly. Burning under her skin.

Her legs loosened, relaxed with the sweet pleasure of what he was doing. She had forgotten to be embarrassed, to be shy. This was Deke, and she was made for him, for his touch.

Her hips lifted, seeking to strengthen the contact. A stronger caress. Almost to the edge. Almost—as she had been before. She could hear her own breathing. Shallow. The occasional gasping response as she edged nearer to what she sought, to where he was taking her. So near. Suddenly the remembrance of his power was inside her body, memory tangled in the honeyed warmth of his mouth. She arched again, trying to force, to hurry the clamoring insanity of her need.

She felt his body shift, the sudden desertion of his lips, and she cried out against the loss. Her hands found and held, pulling him to her. Then his mouth was over hers. Open. And his body. And memory became reality.

She exploded with the first hard thrust, arching wildly into his strength. She was aware of the sounds she made. Sounds she had never made before. Sensations she had never felt before.

Release blossoming upward from their joining, rocking her with its power so that she only wanted to relax into its heat and strength. Carried like driftwood with the force of the tide that roared through her. Light and weightless. Drifting on the surge of its current. But there was no rest. No ebb from the flood of his demand. Still it drove her, hammering into the oversensitized walls of her response. More sensation, more of everything. Wave after wave beating against her senses until she was drowning again in sensation.

Now he would allow her to rest. To savor. But the demand was building again, the hard muscles in his legs moving against the slack, unresisting flesh of hers. Incapable of resisting. Wanting again, and yet wanting release. Freedom from his demand. And instead the spiral built, heat circling upward. Too intense. Too strong. Frightening with the realization of his power over her.

She cried out, arching. Body leaping upward to meet and absorb him. To enclose him, to be captured forever in the amber of her memory. Never to be released. Caught and held like the old enchantresses of mythology held their knights. In thrall. She wanted Deke Summers in thrall.

Perhaps even in the extremity of her passion, she knew, recognized the transitory nature of what he had given her. There were no vows, no commitments, no whispered promises. He was a man who could promise nothing. A brief summer's heat, hot and fierce, burning away all the restraints and conventions by which she had lived her entire life, and then fading, its power enfolded by the cold darkness that surrounded him.

Eventually the sensations shivered away, her skin trembling with aftereffect. Cold, even under the warmth of his body. She was aware again of his weight. Of his skin against hers. Of the hard muscles underlying its hair-roughened texture. Capable again of thought, she put her mouth on his shoulder, lips parted, tongue tracing the warm, salt-sweet flavor of his skin.

"I love you," she whispered. The words had been there a long time, hiding from their own reality in her consciousness.

But there was no reason now to deny. He must know, must now be aware of all she felt.

His big body lifted, sheltering pressure removed from her breasts, her stomach. She wondered if it had been as difficult for him to find the will to separate their bodies as it would have been for her. *They were still joined,* she comforted her sudden fear. *Still joined.*

He was looking down into her face, eyes again shadowed and remote. She wondered if that was only a trick of the lighting. Surely he couldn't be that far from her, not so soon after they had…

"No," he said softly, but his mouth found hers again, and she answered his kiss, allowing nothing of what she felt to remain unrevealed.

Eventually he put his cheek to hers, his weight held on his forearms still, her body covered but not connected. Except where it mattered. *Still joined* echoed again in her heart.

He didn't move for an eternity. She felt the slow softening. The relaxation. Her hands moved over his shoulders, feeling beneath their exploration the forgotten bandage. She hadn't even thought about the injury. He had given her no reason to think about it, to be concerned for him. He had held nothing back except his acceptance of what she had said.

She smiled, fingers still drifting lightly over his back, his breath slow and regular against her throat. He could deny the expression of what she knew, but he couldn't destroy its reality. It was useless to argue with him. Let him say whatever he wished. They both were aware of what was real, of what was between them.

She closed her eyes and put everything else from her mind. Everything but the feel of his body under the slow caress of her hands.

DEKE SUMMERS LAY in the shadowed gloom watching her sleep, remembering what she had whispered. Not in the extremity of desire, but afterward, her voice calm and reasoned. *I love you.* He blocked the power of the words, covering their force deliberately with the horrifying images he had fought for four years. He reminded himself that another voice had whispered that promise from the darkness and then had been destroyed by the explosion which had shattered his life. Another woman, dark haired and dark eyed as this one, her body as softly responsive under his hands, her lips as tender.

He had danced on the edge of redemption for Lila's death for four years. Taunting his enemies. Hiding. Running. Always, carefully, one step ahead. Some part of his rational mind had long ago recognized and acknowledged the game he played. Not with those who followed, but with himself. He had wondered how he would know that it had been enough, when he would finally give himself permission to let it end. To let it all be over. Final redemption for his mistakes.

And it had been ever closer. He had known that. It had been harder to move on. Harder to break away from the fleeting familiarity of whatever stolen life he had slipped into. Becoming harder every day to care any longer what happened to the man who had once been Deke Summers.

Until now. He found his eyes again tracing the sleep-relaxed features of the woman who lay beside him. She had forced her way, she and the child, past the cold, broken shell that was all that had remained of that man. He had thought at first it had simply been a trick of memory, some delicate modification of the punishment he had devised for his own guilt. But she was not Lila. And he knew that. Had known it as he made love to her. With every movement, every whisper, he had been aware that she was Becki Travers. Aware of her strength, her courage, her determination.

But that was not why he had made love to her. Not admiration for her courage or her intelligence, her fortitude. What she offered had drawn him like the remembered warmth of a winter's fire, offering life in the chill of his existence. He could no more have turned away from that promise than he could have prevented his body's physical response.

For the first time he allowed himself to wonder if it might be possible. To love this woman and the boy. To live again.

To find his way back from the edge of that cold darkness which he had always known led to hell.

HIS TONGUE WOKE HER. Pulling her out of the dream images of what he was doing. Had his mouth evoked those images or had he shared somehow the remembrance, been aware of what she was dreaming? Her body was too languid to participate. Exhausted. She lay and let him touch her. Felt her responses build, but there was none of the urgency there had been before. This was only pleasure. Slow and tempered by her satiation. She felt him more intensely, was more aware of each individual stroke and less sensitive to its demand. Relaxed. Accustomed now to the intimacy. Not driven by need nor restrained by embarrassment.

The force shimmered through her body this time, like the waves that flickered over the highways in summer, distorting the clarity of the landscape that was still there behind their curtain of heat. Everything that had lain between them was still there, but overlaid now by lovemaking, the outside world's harsh reality distorted, at least momentarily, by this.

When her body had stilled, spent and mindless, boneless against the bed where they had slept together, he came to lie again beside her. She turned her head, the effort almost too costly, so that she could see his face. He smiled at her again, the slightest movement of his lips, and she felt hers respond.

"Okay?" he asked.

She nodded and at what was in his eyes, crystal blue and warm, her smile widened.

"I like your mouth," he said, expressing the errant thought he had had before.

"I like *your* mouth," she whispered.

He laughed and leaned to touch his lips to hers, gentle and intimate.

"Old married-people kiss," she teased, the unthinking comment spoken as his mouth lifted away from hers.

"No," he said again.

"I'm sorry," she whispered. The cold remembrance was in

his eyes. She didn't know what else to say. She *was* sorry. Sorry that she had reminded him, had broken the connection between them by speaking of the unspeakable. She had not remembered.

"Are you hungry?" he asked, breaking off abruptly and deliberately any discussion.

Her eyes studied his face a moment before she gave in, agreeing to ignore what she had said, what had gone before. And only with his question did she realize that she *was* hungry. It seemed forever since she had eaten.

"Yes," she said.

He got up and found the room-service menu. He tossed it on the bed before he disappeared into the bathroom.

"*Just* like old married people," she said again, but this time under her breath as she opened the folder and began to examine the motel's offerings.

It was not until Deke was placing their order, until she saw the phone in his hand, that she realized she had forgotten to call home the night before. It had been Friday night, and she told her sister she would check with her. Mary had thought it might be Saturday before the men would be in touch, but even so, that was today. There was the chance that they had called last night and left word of their location. She and Deke could even now—

"What is it?" Deke asked. He had put the phone back into the cradle, but he was still sitting on the edge of the bed, watching her face.

"I forgot to call Mary," she said, worried eyes rising to meet his.

"Mary?"

"My sister. My brothers might have called home last night, but with everything that happened... I forgot to call. We could have been there by now."

"If they called," Deke reminded her. "You don't know that they did. A few hours aren't going to make that much difference."

But what she suggested made him uneasy. He didn't like

the possibility that someone else knew where Josh was, might have known now for hours. More than enough time to get to the child. More than enough.

"Why don't you call her," he suggested, trying to keep his voice casual. There was no need to worry Becki. She hadn't wanted the delay in getting to her son any more than he had. Too much had happened the previous night to interrupt the normal thought processes, her instinctive mother's concern.

"How could I have forgotten to call?" she breathed. "How could I have forgotten Josh?"

"You didn't forget Josh. And your brothers may not have been in touch. Call your sister now and see," he suggested again.

He handed her the phone and then punched in the numbers she called out to him. He sat on the edge of the bed, watching her face while she talked. He read relief in the wide brown eyes, raised smiling to his when she knew that her sister had talked to them.

"They're all right," she mouthed.

He nodded, wondering if that was still true. How many hours had passed since they had pinpointed their location for their family? And for who else? He looked up when she leaned across his body to put the phone back in the cradle.

"They were in El Paso. Today they're heading to Carlsbad. They promised to call again tonight if I didn't get in touch. Eight o'clock tonight. Mary will get their number, and then I can call them. She talked to Josh."

He could hear her fear easing with every word. They had been all right the night before, so to her that meant Josh was safe. He didn't like what was happening, but he didn't tell her that. Too much time had passed. Too many people might know, might have *known* their location and their destination, long before he did.

"Deke?" she said, questioning his silence.

"Why don't we eat and then head that way," he suggested. "Now that we have some specific information."

"That sounds good," she agreed, but she recognized something was wrong. Deke's face didn't reflect the soaring relief she had felt, simply knowing that Mary had talked to Josh. It seemed to her that they were now closer to accomplishing what they had set out to do than they had been since they'd left home—getting to Josh before anyone else could.

Soon, baby, she found herself thinking, promising him. *We'll be there very soon.*

Chapter Eleven

She wasn't really aware of the scenery they passed, thinking instead about the route Deke had laid out verbally for her. They would not be able to cover as many miles as she had hoped to before nightfall. She hadn't realized how long they'd slept. They would stop after eight and place the call to Mary. And then it would simply be a matter of using the information her sister provided, to get in touch with Mike and explain some of what was going on, at least enough to warn him and then get to Josh.

She had been repeating that phrase like a mantra since she'd realized Deke was worried. Underlying his surface imperturbability, something was bothering him, and she didn't like it. Deke was uncomfortable with what was happening. Maybe only because, as he'd suggested from the first, he didn't trust Mike. Or maybe because he was afraid they'd be too late.

Resolutely, she denied those thoughts. Nothing was going to go wrong. Deke didn't trust anyone but himself. She knew that. He was simply in a hurry to get to Josh, just as she was. She checked her watch again, realizing with frustration that it was only a little after six.

Deke glanced at her, but he didn't say anything. They had not really talked after they'd left the motel, only the most commonplace exchanges. Not about Josh or the phone calls. Certainly not about what had happened between them. It was as if he intended to ignore the fact they had made love.

She knew that he had never wanted that to happen. She had forced the issue, and she supposed that she shouldn't be surprised if he didn't want to deal with it. It hurt—his failure to acknowledge that the situation between them had changed. They couldn't erase what had happened, but it appeared that Deke was going to do the next best thing by ignoring it.

"Stop worrying," he said finally, the third time she looked at her watch.

"Why shouldn't I worry?" she asked. "You are."

He glanced at her again, meeting her eyes and holding them a moment before he turned his attention back to the highway.

"What makes you think I'm worried?"

"Experience, maybe? Maybe I'm getting better at reading through the mask."

She waited for his explanation, but when the silence continued, she knew he didn't intend to offer one.

"Why don't you tell me what's bothering you?" she suggested.

She thought he wouldn't answer, especially when his eyes remained focused on the road that stretched before them, straight and flat, the colors of the landscape around it the monotonous neutrality of the desert, shimmering with heat and light.

"I don't like the idea that someone knew more than we did," he said.

"Someone?"

"Someone who may have had an eighteen-hour head start on us."

"And that's my fault."

"It's no one's fault. It's just a reality. I don't like the idea that someone might have known where Josh was hours before we did."

"How would they know?" she asked, but she understood what he was suggesting. He had suggested it from the beginning.

"I don't know. I just think…" he hesitated, and angrily she filled in the gap.

"You think someone in my family is giving information to the people who are following you. Following us," she amended.

"I didn't say that."

"You've suggested it. You suspected Mike and Bill, that their trip was somehow connected to all this. That they took Josh. And now? You think they're luring us to meet them? A trap? Is that what you're worried about?"

"It's a possibility," he admitted. It *was* a possibility.

"That's a bunch of crap," she said.

"I know you think that your brothers—"

"Do you trust me, Deke?" she interrupted. She realized that she was holding her breath, waiting for his answer.

"Yeah," he finally said, eyes still on the narrow ribbon ahead.

"Then believe me when I tell you that Mike and Bill are not involved with your enemies."

"Look, I know you don't want to hear this, but all along they've found us too quickly. They have to have some source of information. I'm just afraid that…they might somehow have gotten your brothers' location last night."

"And they might already have found Josh," she said.

"Another possibility."

"Then Mike won't call. We won't know where to go."

"If I'm right, he'll call. They'll want to set up an exchange."

She knew that was, of course, what they'd been attempting when they'd entered her home. A hostage. Someone who would force Deke Summers to finally give himself up, to surrender at last.

Well, she thought bitterly, *I had to ask. Tell me what you're worried about. And he had.*

She closed her eyes, fighting the possibilities he'd suggested. Deke's life in exchange for Josh. That might be what it all boiled down to—what he had told her from the beginning, from the time he'd convinced her to go with him. Only she had never really accepted that might truly be the only option. Deke's life in exchange for Josh.

SHE KNEW BY MARY'S voice that something was wrong, knew it before the first bewildered sentence.

"Did you hear from Mike and the boys?" Becki had asked, trying to keep her voice normal. "Do you have their number?"

"Not a number," Mary said, her anxiety clearly revealed despite the distance. "A message. Mike asked me to give you a message. He said it was important."

Becki leaned against the side of the fast-food restaurant where she was using the phone. Deke had given her a handful of change, dumping the quarters into her outstretched palm, rejecting her idea of calling collect.

"A message?" she repeated carefully. This was what Deke had expected, but the sudden fear the words engendered weakened her knees and churned sickly in her stomach.

"Mike made me write it down so I'd get it right. He said that was important. Do you have something to write on?"

"I've got a pencil. Go ahead." She had dug the pencil out of the bottom of the glove compartment and had torn out the record page of the service manual, prepared to write down Mike's number, which would finally take them to Josh.

"You're to go to a place called Cloud Run. That's a town in New Mexico," Mary said, speaking very carefully. "Monday morning at eight o'clock you have to be at the pay phone on the corner of Everett and Main. The phone's in front of a drugstore. Somebody will call you on that phone with instructions."

"That's it? That's all he told you?"

"Mike said to make sure you understood—nobody but you and Mr. Summers. Don't contact the authorities. No police. No outside agencies. He said that several times. Just you and Summers. Do you understand any of this, Bec?"

"Have you told anybody else about Mike's call?"

"He told me not to talk to *anyone*. That was important, too, he said. Only you. And not to breathe a word to anyone else."

"And you haven't?"

"I just hung up, maybe five minutes before you called. I didn't know what to do until I talked to you. He sounded… He didn't sound like Mike. He sounded scared."

"It's okay." Becki reassured her sister's fear. She was beginning to sound like Deke. *Okay. Everything's okay. What a lie. Dear God, what a lie.* "You know Mike."

"You sound like he did," Mary said, cutting through her assurance. "Pretending to be calm when you're really not. What the hell is happening, Becki? What the hell is going on?"

"The less you know about all this…" she began and then hesitated, recognizing the echo. Deke again. *Keep everybody in the dark. Trust no one.* "Just don't talk to anyone. The boys are all right. I promise you. I'll call you as soon as we make connection with them."

"Who's Summers?" Mary asked.

"A friend of Mike's," Becki lied. Why tell her anything else to drive her crazy? After all, Mary's son was involved in this insanity, too.

"And he's in trouble?" Mary asked.

Becki hesitated, knowing her sister was grasping for some explanation that would make sense of all this.

"Yes," she agreed finally. "He's in trouble."

"And you're not at the beach."

"No."

She heard the depth of the breath her sister took. "You promise me they're all right?"

"As long as you don't tell anyone what you've told me. No one, Mary. Promise me."

"All right," her sister said softly.

"I have to go. I'll call you as soon as I can. Monday night."

"All right," Mary said again. The fear was still there, but overlaid by resignation, by trust perhaps.

She put the receiver back on the metal hook and turned

around to find Deke, cold eyes meeting hers, already aware from her face or posture or from some overheard fragment of the conversation that it had all gone wrong.

"Mike called. We're to go to some place in New Mexico. Cloud Run. We have to be there by Monday morning at eight o'clock. We're supposed to wait at a pay phone for instructions."

Deke's expression didn't change, the information probably only what he'd expected. And then suddenly he smiled at her.

"Right," he said, allowing her to read the sarcasm.

"We're *not* going to wait for further instructions?" she asked, hope fluttering upward from the sickness that had grown since Mary had confirmed Deke's fears.

"Not damn likely," he said. He switched the sack of burgers he held in his left hand to his right and then used his good left arm to pull her against his side. He held her a moment, his mouth against her top of her head. "I'm not going to let anything happen to Josh or to the others. Trust me one last time, Bec. I promise you nothing is going to happen to Josh."

"I NEED TO MAKE A phone call," Deke said.

They had been driving west for the past five hours, since she'd talked to Mary. They both understood the implications of the instructions they'd been given. She realized that Deke had been working his way to a plan, silently considering their options in his head.

"A phone call?" she repeated. It was the middle of the night. And given Deke's admitted lack of ties... They had been told not to call the authorities, but she had already come to the decision that if it came down to a demand for Deke's life in exchange for the others, they would have to get help. Maybe he had come to the same conclusion.

"The best time," he said.

He turned to smile at her, her features barely visible in the darkness. He knew she had been worrying, but he had given her a promise, and in the hours that he'd been driving, always nearer to their destination, he had been trying to work out the best way to make sure it was a promise he could keep. All he needed now was a little assistance.

ALTHOUGH HE HADN'T USED the number in four years, it was intact in his memory. It was a number he had dialed often, several lifetimes ago. He listened to the distant ringing, waiting, anticipating the once-familiar voice.

"Hello."

The response was sleep fogged, a tired man pulled from a well-deserved rest. Deke Summers's lips tilted upward a fraction, knowing that despite the pleasantness of the response, he was being cursed, mentally at least.

"Too much sleep'll slow you down. You know that," he said. "It's almost as bad as old age."

There was silence on the other end for a long time. Deke knew the man he had called would have placed his voice. Too well known to have been forgotten, even after four years.

"Deke?" Luke Ballard whispered. "My God, Deke, is that you?"

"I need some information," Deke said, feeling his throat close against the emotions that lay beneath that whispered question. So many years of friendship. Working together. Trusting his life in this man's hands. And holding Luke's within his own. "No questions asked."

"What kind of information?"

There was a caution in the response, which Deke could hear, but he didn't blame his partner for that. It had been a long time, a lot of water under the dam. A lot of rumors and innuendos.

"A location. A camp. Some kind of training facility. Anything they've got near Cloud Run, New Mexico. There's got to be something nearby, and I need to know exactly what and where it is."

"Something that belongs to the Movement."

"Or something that they would have unlimited and unquestioned access to."

"I'll have to put it through the computers."

"I need it tomorrow. Today," Deke amended.

"Sunday?"

"Don't you have enough pull?" Deke asked, allowing amusement to color the question.

"Yeah," the other admitted, and Deke could hear the answering, slightly embarrassed humor in his voice.

"I heard you'd moved up in the world, once you got rid of that inconvenient partner."

"You in trouble, Deke?"

"I'm *always* in trouble. Don't you remember?"

"You can still come in. We've tried to contact you. I'm so sorry about…"

"No," Deke said. Nothing else.

"You can't run forever."

"Long enough."

Another silence. There was too much they needed to say to each other, and no way to express it.

"Give me a number where I can reach you," Luke said finally, back to business because his friend had given him no choice.

"I'll call you."

"It'll take a while."

"Not for a man with pull," Deke said, his lips lifting again. "And not if you start early. I'll call you."

He broke the connection, holding the receiver a long time, listening to the dial tone, his fingers still on the metal hook he'd pulled down to destroy the connection before there was time for a trace. Old habits.

DEKE HAD PUSHED HARD, determined to reach a vantage point at the top of the ridge overlooking the encampment before sundown so that he could assess the vulnerabilities of the site or of the operation, to formulate some plan of attack.

Luke had provided this location, and its nearness to the town where they'd been told to wait had been verification enough of Deke's suspicions. It was a training facility that, according to the official records, belonged to some survivalist group. The terrain that surrounded it was certainly rugged enough to discourage those who didn't have business here. Too rugged for the merely curious. But Deke had had no doubt that he would find Becki's brothers and the children being held at the camp. Its location was too convenient to be coincidental.

As he had climbed, he had always been aware of Becki determinedly struggling behind him. The slope wasn't that difficult, but the heat and altitude made any activity challenging. He needed to be high enough to see exactly what the setup was, to find the point of attack that would allow him to get Josh and the others safely out of the hands of his enemies.

When Becki reached the summit of the ridge, Deke was already stretched out on his stomach, the binoculars that had been among the supplies he'd bought after he'd made the second phone call trained on the relatively flat ground below.

"Stay low," he cautioned, his attention focused on the scene spread out before him, the sweep of the glasses slow and careful over whatever was down there. Whatever they had come to see. "You'll be visible against the light."

She obeyed without question, easing nearer to the edge of the escarpment. The position he'd chosen was perfect. It was near enough that she could make out a great deal of detail, even without the advantage of the binoculars he was using, and yet high enough to give them a view of the entire encampment.

"That's Bill's van," Becki whispered, recognizing the familiar vehicle parked near the perimeter of the clearing, which seemed to be the center of activity. The van was flanked by several all-terrain vehicles, a couple of which had even been painted over with desert camouflage, and a large panel truck.

Playing soldier, Deke thought when he saw the camouflage. Half of the people involved probably weren't aware of the real purpose of this pseudomilitary operation, maybe not even aware that there were lives on the line, the lives of innocent people caught up in their deadly games. *As there had been before,* he found himself thinking. *Just as there had been before.*

A command tent had been set up in the center of the relatively open area and scattered at its periphery were smaller two-man tents. There was no movement visible around the largest, but it was heavily guarded, and the men standing at the four corners were armed with AK-47s, alert and focused on what they were doing. Since the central tent was the only thing that was guarded, it was an easy conclusion that it must be where the hostages were being held.

He studied the layout and was forced to acknowledge that whoever had designed the security had known exactly what he was doing. This was no amateur operation. Someone with a great deal of experience was in charge of the arrangements, and he had been left with very little to work with. The fall of darkness would offer his best chance at getting to the people who were being held inside, but even that would be a long shot, he was forced to acknowledge. A damn long shot.

"They're inside the big tent, aren't they?" Becki asked.

"Probably," he said. He didn't look at her. He knew that she was trusting him to make this all right. To get Josh and her brothers out without anyone being hurt.

No more broken and bloodied bodies. It was the same promise he had made long ago. No more failures. No more mistakes.

He pushed those thoughts to the back of his mind as he carefully refocused the glasses, tracking the man who emerged from the central tent to address one of the guards. There was something about him that struck a chord of recognition. Not of the individual himself, but an unconscious acknowledgment that he was the leader. The man in charge. He moved with the surety of the man in charge.

"What are we going to do?" Becki asked.

"Wait for night," Deke said. The only shot he'd have, but he didn't tell her that. It was enough that he knew. The only shot.

HE HADN'T COUNTED ON the generator.

They had moved back from the edge of the ridge to eat the

food he'd carried up in the backpack he'd bought. He hadn't been sure at the time he'd made those purchases that they'd be spending the night up here, but he'd come prepared for the possibility. He had bought a sleeping bag, which they could lay open, and the light silver space blanket, for warmth against the desert chill.

He had cautioned Becki against unnecessary conversation, knowing how far sound carried in the thin air, in the starlit silence. He was aware, however, that her eyes would occasionally shift to the shadows where he had chosen to sit, steadily eating the cold provisions. She had barely touched the food, until he'd reminded her that she would need the energy later on. His warning had been enough that she'd gotten down most of the meal, unappetizing as it was.

He fought the desire to hold her. To feel her body under his, warm and alive. Instead, he leaned back against the slowly fading warmth of the rock outcropping and watched her from the darkness. The sun was setting behind her, already far below the horizon, so that her slenderness was silhouetted against the streaked purple of descending night. The first stars were out, spangled like diamonds against the velvet darkness.

"You're going down there," she said, her voice very soft, remembering his warning. It was not a question.

"After they've had time to get settled," he acknowledged.

"To do what? The tent's guarded, Deke. How are you planning to get around that?"

"Improvise," he suggested. He was only a shadow in the dusk, his voice disembodied, his tone as quiet as hers had been. "Take advantage of whatever chance I'm given."

"And if there is no chance?"

"There's always a chance," he said.

She turned away, looking out into the void beyond the rim of the rock face, toward the clearing where her son slept. So near and yet, surrounded by Deke's enemies, so far away. Almost as far as he'd ever been, she thought.

Deke watched as she got up, approaching the edge without the caution of the afternoon, unnecessary now with the backdrop of darkness behind them. She stood on the front of the ridge looking down into the clearing below. He knew she was thinking of Josh. Maybe of how near he was. Nearer to him now than they had been during this entire journey. So close.

"Deke," Becki said. Her voice was very soft, but there was something in her tone, something that had not been there before.

"What is it?" he asked, already moving in response.

"Look," she breathed, her eyes still focused below.

He joined her on the rim, looking down on the destruction of whatever he'd hoped to accomplish tonight. The clearing below was as clearly illuminated as it had been in the heat and light of the afternoon. He could even hear the small hum of the generator that provided power to the floodlights they'd rigged. He wondered briefly how he'd been unaware of its noise before. So much for improvisation. So much for making a move under cover of darkness. There was not a shred of shadow in the glare of light that bathed the circled tents below.

"No place to hide," Deke said softly.

At what was in his tone, she turned toward him, pulling her gaze away from the brightly lit scene spread out at the foot of the ridge. His face was still and set, the tension in his jaw obvious even in the darkness.

"It's all right," she whispered, putting her hand on his arm. "We'll think of something."

At her touch, the line of his mouth moved slightly, and then she felt the clenched muscle that rested under her fingers relax.

"We'll think of something," he agreed, and he smiled at her.

She couldn't see his eyes in the shadows, but she shivered at the coldness of his tone.

THEY HAD LAIN DOWN together, opening the big sleeping bag and sharing the covering of the light blanket. Deke had again crossed his hands under his head, looking up at the panorama of stars, clearer here in the desert darkness than anywhere else on earth. She had turned on her side, her head pillowed by her arm, so that she could watch him. He hadn't mentioned going down into the encampment again, because they had both known the hopelessness of that. They still had time. Several hours until they were supposed to be back in town, patiently waiting for their instructions. She knew Deke was thinking about what he could do tomorrow.

"We have to call somebody," she said.

There was no movement from the man beside her.

"We have to get help. You'll have to trust someone," she argued, wondering if what she was saying was having any effect on the man Deke Summers had become. She had accused him before of paranoia, but she knew that the danger of the dark forces he fled was real and terrifying. Now they had Josh. And her brothers. This wasn't something they could handle themselves, no matter what Deke thought.

"Deke?" she whispered, wanting some sign that he was at least thinking about what she'd suggested.

He turned his head. She wondered if her features were as hidden by the darkness as his. Changed into something— someone—unfamiliar by the play of light and shadow, touching the hard planes of his face with mystery.

He lifted on his elbow, leaning slowly toward her, giving her an opportunity to stop him. To tell him that this was not the time and place. That she was too concerned with the fact that Josh was sleeping, hostage, a few hundred yards away. Not the time for lovemaking. The time, instead, for something else. For fear or caution.

But that was not what was in her heart. She needed his warmth. She needed, as much as she ever had before, the alive solidity of his body over hers.

"Yes," she breathed into his waiting stillness and watched his mouth lower to cover hers, his tongue moving inside. There could be nothing, she thought, more life affirming. Nothing closer to the act of creation. Procreation. And the thought of Deke's child was suddenly in her mind. A child who would be as beloved to her as Josh. There were many reasons why that child should never be conceived, but none of them was as compelling as the thought, half memory and half fantasy, of carrying Deke Summers's baby.

He let his fingers touch her throat. She was so warm, and the coldness had already begun to grow outward from the hard center where he had kept it contained for four years. The knot of black ice, created by guilt and regret, by the horror of all the deaths, had once begun to melt in the heat of what they had shared. Of what she had given him. He put his lips against the pulse that his fingers had found and closed his eyes, blocking everything but the warmth of her body moving under him. Welcoming.

They had not had to deal with the awkwardness of clothing before. Her fingers too slow over the buttons of the borrowed shirt and then against those of his jeans. His hands struggling with the soft knit of her shorts, distracted by her mouth. Distracted by memory. By the remembrance of the welcoming heat of her body closing around him. Taking him. Pulling him into her hot wetness. Hot and wet because she wanted him. There was no cold darkness in Becki Travers's soul. Warmth and light and joy. Welcoming. Making him believe, at least for a time, that this was possible. As he had always known it was not.

But he fought to hold the coldness at bay tonight, pushing hard into the heat of her passion, her body lifting to meet him, to enclose him. His palm was under the full curve of her breast, and his lips had found the softness at her temple. Her hair still smelled of flowers. Despite all that he had dragged her through, the warmth and sweetness were still there. And this was the memory he had wanted. Her body entwined willingly with his. No coldness and no shadows. No aching darkness. Only the pulsing intensity of her hips arching to meet the driving thrust of his.

He felt her response begin, and this time he rode on the same wave that surged with shivering force through her frame. No need to wait. No need to restrain his response. Meeting hers. Joining it. Deliberately allowing it to overwhelm his control. Lost in sensation. All other knowledge destroyed, buried, forgotten in what it meant to make love to her.

No noise. Some fragment of rational thought intruded. He bit his tongue, tasting the copper-salt tang of his own blood. The hard convulsions rocked his resolve. He wanted to scream against what he knew. What he had always known. But that was too dangerous. *For Josh,* he reasoned silently. His head lowered, his lips finding the sweating dampness of her neck. Her hair, still flowers, drifted against his cheek, catching in the stubbled beard. He could hear his own breathing. Panting. Aching lungs gasping thin air. Too loud in the desert stillness. Too loud.

Her fingers drifted over his shoulder, downward, caressing.

"Shh," she whispered, her mouth opened against his face, the warm sweetness of her breath over his skin. "Shh. It's all right. It's okay." Comforting him.

He pushed upward enough to see her face. The fragile bones relaxed, softened. Her clear skin translucent with the flush of passion. Dark eyes reflecting the silvered desert sky above them. He had wanted this memory. This image.

"I love you," she said again. His face didn't change. There was no response to what she had said in the cold, stone-set features. Nothing in his eyes, but they held hers a long time before, again, slowly, his mouth began to lower.

WHEN SHE AWOKE the next morning, the first hint of dawn was beginning to crimson the darkness. She turned, aware of hardness beneath her body, which was stiff and aching, not only from the rocks. She looked for Deke and found him, fully dressed once more, lying prone at the edge of the ridge, the binoculars again trained on the camp below.

She shivered suddenly in the chill of the desert morning, a cold she had not been aware of before. Without throwing off the light blanket, she found her clothing and began to dress, her movements hidden and awkward. She stole glances at the figure of the man who had slept last night entwined with her.

So distant now. Out of her reach. Deliberately distant, she found herself thinking.

When she was dressed, she slipped out of the disordered nest of blanket and sleeping bag and stretched out beside Deke at the lip of the rim, looking, as he was, at the scene below. There was as yet no movement in the clearing. The guards were different, she thought, but nothing had changed in their vigilance. Nothing had changed at all.

"Now what?" she whispered. She allowed her eyes to move to the figure beside her. The strong brown hands were fastened competently around the glasses. She had first been attracted to his hands. To the sunlight glinting in the crisp hair that covered the tanned forearm. Nothing had changed.

Deke lowered the glasses, his eyes still focused before him for a few seconds, and then he turned to face her. His features were as carefully controlled as when, long ago, he had been only her neighbor. There was nothing in his face of what had happened again between them during the night. Nothing of the long hours they had made love. Nothing but cold, pale blue.

Deke had finally allowed himself to look at her. Her hair was disordered and there was a smear of dust on her cheek, but the dark eyes were still trusting. Trusting him to do what he'd promised. Not to let anything happen to Josh.

"We're going to need some help," he said softly, his voice relaxed. "I think it's time to call in the cavalry." He forced his smile, still watching the dark eyes, waiting for her reaction.

She was surprised by his admission. She had known this was not something Deke could handle on his own. There were too many of them, the precious hostages too heavily guarded. She nodded, feeling relief sweep through her that he had finally decided they had to trust someone. If they were going to get her brothers and the boys out of this, they were going to need help. Thank God Deke had realized that, too.

"So what do we do?" she asked.

"Not we," he said. "I have to stay here in case they decide for some reason to move them. In case anything unexpected happens."

"Then…?"

He fingered a folded slip of paper out of the breast pocket of the borrowed shirt. "This is the number of my former partner. His name is Luke. He knows a little about what's going on."

"That's who you called? And he agreed to—"

"I didn't ask him for anything but information."

"What do I tell him?"

"That he was right about their location. Describe the hostage setup to him, tell him we need help to get them out safely, and then let him take it from there. It's his job, his profession. He has access to the resources that will allow him to carry this off."

She nodded, and then she knew she had to ask.

"It won't be like before?" she whispered, remembering what he'd told her about the botched raid and the other children.

"Not like before," Deke promised. "Luke won't let it be. I won't. There won't be any mistakes, Becki, I swear to you."

She nodded again.

"Can you find the car?" he asked, thinking of the long walk they had made the day before in the gathering darkness.

"Of course I can find the car."

"Then you better get started," he said, smiling at her. "And come back with the cavalry."

She leaned toward him, soft lips parted. Waiting for his kiss, for some sort of acknowledgment of all that lay between them. There were so many things that he wanted to say, but he had never been good at that. Another of his many failures. Again he could find no words to tell the woman he loved what he was feeling. There was nothing he could tell her—at least not with words.

His mouth met hers instead, his hand over the curve of her cheek, the line of bone fitting again into his palm. He didn't allow his tongue to invade, only the soft brush of his lips against hers. *Old, married kiss*. Memories. Her body beneath his. Warm and welcoming.

"Be careful," he whispered, withdrawing.

She nodded, her throat tight with so many things that were unsaid. He didn't want to hear them. She knew that. He was thinking about other things now. About Josh. The situation. There would be time for the other when this was over. It was encouraging that he was willing to make contact with his partner. A return to normality, so maybe...

"Go on," he ordered, his mouth still near enough that she felt the breath of the command.

She eased back from the edge of the escarpment they had been looking over, careful, as he had taught her, not to become a silhouette against the dawn sky.

When she was a safe distance away from the edge where he lay, the glasses once again raised to his eyes, she turned and began to move faster down the rocky slope, pebbles rolling and tumbling under her hurrying feet. Back to where they had left the car. And she didn't allow herself to look back.

Chapter Twelve

Becki stopped on the outskirts of the small town, pulling the car up in a spray of dust next to the first pay phone she found. She held the receiver to her ear with her shoulder, right hand inserting the coin into the slot while the fingers of her left struggled to unfold, without dropping it, the paper Deke had given her.

The significance that it was blank didn't register for a second, and she turned it over, still searching for the number, the dial tone in her ear demanding. Puzzled, she turned the paper back over, holding it at a different angle to the clear morning light, thinking she must have missed the penciled markings.

Nothing. The small scrap of white held no telephone number, she finally realized. No one to call.

Still, it took a moment before the realization of what Deke had done sank in. He had never intended for her to call in the cavalry. Whatever plan Deke Summers had for dealing with the situation was already being put into effect as she stood here in the early-morning quietness of this tiny New Mexico community, safely out of the way of whatever was happening.

She put her forehead against the cool metal of the phone box, closing her eyes tightly, but there were no tears. Instead there was a cold, black numbness because she knew what he intended. To carry out the only promises he'd ever made to her. *Not like before. No more dead children. And no one else's life sacrificed for his.*

Suddenly she threw the receiver as hard as she could into one of the scarred Plexiglas panels surrounding the telephone.

"No," she said, her useless protest almost a scream. "No, damn it. No." The receiver bounced harmlessly and then fell to dangle, swinging, from its silver umbilical cord.

There was no response to her cry from the sleeping town, untouched by whatever was happening in the rugged beauty of the nearby mesas. As ordinary as the little Alabama town where she had once lived, watching violence through the distorted, distant kaleidoscope of the nightly news.

Turning, she ran back to the car, knowing that whatever she did, it was probably already too late.

AGAIN DEKE HAD CHOSEN his position carefully, depending on his long years in law enforcement, his military training. This was too important to screw up. A promise.

He watched the figures in the encampment, much closer now. He wanted to deal only with the man he had recognized instinctively as the leader. The man in charge. It would be safer that way, negotiating with someone who was in a position to make the decisions. Fewer things could go wrong, fewer people to make mistakes.

He could see the shadowed outlines moving within the central tent. The smaller stature of the boys was obvious even through the canvas. He wondered briefly which of the small shapes represented Josh, and then he blocked the thought, knowing that it didn't matter.

Suddenly there was something on the periphery of his vision, and moving only his eyes, he tracked across the clearing the path of the man he had been waiting for. The commander walked with a sure, quick military stride, his step full of confidence. *And why shouldn't it be,* Deke thought. He had planned for every contingency, the hostages as professionally guarded as Deke himself could have arranged.

He took a deep breath, knowing there would be no turning back once he'd begun. This was not the ending he had always envisioned, but it was the hand he'd been dealt, and given the odds, he knew he had no option but to play it out.

"We need to talk," Deke shouted, pitching his voice to reach the encampment. The backdrop of the rocks he had hidden in did just what he'd expected, projecting the sound and at the same time distorting his precise location. The echo behind the word "talk" bounced softly among the surrounding boulders.

The leader turned in his direction, his face reflecting surprise, which was quickly controlled. The thin line of his lips moved fractionally, a satisfaction he didn't hide.

"Summers?" he called, but the surety was in his voice as it had been in his smile.

"Yeah," Deke acknowledged.

"What do you want to talk about?"

"Let them go," Deke shouted, allowing nothing but confidence to color his own tone.

"You come in. Then they can go."

"Let them go, and I'll come in. Nobody gets hurt."

"My theater of operations, Summers. My rules."

"Then all but one. Everybody allowed into the van except one. I walk in as he walks out. Your choice."

Again the brief, quickly controlled reaction of the thin lips. "My choice," he agreed.

Too easy, Deke thought, feeling a shiver of premonition along his spine. *Too easy.* He wished he hadn't suggested the single hostage, but it was the classic solution for the situation. It minimized the danger. One person vulnerable rather than all of them, and if anything went wrong...

Nothing would go wrong, he vowed. *Nothing would screw this up. A simple exchange.* As one of Becki's brothers walked to the van, he'd go in, give himself up. His hands in the air, gun held high where everyone could see it, a clear target. He knew their weapons would be poised to shoot him or at least to shoot the gun out of his hand if he began to lower it. Then when everyone was in the van, he'd throw the weapon to the side, surrendering himself into their control. There had been no discussion about those details. They both knew how the game was played.

He became aware that the hostages were being led out of the tent. The four boys, blinking in the sudden glare of sunlight, were surprisingly small, moving hesitantly on tanned legs which looked pipe-stem thin, protruding from beneath their cotton shorts. Josh put his hand up, shielding his eyes and one of the guards pushed it down. Bewildered, the child looked up at the man, puzzled by the unexpected hostility.

The uncles were almost as subdued as the children, as unfamiliar with this situation and as unprepared. The younger brother, the one Deke had met, showed evidence of blows to the face: bruises, some swelling and the skin broken in a couple of places. Apparently he had had to be coerced into making the phone call to his sister.

Another life touched, marked forever by Deke Summers's darkness. Like the bewildered fear that was now in the face of the bright, confident little boy who had once lived next door to a man named John Evans. Another lifetime ago.

There was a brief but serious discussion between the commander and one of the "soldiers," who appeared to be expressing his feelings passionately. Deke watched the apparent resolution of that, indicated by a slight nod of the commander's head. He could hear only an indistinguishable murmur of the instructions being given to the hostages. Unexpectedly there was argument from the two brothers. Anger. Deke hadn't anticipated any resistance from them. The muzzle of a rifle was suddenly against the chest of Becki's youngest brother, pushing him away from the confrontation with the man in charge.

Objecting because he had been told to stay behind as the others moved toward the van? Deke wondered. *Just do it, damn it,* he urged silently, trying to will Mike's compliance. *Whatever the hell you're told to do. Too late to play hero. Just do what you're told. Follow orders.*

The situation was escalating, but Deke was still having a hard time making out the words they were saying to each other. And then finally, under the repeated prodding of the muzzle, Mike was forced to turn and move off, walking beside the others. All but one of the group heading to the relative safety of the van. All but one.

The small dark-haired boy stood uncertainly by the commander. His eyes moved, searching for some explanation from the strange adults who surrounded him as to why he'd been left behind. Deke felt his throat close at the aloneness projected by the solitary figure of the child. This was the choice the commander had made. The single remaining hostage was Josh.

Deke closed his eyes, fighting the rush of feeling, trying to tamp it down again into the familiar, cold darkness. This had always been the choice. He had known that from the beginning, and somehow, he admitted, it was even fitting that it would be played out this way. At least he would remember exactly what he was dying for.

Deliberately he turned his blurring vision away from the child who had tried so hard to make some connection with the empty, embittered man he had become. Josh couldn't know that the connection had always been there, from the very beginning. From the first moment he had looked into those same dark eyes that had haunted his dreams for four years. Like the child she had so desperately wanted. The child he hadn't been able to give her. His son.

And with that word, the images of Becki Travers invaded, destroying again with the memory of her sweetness the familiar ghosts. His son. That, too, might have become reality had he not been who and what he was—Deke Summers, with all the blood on his soul that must now, finally, be paid for.

The others had reached the van. Only Mike was still outside, standing as he had been instructed by the opened door, waiting for the small figure to walk across the clearing and back to the familiar safety of home. A simple journey that was light years beyond the reach of the man who was standing now in the elongated shadows of the surrounding rocks. Also waiting for Josh to begin the journey which would end his.

The others had moved away so that the two stood alone before the tent. Just the boy and the commander. Almost unconsciously the militia leader put his hand on the raven silk of Josh's head. At the touch, Josh glanced up again, and then his gaze moved to find whatever the man standing beside him was looking at so intently across the clearing.

Josh's recognition was instantaneous, the connection as strong as always. Without his conscious volition, Deke Summers's hard mouth tilted upward in response to the joyful smile that had lit the small countenance.

The man beside the child said something. Josh looked up at his captor, and then again, almost regretfully now, at Deke. He took a hesitant step toward the van and knowing that was his signal, Deke began to cross the desolate expanse that separated him from the men who had hunted him so long.

He walked slowly, head up, his arms held high in the air, right one gripping the handgun he had never intended to use. He didn't look at the men who were waiting for him, who had been waiting a long time for this day. Instead, the blue eyes watched the child who trudged toward his uncle, small reluctant feet kicking up dust with each step.

They were about halfway toward their respective goals when the boy, perhaps far enough away from his captors to feel some sense of freedom, turned and began to run toward the tall, blond man who was advancing steadily toward the central tent.

Deke was aware of every movement. It all was happening in slow motion and yet far too quickly, everything spinning suddenly out of control. The powerful guns beginning to focus on the small figure running in the wrong direction. The armed men reacting with fear, with a need to protect themselves from the unexpected. And that was what Deke was afraid of. Just as before. Frightened men reacting without thought that this was only a child. No threat to them. No threat to anyone.

Distantly, in the soundless vacuum of horror that had suddenly surrounded him, Deke heard Mike shouting, calling the boy's name, urging him to complete the proscribed journey to the van, but those pleas were in vain. Josh, perhaps terrified by the resulting clamor around him, continued to run toward the man *he* had chosen, the man who somehow now represented safety and home. But this was not what was supposed to happen, and the guns continued to track.

Not again, Deke thought. *Please God, not again.* The child was moving very quickly, but Deke could see all the details, vividly illuminated by his own terror. The spurts of dirt, shooting up and then falling behind the small, scuffed sneakers. Shining black hair flying back from the smooth oval of his face. Dark eyes too wide. Frightened.

"No," Deke shouted, not sure to whom the command was addressed. It had no effect on the panicked boy. No effect on what was happening. *No more,* he prayed again. *Please, God, no more.*

Deke threw the gun away, holding his empty hands higher, palms toward the militiamen, fingers spread wide, hoping they would see the gesture and realize that even with the boy beside him, the last remaining hostage, he presented no danger to them. *He* was the sacrifice, a willing one. Not the child. *No more broken and bloodied bodies.*

Josh was almost there, almost to him, and Deke found himself waiting helplessly for the shots. He knew he would see their impact on the fragile body, jerking with the force of the bullets long before he would hear the noise. And he waited still, silhouetted against the backdrop of the red rocks, knowing that any movement from him would surely precipitate the deadly fusillade that would catch the running child between them. He forced himself not to move, hands held high as two small arms wrapped around his thigh. Wrapped and held. A small face pressed sobbing against his leg.

Deke's eyes met those of the man who had mercifully not given the order to shoot. The man who had held their lives in his hands and who had chosen not to react to the boy's unexpected divergence from their agreement.

"Please," Deke said simply. He waited a long time. The

clearing was absolutely silent except for the muffled crying of the child.

Finally the man nodded. "Hold your fire," he ordered.

There was an infinitesimal relaxation in the tension that had built unbearably since Josh had broken course. Slowly Deke allowed his right hand to move downward, still spread, still open and unthreatening. When it was level with the small head, he cupped it around the back of the child's skull, feeling the baby-fine hair under the callused roughness of his palm.

"It's okay," he promised softly.

The clutching fingers released their frantic grip on Deke's jeans. Eventually, the boy's face was raised, the tracks of his tears marked poignantly on the ashen, dust-smudged cheeks.

The smile that touched Deke Summers's mouth was the same one he had given Becki in the shower. For the first time it was full of welcome for the boy he had held, always, at arms' length, any affirmation of what he felt for him unallowed. Until today. Today it was all there in his eyes. All the love and acceptance that Josh had once hoped for.

With the unquestioning forgiveness of childhood, the little boy's mouth quivered into an answering grin.

"It's okay," Deke said again, moving his hand to ruffle the dark hair. "Everything will be okay."

Too young to question the existence of miracles, Josh raised his arms in silent entreaty to the man he had worshiped from afar. Deke's eyes moved to the silent watcher and again the thin lips tilted in sardonic amusement, but he nodded. Permission granted.

Deke Summers bent and carefully enclosed the body of the child, lifting him. Josh's arms tightened around his neck, and his face found, naturally somehow, the protective niche between Deke's neck and wide, strong shoulder. The blue eyes closed, as Deke fought the urge to squeeze too tightly. To try to hold on to the trusting body of the little boy who wanted to be held. But there was only here. Only now. Too brief.

"You can't stay with me, Josh. You have to go with your

uncles," he said finally, explaining the unexplainable. "Your mom's waiting for you."

"Mom?" Josh said, raising his head to authenticate from his hero's face the accuracy of that surprising information.

"In town."

"And you'll come later?" Josh asked. His gaze moved back and forth between the blue eyes and the half-healed gash on Deke's neck, his small, grubby fingers gently touching the cut, worrying.

"As soon as I can," Deke said. "But you have to go now. For me, Josh. When I put you down, you have to go straight to your Uncle Mike. No turning back this time. Do you understand?"

The dark eyes held a moment, sensing something behind the calm instructions. *As sensitive as his mother. And just as strong,* Deke prayed. "Will you do that for me?"

Josh nodded, and then the thin arms locked suddenly again around Deke's neck. The smooth cheek was against the stubbled roughness of the man's, and then the little boy turned his head, soft lips finding the rigidly held corner of Deke Summers's mouth.

Deke bent, forcing his mind away from all the might-have-beens and put the child carefully back on the ground.

"Go on now," Deke whispered, and again Josh nodded.

"You'll come as soon as you can?"

"As soon as I can," Deke said.

The boy turned away, and Deke straightened to stand upright again. They all watched, still unmoving, as the child crossed the glare of hot sand. When he reached the van, his uncle bent and scooped him up. Mike's eyes, dark and too reminiscent of his sister's, met the serenely calm gaze of the man who stood alone at the edge of the clearing. He nodded and saw the small reactive movement at the corners of Summers's mouth.

Then as Mike climbed into the passenger seat of the waiting van, Deke began to move forward again, to finally complete the journey he had always known was inevitable.

THE CARAVAN OF PATROL cars met the van only a few miles out of town. Becki's shout when she saw the familiar vehicle startled the sheriff, but he reacted far more quickly than she would have expected, given the agonizing slowness she had felt his response to be when he'd first heard her story.

She jumped out, almost before the car had rolled to a stop and was enfolded again in the arms of her family. She couldn't stop hugging Josh, and she couldn't seem to stop crying. Despite her relief that her brothers and the children were safe, the reunion was brief because the thought of finding Deke was now paramount.

She walked quickly back to the waiting lawmen, her arm still tight around Josh's shoulders because she couldn't bear to let him go. Her hurried recitation of Mike's story sounded garbled even to her own ears. Apparently, however, it was coherent enough, because it was only seconds later that the cars, sirens screaming and lights flashing now that there was no need for caution, roared again down the two-lane road that led to the training camp, followed closely by the van.

There was no one there. The tents were still standing, but the vehicles had disappeared, as had the disciplined men who had stood such diligent guard over their hostages. The terrain stretched barren and lifeless as far as the eye could see.

Becki said nothing, hoping, as she watched the deputies' careful examination of the site. It seemed to take them an eternity, and finally the sheriff returned to where the small, subdued group stood waiting, even the children responding to the return to the camp with unnatural restraint.

"Ms. Travers, I'm sorry, but it appears we're too late," the sheriff said. He pushed the sweat-stained Stetson hat back away from his forehead, his fleshy face perspiring in the desert heat.

"They have to be close. There hasn't been enough time for them to get very far. Someone will know where they've taken him," she argued. She wanted them to do something. Anything. Anything besides stand around and look uncomfortable, eyes meeting and then sliding away from the knowledge they believed she wouldn't understand, didn't know.

"With all-terrain vehicles they could have gone anywhere. They'd be able to avoid the roads, and that means there's a hundred different directions they could go. They could have split up. And there ain't no way to track them in this kind of country. I can put out an APB, but eventually they're either going to hole up somewhere or change vehicles. If only half of what you've told me about their organization is true..." He didn't complete the opinion, but he didn't have to. The small shrug of his shoulders was indication enough of what he believed.

"Get some helicopters," she ordered, feeling her frustration build with his dispassionate appraisal. "Call the state or the military or somebody. Get some help, damn it. Do something. A man's life is at stake."

"I can request help 'til I'm blue in the face. That don't mean I'm going to *get* it in time to do any good."

"You won't know until you ask," she argued.

"I intend to ask, but without some kind of idea about their destination—"

"The locals," she demanded. "Somebody here knows something. Contact the local minutemen or militia or whatever the hell they call themselves here. Somebody knows where they've taken Deke Summers."

His eyes met those of his deputy again, and his lips pursed slightly. "You may be right, Ms. Travers, but that don't mean they're going to tell *us* anything."

"And the locals weren't involved in this," the deputy added.

"How do you know that?" she asked, dark eyes flashing to his, cold with her sudden suspicion. His gaze shifted away.

"*You're* involved with them," she accused.

"No, ma'am. Not in what happened here today, but I know the people that built this camp, and I can tell you that nobody local was involved in what went on out here. This was an operation run by outsiders. They came for just one reason, and I guess you know what that was.''

"And now they're gone," she suggested bitterly, "and that's it?''

"Yes, ma'am. They're gone," he repeated.

"And you don't intend to do anything? You don't even intend to look for them?" she asked, turning back to the sheriff.

"I told you I'll put out an APB. That's our best shot. We'll hope somebody will notice something suspicious. But as for roaming through this country looking for a couple of needles in this particular haystack, then no, ma'am, I ain't. I don't have the manpower. I'll inform the state and if they want to mount a search..." Again the sentence drifted, incomplete.

Becki held his eyes a moment, realizing that she wouldn't change his mind. "All right, if you won't do anything, then we will," she said. She walked away from the cars toward the center of the encampment. She was aware that Mike followed her, aware, too, of the departing patrol cars. She wondered briefly if the sheriff would even make the small efforts he'd promised. She pushed that thought away, knowing that she couldn't do anything about his seeming lack of concern. If she had to, she'd find Deke by herself.

The tent was empty. The central table held a few dishes, the remains of the food they'd contained hardening in the dry air. There was nothing else. No papers. No maps. Nothing left behind to indicate where the men who had taken Deke had come from or where they had gone. Nothing.

Mike put his arm around her shoulder. The human touch was comforting and she leaned against him, remembering how it had felt when Deke had held her against his body, allowing her to draw strength from his. And now...

"It's too late, Bec," Mike said.

Angrily, she jerked away. She didn't want to hear this. More of the same defeatist crap the sheriff had spouted.

"It's not too late," she said. "An hour at the most. That's all the head start they've had. We can still find them. Deke's not going to just give in. He'll keep fighting. We just have to find—''

"He threw his gun away. He gave himself up to them in exchange for our freedom. It's what he intended to do. They had already decided on the one who..." Mike hesitated, and then, like the deputy's, his eyes fell away from hers.

He didn't need to finish the thought. She knew.

"The guy in charge?" she asked bitterly.

"A kid. Some kid they called Richard. He wanted that 'honor' pretty badly," Mike said bitterly. "He seemed to feel he had some right to...be the one to do it. That's what he said. Some kind of payback.''

"Richard," she repeated softly, shaking her head, remembering the dark night and the man Deke had chosen not to kill. So ironic. So damned ironic. "Richard," she said again.

It was unfair that someone Deke had deliberately chosen to spare would now be allowed to take his life. Might already have carried out the execution he had described to her. Might already have...

The rage that had caused her to throw the phone when she'd finally realized what Deke intended was back, boiling uncontrollably through her body. There was nothing she could do. She didn't know the country or the direction they'd headed. Nothing. And no one else seemed to care. No one cared.

Furious with her inability to change anything, she suddenly swept the dishes off the table, a single swing of her arm across the surface, watching them fall and bounce on the canvas floor of the tent. Only one glass broke, and that because it struck with a sharp ping against the lip of one of the thick white plates. She wanted it all to break into a million pieces, as she was breaking inside, but instead they fell almost silently against the softness of the tent floor. She watched them settle, the liquid that had been left in one of the glasses spreading in a small silver puddle over the treated canvas.

She pushed against the edge of the camp table, lifting with both hands until it turned over, landing against the wall of the tent. Then there was nothing else to fight against. Nothing else of theirs she could hurt or destroy. The small, senseless protest was over. She found she was crying, dry, hard sobs that hurt her throat and chest. Nothing to do. No target for her anger. She wanted to tear down the tent they had erected, but like the dishes she'd tried to destroy, that wouldn't change anything. It was already too late. They had waited too many years to get their hands on Deke Summers. They weren't going to screw it up now. Too late. She couldn't stop whatever was happening. Had already happened.

She didn't resist when Mike's arms wrapped around her, holding her, allowing her to cry out her despair against his body. They stood together in the shadowed interior of the enemy tent. *They'll put the muzzle of a rifle…* The phrase echoed unwanted in her heart. His life for Josh's. A sacrifice she knew he had willingly made. She acknowledged her gratitude and knew that, as she had before, she'd eventually learn to deal with this loss. But not yet. Not for a long time would she forget what she felt for Deke Summers.

BECKI WAS AT HER grandmother's, after another Sunday dinner, when she discovered that the prayer she had offered so fervently for the past three weeks wasn't going to be granted. She leaned against the coolness of the floor-length mirror attached to the back of the bathroom door and felt the tears slip out.

Her period had been late, although she hadn't really been aware of it for a while after their return from New Mexico. When she *had* realized, she had tried to tell herself it was simply the result of all the stress, but the small hope had grown with each passing day. It hadn't seemed so much to ask for. Deke's child. But now, finally, she knew that wasn't to be. It seemed that nothing was left of the man who had touched their lives, hers and Josh's, except memories.

Someone knocked on the door, softly, but given the fact that this was the only bathroom and considering the number of people crowded into the old house, she knew she would have to respond. She sniffed, wiping away the tears, and then, using the mirror, attempted some quick repair.

The soft knock demanded again. "Bec?" her sister said. "You okay?"

Deke's word. "I'm okay," she whispered.

"Then let me in," Mary demanded.

Becki opened the door and watched as her sister's concerned eyes traced over her features. Apparently she hadn't been very successful in her attempts to hide the tears. Mary stepped inside and closed the door behind her.

"Would talking help?" she asked.

"Not really," Becki said truthfully, but because the love was so clearly visible, she put her arms around her sister and hugged her. She stepped back, almost embarrassed by her display and said again, "I'm okay."

"How's Josh?"

"Waiting. At least I think that's what he's doing. I've tried to tell him that Deke isn't coming, but I don't seem to be having any effect. He doesn't believe me."

"That's...awful," Mary whispered.

"I don't know. Maybe it's better that way. Eventually he'll forget. It'll just be one more thing some adult promised and then screwed up. Who knows what's easiest?"

"Is that what you're crying about?"

"No," Becki said, smiling. "At least, not this time."

"Look," Mary said softly, "eventually you'll—"

"Don't. Just don't. Whatever you're about to say, just don't say it. It won't help."

Mary studied her face a moment and then nodded. "All right. No big-sister advice. But I care. And I'm grateful. Mike told me some of what happened. Enough to know that Summers didn't have to do what he did."

Becki took a breath, thinking about the enigmatic man she had known so briefly, and then she said, "I think maybe he did. Because he was the kind of man he was. I think he had to do exactly what he did."

Mary nodded.

Suddenly Becki wanted to share the sense of loss, that no one else might understand was a loss. Only a cold emptiness where she had imagined Deke's child to be, longed for it to be. She had visualized, through the long, dark hours of the nights she didn't sleep, his child growing safely inside her body. Maybe it would help just to tell someone.

"I just discovered I'm not pregnant," she said. No explanation.

"And you wanted to be?" her sister asked carefully.

"More than anything," she admitted.

They said nothing for long moment.

"That would have complicated the hell out of your life," Mary said finally, smiling, sharing feminine understanding. "At least..." Mary began and let the sentence die because she knew her sister didn't care about any of the complications. "I'm so sorry, Bec," she said. She leaned to put her lips against her cheek. "So sorry."

They moved away from each other, still slightly embarrassed by the shared confidences.

"You're not shocked?" Becki asked, trying to read the truth in Mary's eyes. "Disappointed in me?"

There was some subtle shift in her sister's eyes, some response that she hadn't expected.

"Because you slept with him?" Mary asked. At Becki's nod, she shook her head. "I'm not shocked."

"It seemed so right, with everything...that was going on. It *was* right. I loved him so much."

The tears had begun again, and she blinked to clear them, seeing the sudden answering moisture in her sister's hazel eyes.

"I know," Mary said. "You don't have to explain. Sometimes things happen that you don't plan on, don't expect."

Becki nodded.

"That's really what happened with Vernon," Mary said, her voice very soft. "I didn't intend anything...like that. And then the week Joel was gone...it just happened."

"Vernon?"

"I know he's not... I do know what y'all think about him, but he's good to me. And I was lonely. You know? Just so damn lonely." Mary's voice faded, the confession suddenly too hard.

"I know."

"There was no reason for him *not* to stay. No one would ever know, he said. He wanted to. And I wanted him to. And there was no reason... It was nobody's business but ours."

"The nights the guys were gone?" Becki said, the remembrance of Mary's sleep-filled voice the morning she had called from Louisiana suddenly strong in her head. Her sister's hand over the phone, speaking to someone in the background. "Vernon was with you then?"

"Shocked?" Mary asked, her question a little bitter at what she thought she heard in Becki's voice, given the confession her sister had just made.

"He was with you the morning I called."

"You called at the crack of dawn. Of course, he was still there."

"And that's who you were talking to?"

Mary shook her head, puzzled. She probably didn't remember putting her hand over the phone, answering Vernon Petty's harmless question.

"He asked you who was calling, didn't he?" Becki asked, finally putting it all together. Deke hadn't been wrong, but then neither had she. It had *not* been her family providing information to the enemy. At least, not directly.

"I think so. I really don't remember. What does it matter?"

"And you told him it was me."

"Probably. If he asked," Mary said.

"And you told him where Mike and the boys were when Mike called you Friday night."

"Of course, I told him. Why not? The call came while we were... What does it matter?" she asked again, her tone defensive now.

"He must have traced my call that morning, asked the phone company where the collect call you'd just accepted had originated.'' Becki was thinking out loud now, still piecing it together. And it had been Vernon's little service station where she and Deke had stopped to make the call to her mother. Finally it all made sense. ''Vernon saw the car. That's how they found us at Wal-Mart the first time. Vernon told them what car to look for.''

''Becki?'' Mary said when she finally ran down. ''Just what are you accusing Vernon of?''

''That son of a bitch,'' Becki said instead of answering. ''That redneck son of a bitch. It was Vernon all along.''

Chapter Thirteen

The small station was empty. That had been obvious some-how, although there was no For Rent or For Sale sign, only the chain and padlock securing the front door. Becki peered in through the window to the right of the door and then crossed the narrow planks of the small porch. She stepped off at the end, looking in windows as she made her way around to the back.

She didn't really know why she had come or what her in-tentions were, now that she was here. The thought that con-fronting Vernon Petty might be dangerous had occurred to her, but it hadn't prevented her getting into the car and driving several miles to the other side of the Sunday-afternoon-idle town for that confrontation.

The door in the back was open, swinging slightly in the occasional breath of hot air that also stirred the lush weeds that had proliferated with the owner's absence. She pushed the door with her fingertips, creating a wider opening, and then hesitated before stepping across the threshold. She didn't know what she was afraid of. She could see inside. There were only shadows in the darkened interior. Smells. Years-old fumes of gasoline and floor-cleaning compound. The musty aroma of an unoccupied building.

She walked into the small back room, an office, she realized, although it had been stripped of furniture. There was appar-ently nothing left of the man she had come to find. Nothing of the man who had courted her sister. The man who had been indirectly responsible for Deke Summers's death. Nothing.

She walked across the wooden boards, her heels echoing strongly in the enclosed space. She allowed her eyes to trace over the walls, realizing that what was left on them had been put up long before Petty had bought the business. A couple of travel posters, the heavy stock they had been printed on yellowed now, the people and scenes they portrayed subtly out of date. Someone had laminated a map of Alabama and the bordering states, the gold star which marked the location of the station still dimly gleaming, protected through the years by its overlay of plastic. She turned, admitting finally that this had been a wasted trip. Foolish. There was nothing here. The one enemy she'd been able to identify had disappeared, fading back into the nameless, faceless void of ideology that connected them all.

It was only as she headed to the door through which she had entered that she realized there was something on the opposite wall that was different. The paper was starkly white, new and therefore, in contrast to the aging posters, noticeable. She walked over to stand before the picture. Computer generated, it was a black-and-white photograph. A slashed-across-the-middle circle had been imposed over the features of the man she loved. Printed across the circle was the single word *EXECUTED*. And a date. The day they had left New Mexico.

She stared unseeing at the picture a long time, all the memories running through her head like the images of a video on fast forward. It had all gone too quickly. Fragile and fleeting. If anything, that was the legacy Deke had left her: the knowledge that life was so damn fleeting.

Her fingers were remarkably steady as she tugged the blue plastic map pin out of the wall. She didn't know why she wanted to take the picture with her. Her mind recognized the impulse as macabre. Morbid. But somehow she couldn't leave it here—Vernon Petty's trophy. She stuck the pin back in the wall and carefully folded the paper.

She closed the door behind her when she left, and she didn't allow herself to look at the phone booth from which she'd made that early morning call to her mother. These were not the memories she would cherish. Only the others—the few, brief moments when she had been allowed to touch the real man behind the created identity.

When she'd climbed back into her car, she slipped the folded paper into the side pocket of her purse. She turned the key and resolutely dry-eyed drove back to her grandmother's to pick up her son, to get on with the business of living each fleeting, precious day to the very best of her ability. Somehow that had become a responsibility. And a promise.

IT HAD BEEN THE HOTTEST day of the summer. It was August, and the afternoon temperature had climbed several degrees above one hundred. At dusk Becki Travers stepped out of the comfort of the air-conditioning onto the small deck that backed her house. She set the cat bowl down in its customary spot. She had filled it with tuna—not the feline kind—real tuna.

"Here, kitty, kitty, kitty," she called. They hadn't seen the ginger tabby since their return. Almost six weeks now. Mentally, she had acknowledged that he had probably moved on to a more dependable source of food or had gone back to the wild. She had even, mother rational, told Josh that, but somewhere in her heart she hadn't completely accepted it. And so occasionally she went through the motions of trying to lure him home.

"Here, kitty, kitty," she called again, eyes tracing across the edge of the woods that backed the yard, hoping for the proud swagger of a faintly ringed tail, moving out of the undergrowth.

The phone rang, the sound distant through the closed door, and she hurried inside to answer it.

"Hello," she said, balancing the receiver against her shoulder while she slipped the spoon she used to scoop out the tuna into the cooling dishwater in the sink.

"Rebecca Travers?"

"Yes," she said, trying to place the voice. It was not familiar and not Southern.

"My name is Ballard, Ms. Travers. I'm with the ATF. I'd like to talk to you."

"About what?" she asked. She had always expected someone official to call, to question the events of June.

"About Deke Summers," the voice acknowledged.

Despite the fact that it was only what she'd expected, her reaction was strong. Too emotional. She fought it, determined to keep her voice steady.

"All right," she managed.

"I hate to ask, Ms. Travers, but would it be possible for you to come in to Birmingham? I think that might be better than our calling on you at home."

"Better? Do you mean safer?" she asked, suddenly apprehensive.

"You're in no danger, Ms. Travers. Not any more. I just thought it might cause less…comment if you came here. If it's convenient. I'm afraid I'll only be in town a couple of days. Would it be possible for you to come in tomorrow?"

Less comment. She didn't know how much of the story was common knowledge, but she knew how small towns worked. She thought about that. About Josh.

"All right," she said again.

After they had made the arrangements, she hung up the phone. She finished clearing the kitchen, a routine not demanding concentration. As she worked, she found herself dreading the interview. At least she could give them her information about Vernon Petty. She recognized, as Mike had told her when she'd shared her discovery of Vernon's role, that it would be difficult to prove what he had done. There was no doubt in her mind of his guilt, of course, but more cynical now, she didn't really expect the authorities would pursue her gut reaction. All she could do was give the information to the man who had phoned tonight.

It was much darker when she stepped out on the deck to call Josh in for his bath. The sky was purple, the shadows giving a sense of mystery to the familiar backyard. Josh was sitting on the second step, his glass insect jar beside him. There were no fireflies imprisoned there, and she pushed it to the side with her bare foot and sat down on the top step, directly behind him. Josh leaned back between her legs, and she bent forward to put her arms around his chest, hugging him to her body.

"What are you doing?" she asked.

"Waiting for the stars to come out," he said, and his head tilted back, eyes raised skyward.

She looked up, remembering, despite her intentions, another sky, its darkness spangled with a million diamonds. Now there was only the evening star, already brilliant against the backdrop of approaching night.

"Star light, star bright," she whispered.

"First star I see tonight," Josh added.

Smiling, she went on, not really thinking about the words, convenient in her memory, stored there in childhood. "I wish I may, I wish I might..."

"Have the wish I wish tonight," they finished together.

She squeezed Josh tightly, suddenly wishing she could hold him forever, all the while knowing that her job was to let him go. To prepare him to function without her. To make Josh the same kind of strong man—

"What did you wish for?" he interrupted her thoughts. He put his arms around the outside of her knees, pulling them against his ribs.

She couldn't tell him that she hadn't really made a wish, other than that forbidden one—to keep him a child forever, small enough that she would always be able to protect him, to hold him. She tried to think of something, not willing to reveal that she was too cynically adult to believe any more that wishes made on stars came true.

"That Wimsey would come on home," she offered.

"That was a good wish," Josh complimented.

"Thank you," she said. The top of his head was just under her chin, and his hair smelled of the summer, dust and sunshine, little-boy sweet. "What did you wish for?" she asked, not because she wanted to know, but just to hold on to the moment, the quiet, perfect magic of being together as the stars drifted out.

"If I tell you what I wished for, it won't come true."

"You asked me," she argued. "And I *told* you," she said, laughing.

"*I'm* not to blame if you don't know the rules," he said reasonably.

"Was yours a good wish, too?"

"The best," he said softly. "The very best."

She bent her head to drop a kiss on the sun-warmed softness of his hair, suddenly afraid that she knew what Josh had wished for.

IT TOOK HER A LONG TIME to go to sleep. Worrying about Josh. About the interview. Remembering. The memories drifting upward, unbidden, appearing suddenly out of the lonely darkness, just as the stars had tonight. Just suddenly there against the sky.

When the dream woke her, she didn't know how long she had been asleep. The images were still in her head, strong and terrifying. Nothing she had really seen. Except in her dreams. But that didn't make the nightmares any less vivid.

She raised her hand to wipe away the tears. Her grandmother always said that grief would manifest itself somehow. Even those who didn't seem to make any outward show were still dealing with their loss. And that sometimes it was harder for those who didn't have the luxury of grieving openly.

She turned on her side, looking toward the windows. There was no sign of morning. Hours of night to be gotten through again, always the hardest.

In the stillness, she gradually became aware of a sound. Soft enough that it would never have awakened her. Familiar and yet out of place.

Tentatively, hardly daring to breathe, she allowed her fingers to move in the direction of the sound and knew with sudden wonder that she hadn't been mistaken. She ran her hand lightly over the warm fur. There was a small *hrump* of reaction, a shifting of position, stretching. And then again, the cat's breathing settled into the familiar, softly rhythmic purr of contentment.

Wimsey was back, and although she wasn't sure, she thought she detected the pleasant scent of tuna surrounding him. And she lay awake a long time in the less-lonely darkness, thinking about the faith of childhood and wishes made on stars.

THE MAN WHO STOOD UP from behind the table in the room where they had sent her was slim and black, city elegant, dressed in a charcoal gray suit over a starched white shirt, a silk tie. Despite the air-conditioning, a dew of perspiration was shining on the smooth ebony of his forehead, and she fought her automatic smile at his attire, given the heat and humidity. She had not dressed up, choosing instead a cotton sundress that left a lot of tanned skin visible.

"I'm Luke Ballard, Ms. Travers," he said. He pulled out a leather case, flipping it open with a practiced twist of his wrist to reveal the ATF identification it contained.

"How do you do, Mr. Ballard," she said politely, extending her hand, which was lost in his. *Deke's ex-partner,* she realized, and then knew that she should have guessed who they'd send.

Cool and in control, far more poised than he was, Luke Ballard thought, assessing. He hadn't expected that. He had thought she might still be suffering from the effects of all that had happened. Emotionally on edge. But if she was, she was hiding it very well, brown eyes as direct as he'd expected them to be.

"Deke Summers was my partner," he said, images from that long friendship suddenly too clear in his own head. "For a lot of years."

She smiled at him, waiting through the silence. Not rushing him. A comfortable woman to be around, he acknowledged, and he wondered if that had been part of the reason Deke had been attracted.

"Would you like to sit down?" he invited.

She pulled out the chair on the opposite side of the table and sat down in it, her purse held in her lap, the picture of a Southern lady, despite her exotic coloring and the black sundress. He had been told she was a teacher, high-school English, but she didn't look like any teacher he'd ever had, Luke thought in quick amusement.

He sat down again, nervous fingers finding the pen he'd been jotting notes with while he waited. She let the silence grow, and finally he looked up. She was watching him with those calm eyes, waiting for him to reveal the reason he had brought her here.

"Deke and I worked together for nine years, except occasionally when he went undercover. *Especially* when he went inside the Movement. That wasn't something I was exactly...suited for," he said, smiling again, remembering all the less-than-subtle jokes.

Again, she answered the smile.

"It took a while for us to be friends," he continued, still remembering. "Given our backgrounds. Deke grew up hardscrabble poor in Tennessee, and I was ghetto tough and proud of it. But once we were over all that..." He was forced to stop, his throat tightening unexpectedly. He hadn't known this part would be so hard. The other he'd prepared for, but this—somehow he had expected this to go smooth as glass. It was a story he'd told a hundred times since Deke had disappeared. There had been a lot of people interested in the phenomenon of Deke Summers.

"I knew he was planning to quit—at least quit the undercover work. Take a desk job, something safe. As safe as what we do ever gets," he amended. He paused again, taking a breath. "And then everything went to hell. The botched raid. That wasn't Deke's fault. That came out in the hearings, but of course, those were a couple of years down the road. And then the witness-security slipup. His wife's death."

"Slipup?" she repeated.

"Deke always thought someone inside had betrayed their location, but we never found any evidence of that. *If* that information came from the inside, it almost certainly happened by accident."

She didn't say anything, remembering all the times she'd accused Deke of paranoia, mentally accused him anyway. And she had been wrong. Maybe it was a slipup, but considering all that had happened, somehow she doubted it.

"I tried a lot of times through the next four years to contact Deke, to talk him into coming in. We could have kept him safe. I swear we could. And then finally...I realized he didn't want to be safe."

"Didn't *want* to be safe?" Becki repeated carefully.

"You hadn't figured that out," he said, a statement, not a question. "But then, it took *me* a long time to understand what was going on inside his head, and I knew Deke Summers better than anyone, a lot longer than you did." He paused, and then he asked her the question that had finally occurred to him. The obvious question. "If you wanted to hide from people who mostly live in rural areas, where would *you* go, Ms. Travers?" he asked softly.

The brown eyes held his, her obvious intelligence dealing with what he'd just suggested about the man they both loved. He wasn't surprised when she refused to answer him, even when he saw the realization in her face.

"You'd go into some city," he went on, answering his own question. "You'd hide in the urban maze, blend into the faceless throng. You'd stay in cheap hotels that rent by the month in the biggest metropolis you could find. What you *wouldn't* do is live in the heart of country that holds the largest portion of the very folks you're trying to avoid." He paused and then added the hardest part, hardest for him to have accepted. "Not unless you *want* those folks to find you."

Still she held his eyes, and finally she asked, her voice softly reasoning, "And how would you make a living in that city? With no ID? No social security number?"

"Same way," he said, shrugging off the question. "Odd jobs. City people need carpentry work, too. Be a handyman. Wash windshields, if you had to. Hold out a tin cup."

"Somehow," she denied, "I can't see Deke living like that."

"*Living*," he echoed. The salient part.

"Are you suggesting…" She stopped, unwilling to put the idea into words.

"Deke Summers thought he had a debt to pay for everyone who'd died. Some kind of blood guilt he had to work out. So he never *completely* disappeared."

"That's…" She hesitated again, and he completed the thought.

"Crazy?" he suggested. "Maybe. Enough had happened that maybe he had a right to be a little screwed up. And if not, maybe being hunted like an animal for four years would—"

"Deke Summers was the sanest man I've ever met," she interrupted, defending. "*Despite* everything that had happened to him."

It was his time to be silent. Considering.

"Deke always thought everything was his fault," he said, sharing things he hadn't intended to tell her, because he thought she needed to know. It might make it easier for her. "He was always responsible. And if things went wrong, he was the one who was supposed to pay the piper. Everything was his responsibility—to see it right. Part of that came from having a drunk for a daddy. Deke's mama died when he was eight. Worn out, I guess. Worked to death. Mistreated. Deke hadn't been old enough or big enough to protect her, not from anything, and he always felt that was his failure. And then those children in that compound in the Smokies died, and that became his failure, too. And finally—"

She stood up abruptly. "I don't want to hear this, Mr. Ballard. I'm sure you think you're being kind. Or helpful. Something. But I don't need an assessment of Deke Summers's character. Maybe he did have a sense of responsibility. Out of proportion, perhaps, to what he could control.'' She paused, and then shook her head, ''But considering the world today, I'm afraid I don't find a sense of responsibility something to criticize. He saved my son's life because he felt responsible for it. I don't intend to sit here and listen to you try to tear down—''

''Hold on, Ms. Travers. I'm not tearing anybody down. Especially not Deke. I'm trying to explain to you why I believe he lived the way he did the last few years. I didn't mean any disrespect.''

The angry rigidity of her body softened somewhat, and finally she nodded, but it was obvious that she didn't intend to let him share any more of the insights on Deke Summers that had taken him a dozen years to figure out.

''I know the name of a man who was involved in what happened,'' she said. ''Someone who furnished information to Deke's enemies. From back in Muscova.''

He didn't say anything.

''If you're interested,'' she added, her eyes accusing him of not being interested enough.

''Vernon Petty,'' he said.

''Yes.''

''We know about Mr. Petty's activities.''

''Did you arrest him? Is that why...'' She stopped, because he had begun to shake his head. ''Why not?'' she asked. ''If you knew about him?''

''Because our information came from an informant. If we acted on it, there were some pretty substantial risks involved. We decided punishing Mr. Petty wasn't important enough to justify those risks.''

''Not *important* enough?'' she repeated, not bothering to hide the bitterness.

There was a long silence while he thought how to tell her. This was the part he had known would be hard. There was no way to make it any easier. He hoped that eventually she'd forgive him.

''We got a lot from this particular informant. More than just information. He wasn't even ours. He was an FBI agent working undercover in a special unit, some kind of commando-group crap they'd put together. We got real lucky, Ms. Travers. Lucky about a lot of things, things we don't intend to jeopardize in order to arrest the Vernon Pettys of this world.''

The wide, brown eyes were cold for the first time, the bitterness that had been in her voice reflected in them, too.

This was no less than what she had expected. Obviously her definition of lucky and his didn't coincide.

"I see," she said. "Then if there's nothing else, Mr. Ballard, I think you'll have to excuse me. I have some shopping to do. I'd hate for this to be a *completely* wasted day."

He stood also, watching her walk across the room to the door.

"Would you feel strongly about relocating, Ms. Travers?"

The question stopped her, as he'd intended.

"Relocating?" she repeated, puzzled. He had told her they were no longer in danger. Why was he now suggesting that she needed to relocate? Because they hadn't arrested Vernon Petty?

"To a major city somewhere."

She shook her head. "I'm afraid I don't understand."

"The FBI agent I told you about used an alias, of course," he said.

A small, puzzled crease had formed between the dark wings of her brows. He could tell she didn't understand what he was trying to work around to. And he had to admit he wasn't doing a very good job of helping her.

This wasn't fair, Luke thought again. They had all known it wasn't fair, but it had seemed the best way. To ease her toward the truth, not just to spring it on her, so he added a little more information.

"The name he chose to use was Avery. Richard Avery. Does that name mean anything to you, Ms. Travers?"

"I don't know what—" The words were cut off. Some thought began to move behind the dark eyes. "Richard?" she said. "There was a man named Richard with the people who took Josh. Mike said he was to be the one…"

There was another long silence. He let her think about what he'd told her. Deke had said she was smart, and apparently he had not been mistaken. Her eyes glazed with tears, but she blinked, gathering control. She opened her purse and took out a folded sheet of paper. She walked back to the table, and unfolding the picture she had taken from the service-station wall, she slid it across to him.

"Could that *possibly* be what don't you intend to jeopardize, Mr. Ballard?" she asked.

Luke looked down at the picture of Deke Summers and the message that had been posted on the electronic bulletin boards all over the country, sent out to the far-flung members of the elusive Movement. To all the groups who had hunted this one man so long. EXECUTED. And with that message, the hunt for Deke Summers had finally come to an end.

He looked up into her eyes, starred with tears. Waiting to have confirmed what he had brought her here to tell her.

"That's *exactly* what we don't want to put at risk."

"Deke's alive," she said softly, her voice without emotion, but what she felt was all there in the dark eyes.

"We couldn't let you know," he said, trying to explain the reasons for what they'd put her through. "We had to make sure they really believed he was dead. Deke was determined not to endanger you or your son again. He *had* to know they were convinced the execution had been carried out."

"And if they hadn't been? What then?"

"If Deke had had any doubt the hunt was over," he said, "you would never have been called." He shook his head, still unable to believe how lucky they had been. "The whole thing was just a fluke. Or a miracle. The agent took an incredible risk, a spur-of-the-moment chance that shouldn't have worked."

"How did he convince them that Deke was dead?"

"Normally, one man would never have been given the sole responsibility, but it all came down before they were ready.

You and Deke hadn't waited for their phone call. Suddenly Deke was there, hours before they'd expected to deal with him. And they realized that as soon as they released the hostages, your brothers would alert the authorities in Cloud Run and someone would come out to the camp. They had to get out of the location. The decision was made, giving in to Richard's rather frenzied requests to let him handle the execution and then dispose of the body somewhere in the desert. It was the one deviation from normal procedures the commander made. To put one man in charge of that operation. To be fair, however, by the time he allowed that, Deke was no longer much of a threat to anyone.''

"What had they done to him?" she whispered.

"Enough that they weren't worried about one man being able to handle him," he admitted. She didn't need to know any more than that. Deke would probably kill him for telling her anything.

She swallowed, fighting down the sudden sickness.

"It's okay," he said. "It's all over. Deke's safe. And he's going to stay that way. We've monitored their communications for over six weeks. There hasn't been a hint of suspicion. A week ago the man they knew as Richard Avery 'died' in a tragic automobile accident—one that was staged by some of our experts. None of the computer traffic has even mentioned the coincidence. No one's suggested his death was anything out of the ordinary. Apparently, they bought it all.''

"And now what?" she asked, hoping.

"I guess that depends on you," he said. "On what you want.''

SOMEHOW, SHE HAD EXPECTED that he would have changed more during the eternity she had existed without him. She was aware that Luke Ballard had closed the door to the room where Deke had been waiting, allowing them privacy, but she didn't seem to be able to manage the short distance across it.

There was a lightweight removable cast on his right wrist. His hair was shorter, a little darker perhaps, without its daily exposure to the strong Southern sun. There was something different about his nose, no longer perfectly straight, but subtly out of alignment now. But the tan had not completely faded, and his eyes, of course, hadn't changed. Palely luminescent, shadowed by the thick lashes. Watching her reaction.

She had no idea what he intended. They had never talked about the future, because he had never had one.

"Luke thinks this is an opportunity to really start over," Deke said. His eyes hadn't left her face. "But the name I have to give you—if you decide you want to take it, you and Josh— it still won't be my name. Somebody else's identity. Another town. Away from your family. I understand what I'm asking you to give up. And how little I have to offer in exchange."

He stopped, and she thought maybe that was all he intended to say. More sentences than she'd ever heard him put together before. She hadn't expected romantic language. Deke Summers wasn't the kind of man who whispered sweet nothings.

"But I'll always be there, Becki. For both of you. And I'll keep you safe. This time…" The deep voice faltered suddenly. And then, because he was the man he was, he found the courage to make the promise he thought she wanted. "This time, I promise to do it right."

She heard the unspoken thought, and so she said it for him, understanding far more than she had before. She'd have to apologize to Luke Ballard.

"And this time, everything will be perfect," she suggested. "No mistakes allowed."

She felt her eyes fill because she loved him so much. And because she recognized the incredible courage it would take for Deke Summers to begin again.

"I want you to understand that I'll always love you for that, Deke. For *wanting* everything to be perfect for me and Josh."

Then, because she knew the things she needed to say were hard, she smiled at him, slightly tremulous, but still a smile.

"But life doesn't come with those guarantees, Deke. And you can't make those promises," she said softly. "They aren't up to you. Bad things happen to good people, to people who don't deserve them. You and I both should understand that by now. Illnesses and accidents. Betrayals. Disappointments. They happen, despite our best efforts. And even *with* our best efforts, we're going to make mistakes. I will. And you will. Because we're human.''

The silence stretched between them. Finally, he took a breath, deep enough that it was visible.

''I know...'' he began, and then stopped. It was so hard to put it all into words. He had practiced the other, what he wanted to say to her. What he thought she would need to hear. It would be far easier not to explain the rest, but he knew he had to try. *That* was what he had really done wrong before. Somewhere in his heart he had always known that.

''I know I have some problems,'' he acknowledged. Something else Luke had convinced him to do. To get some help dealing with what had happened. To stop denying that he needed help.

''That's okay,'' she said quickly. ''I have some problems too. Everybody has problems. It's how we cope with them that's important. How we live our lives. That's what matters. You taught me that.''

''I taught you?'' Deke repeated, shaking his head. He knew there was nothing in his screwed-up existence that could teach Becki Travers anything about how to live her life. She was the one who had done it all right.

She smiled at his tone. ''Maybe not consciously,'' she admitted. ''But still, it was a lesson I learned from you. That every day is precious. That it all goes so quickly. That there's no time for living in the past, for dwelling on the mistakes we made yesterday. You can't live that way any more, Deke. Not if you want to live with me and Josh. No old failures. No ghosts. We'll make enough mistakes trying to do it right day by day. And we won't have time to look back. You can't promise us that life will always be good, Deke. No one can. Not health or wealth or happiness. No guarantees about any of those.''

She smiled at him again, hoping he understood. It wasn't

his job to make the world they lived in right. Not his responsibility. His expression hadn't changed, and she realized suddenly that she hadn't answered his question. She wondered how he could not know what she wanted—for Josh and for herself—but maybe he didn't.

"But if you're willing, Deke, I'll accept the other. The promise to always be there. Just *be* there. When I wake up at night, I want to hear you breathing beside me. I guess that's the only promise I want from you. The only one you can really make."

"As long as I live," he vowed softly.

And as he had once before in a darkened parking lot, he opened his arms, welcoming her home.

Epilogue

It was late when she got back to her mother's house to pick up Josh, late enough that she allowed herself to be talked into having supper with her parents. She realized belatedly that she hadn't eaten anything since breakfast. In light of all that had happened, she hadn't thought about food, but her mother's chicken pie was justifiably famous, and she didn't resist the familiar urging to stay and eat. *There's plenty,* her mom had tempted—ritual—and of course, there was.

It was almost dark, twilight deepening and the sky shading to purple, when she and Josh finally got home. Almost exactly the same time of day, she thought, when they had sat together on the back steps and made wishes on the evening star. At least, she amended, Josh had made a wish.

She had hugged the knowledge of Deke's return to her heart on the way home from Birmingham, thinking about the best time to explain everything to her son. She had finally settled on bedtime, the time set aside for all their important discussions, the time for whispering secrets too precious to be shared with anyone else. It seemed perfect for this revelation.

"Run your bath," she told Josh, "while I give poor Wimsey his supper. He probably thinks we've deserted him again."

Standing in the kitchen a few minutes later, she could hear distantly, over the whir of the can opener she was using, the sound of bathwater running in the old-fashioned porcelain tub.

She unlocked the sliding door and pushed it open, expecting

the ginger tabby to be perched on the railing, tail flicking impatiently as he waited, yellow eyes accusing because of the delay. There was nothing there. No Wimsey.

She set the bowl down in its customary spot and walked to the steps, looking out into the shadowed yard. She knew it would take a moment for her eyes to adjust to the gathering darkness, so she waited, letting the pleasant night sounds surround her. Gradually the area of the yard where the woods always threatened to encroach began to become more distinct. And from the less indiscernible darkness the two shapes took form.

Deke was sitting on the ground, his back against Josh's tree—the same tree where he had hidden the night the nightmare had begun, waiting to rescue her from a man they had called Richard. The scarred tom was twining around the bent, jean-clad legs of the seated man.

She stepped quietly back to the sliding door and pushed it open a little.

"Josh," she called, pitching her voice strongly enough to reach the bathroom and yet not too loudly. They were certainly isolated out here, especially since the house next door had not been rented, but she knew that coming back to a place where he might be recognized could be dangerous for Deke. She wasn't willing to take any chances.

Josh appeared in the doorway to the kitchen. He had removed his shoes and socks, but he hadn't yet undressed.

"Do me a favor," she said.

"Okay," he agreed without question.

"Wim's out in the Bat Cave, and he won't come up to eat. Want to go get him for me?"

"Sure," Josh said.

She moved aside enough to allow him to slip through the sliding door. Standing in the light filtering from the curtained opening behind her, she watched him cross the darkened lawn, and despite the shadows she could tell when he stopped in surprise, a few feet away from the seated man.

The cat deserted his original object of affection to touch his broad head under Josh's fingers. She waited, wanting to give them privacy, but still wishing she could know what he and Deke were saying to one another. The bond she and Josh had shared for so many years had now been expanded, and despite the small tug of loneliness she felt, she knew that she could never provide her son with the things Deke could give him, wanted so desperately to give. And so she smiled and stayed where she was, watching them together.

"Hey," Deke said softly. Somehow it had been easier before, in the enemy encampment, all the barriers he had erected through the years instantly destroyed by what was happening.

"Hey," Josh said.

The silence stretched between them, strained and a little uncomfortable.

"Mom sent me to get Wimsey," the child explained, reaching down to caress the circling cat.

"Butch," Deke corrected. "At least—that's what I always called him."

"He ran away while we were gone," Josh said. He squatted, balancing on bare toes to rub the cat. The dark eyes were now on a level with the steady blue ones. "But Mom wished him back."

"Wished him back?" Deke repeated carefully.

"Wished on a star that he'd come on home," Josh explained. His eyes lifted briefly to the growing darkness overhead and then came back to the man's.

"Did you help wish him back?" Deke asked. Despite his intent, the question was tinged with amusement. It had been a long time since he had been around anyone who believed wishes came true, but somehow he didn't find it hard to imagine that Becki Travers would.

"No," Josh admitted. "I wished *you* back."

In spite of what he had always known about the child's feelings, the comment caught him unaware, broadsided by its honesty.

"Thanks," Deke said finally, speaking around the unfamiliar knot in his throat.

"You're welcome," Josh said politely. "Would you like to come inside our house, John? I don't think Mom would mind. I can ask her."

"Deke," he corrected. "I know it's confusing, but my real name is Deke."

"Yeah," Josh said. "Mom told me, but I forgot. When I prayed for you, I always said John Evans. I guess God knew who I meant, though. He's supposed to know everything. And you're here," he added, the most compelling argument for the Lord's omniscience.

"I guess He does," Deke confirmed softly. He couldn't think of another soul in his entire life who might have prayed for him. Maybe his mother. A long time ago. And Becki, who apparently still believed in miracles; who thought that despite what he was, he could be the kind of father her son deserved.

"Your mom and I thought we might do something about helping you keep all the names straight," Deke said carefully, watching him rub the soft fur along Butch's spine the wrong way. The tom didn't seem to mind, butting contentedly against the child's hand. "Mine's probably going to change again. I can't explain all the reasons why, but..." He paused, wondering how much to say. He didn't want to mess this up. It was too important.

"It's okay," Josh said when Deke hesitated. "Whatever you want me to call you, it's okay. I can remember."

"I thought maybe...we might try Dad," Deke said. His deep voice was almost a whisper, almost fading into the harmony of the tree frogs, floating from the woods behind them. Nothing he had done in his life had taken more guts than giving voice to that suggestion.

"Okay," Josh said softly. His fingers had deserted the tabby who twisted now between Deke's ankles. "Or maybe Daddy?" Josh offered tentatively. "That's what my cousins call their dad. Do you think that would that be okay?"

"Yeah," Deke agreed. "I think that would be...just about perfect."

Again the silence grew, more comfortable now. Familiar.

"Grandma sent us some rice pudding," Josh said finally. "It's just what was left from supper, but there's plenty. You want to come inside?" he invited again.

More than life itself, Deke acknowledged, but of course, that wasn't what he said.

"Okay," he agreed, pushing up from the ground. He had forgotten to protect the wrist they had broken, and the sudden pain was enough to fight the pull of emotions that had threatened to overwhelm him. He took the couple of steps that separated him from the boy and felt the trusting fingers slip into his big hand. As they crossed the grass, Deke looked up to find Becki watching them, waiting, surrounded by the small circle of light that he finally understood was powerful enough to defeat even his darkness.

A miracle.

Harlequin® Historical

If you're a serious fan of historical romance,
then you're in luck!

Harlequin Historicals brings you
stories by bestselling authors, rising new stars
and talented first-timers.

Ruth Langan & Theresa Michaels
Mary McBride & Cheryl St.John
Margaret Moore & Merline Lovelace
Julie Tetel & Nina Beaumont
Susan Amarillas & Ana Seymour
Deborah Simmons & Linda Castle
Cassandra Austin & Emily French
Miranda Jarrett & Suzanne Barclay
DeLoras Scott & Laurie Grant...

You'll never run out of favorites.

Harlequin Historicals...they're too good to miss!

HH-GEN

HARLEQUIN®

I N T R I G U E ®

★Cheyenne Nights★

by Carla Cassidy

As little girls the Connor sisters dreamed of gallant princes on white horses. As women they were swept away by mysterious cowboys on black stallions. But with dusty dungarees and low-hung Stetsons, their cowboys are no less the knights in shining armor.

Join Carla Cassidy for the Connor sisters'
wild West Wyoming tales of intrigue:

SUNSET PROMISES
(March)

MIDNIGHT WISHES
(April)

SUNRISE VOWS
(May)

Look us up on-line at: http://www.romance.net   CHE-3/97

LOVE *or* MONEY?
Why not Love *and* Money!
After all, millionaires
need love, too!

How to Marry a
MILLIONAIRE

Suzanne Forster,
Muriel Jensen
and
Judith Arnold

bring you three original stories
about finding that one-in-a million man!

Harlequin also brings you
a million-dollar sweepstakes—enter
for your chance to win a fortune!

 HARLEQUIN ®
®

HARLEQUIN® Temptation.

and

HARLEQUIN®

I N T R I G U E ®

Double Dare ya!

Identical twin authors Patricia Ryan and
Pamela Burford bring you a dynamic duo of
books that just happen to feature identical twins.

Meet Emma, the shy one, and her diva double,
Zara. Be prepared for twice the pleasure and
twice the excitement as they give two
unsuspecting men trouble times two!

In April, the scorching **Harlequin Temptation** novel
#631 **Twice the Spice** by Patricia Ryan

In May, the suspenseful **Harlequin Intrigue** novel
#420 **Twice Burned** by Pamela Burford

Pick up both—if you dare....

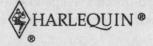

HARLEQUIN ®

It's hot...and it's out of control!

BLAZE

Beginning this spring, Temptation turns up the
heat. Look for these bold, provocative,
*ultra*sexy books!

#629 OUTRAGEOUS
by Lori Foster (April 1997)

#639 RESTLESS NIGHTS
by Tiffany White (June 1997)

#649 NIGHT RHYTHMS
by Elda Minger (Sept. 1997)

BLAZE: Red-hot reads—only from

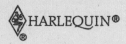 **HARLEQUIN®**

Not The Same Old Story!

 **HARLEQUIN PRESENTS®**
Exciting, emotionally intense romance stories that take readers around the world.

 *Harlequin Romance®*
Vibrant stories of captivating women and irresistible men experiencing the magic of falling in love!

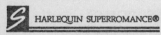 **HARLEQUIN® *Temptation***
Bold and adventurous— Temptation is strong women, bad boys, great sex!

S HARLEQUIN SUPERROMANCE®
Provocative, passionate, contemporary stories that celebrate life and love.

 **AMERICAN ROMANCE®**
Romantic adventure where anything is possible and where dreams come true.

 **HARLEQUIN® INTRIGUE®**
Heart-stopping, suspenseful adventures that combine the best of romance and mystery.

LOVE & LAUGHTER™
Entertaining and fun, humorous and romantic—stories that capture the lighter side of love.